EVERYONE IS BEAUTIFUL

Piling everything she owns into her car, Lanie leaves family and friends behind — all so her husband can be a professional musician. But Lanie suddenly realises that she once had dreams too. If only she could remember what they were. Fifteen years, three babies and many more pounds after she said 'I do', Lanie longs to feel like her old self again. It's time to fish her va-va-voom out of the nappy bin and find the woman she was before motherhood — harder said than done, when by finding herself she seems to be losing everything else in the process.

from Vassar
ssar College
an MA
of Houst
or for
t, an
colle
the
Fic
tea
n

o

KATHERINE CENTER

EVERYONE IS BEAUTIFUL

Complete and Unabridged

ULVERSCROFT
Leicester

First published in Great Britain in 2010 by
Piatkus
an imprint of
Little, Brown Book Group
London

First Large Print Edition
published 2011
by arrangement with
Little, Brown Book Group
An Hachette UK Company
London

The moral right of the author has been asserted

British Library CIP Data

Center, Katherine.
  Everyone is beautiful.
  1. Wives- -Fiction. 2. Self-realization- -Fiction.
  3. Large type books.
  I. Title
  813.6–dc22

ISBN 978–1–4448–0884–1

Published by
F. A. Thorpe (Publishing)
Anstey, Leicestershire

Set by Words & Graphics Ltd.
Anstey, Leicestershire
Printed and bound in Great Britain by
T. J. International Ltd., Padstow, Cornwall

This book is printed on acid-free paper

For my husband, Gordon Center,
who is the reason I believe so
much in love.

1

The day I decided to change my life, I was wearing sweatpants and an old oxford of Peter's with a coffee stain down the front. I hadn't showered because the whole family had slept in one motel room the night before, and it was all we could do to get back on the road without someone dropping the remote in the toilet or pooping on the floor.

We had just driven across the country to start Peter's new job. Houston, Texas, to Cambridge, Massachusetts. I'd had the kids in our ten-year-old Subaru the whole drive, two car seats and a booster across the back. Alexander kept taking Toby's string cheese, and the baby, except when he was sleeping, was fussing. Peter drove the U-Haul on the theory that if it broke, he'd know how to fix it.

On the road, I was sure I had the short end of the stick, especially during the dog hours of Tennessee. But now Peter was hauling all our belongings up three flights of narrow stairs, and I was at the park, on a blanket in the late-afternoon shade, breast-feeding Baby Sam. Peter had to be hurting. Even with our new landlord helping him, it was taking all day. And I was just waiting for him to call on the cell phone when he was ready for us to come home. Or as close to home as a curtainless apartment stacked high with boxes could be.

We'd been at the park since midmorning, and we were running low on snacks. Alexander and Toby were galloping at top speed, as they always did. I'm not even sure they realized they were in a new park. They acted like we might as well have been at home, in Houston, the only place they'd ever lived. They acted like the last five days of driving hadn't even registered. I, in contrast, was aching with loss.

I didn't like this park. Too clean, too brand-new, too perfect. The parks at home had character — monkey bars fashioned like cowboys, gnarled crape myrtle trunks for climbing, discarded Big Wheels with no seats. And we'd known them backward and forward — every tree knot, every mud hole, every kid.

This park, today, felt forced. It was trying too hard.

I surveyed the moms. Not one of them, I decided, was a person I wanted to meet. And just as I was disliking them all and even starting to pity them for having no idea what they were missing, park-wise, Toby — my middle boy, my sandy-haired, blue-eyed, two-year-old flirt — watched a younger kid make a move for the truck in his hand, and then, unbelievably, grabbed that kid's forearm and bit it.

The little boy screamed as Toby pulled the truck to his chest. 'My truck!' Toby shouted. (He always pronounced 'truck' like 'fuck,' but that was, perhaps, another issue.)

And then, of course, all hell broke loose.

I jumped up, startling the baby out of a nap and off my boob. I ran across the park, wailing baby on my shoulder, shirt unbuttoned, shouting, 'Toby! No!' Toby saw my horrified face and instantly started to cry himself — though he was no match for the little kid he'd bitten, who was now screaming like he was on fire. His mother, too, had sprinted from her perch, dropping her purse on the way, and was now holding him as if he'd been shot. 'Is it bleeding?' she kept asking the boy. 'Is it bleeding?'

It was clearly not bleeding. Isn't that the number one rule of parenting? Don't Make Things Worse?

All the other parents, meanwhile, had gathered around us to see what the heck was going on. My shirt was hanging open, the baby was still shrieking, and I remembered from one of those parenting books I used to read — back when I used to do that type of thing — that when a child bites, the parent of the biter must give attention to the bitee. I turned toward the little boy and reached out to comfort him, and, at the same moment, his mother actually tightened her grip on him and rocked away from my hand so that I missed him altogether. As if I myself had done the biting. As if I were about to attack again.

I regrouped. 'I'm so sorry about that, sweetheart!' I said to the boy, who was not, you might say, in a listening mode. Next, I tried his mother. 'I'm so sorry!' I said. 'He's never done that before!' She was staring at me, but not at my eyes, and it took me a second to realize that it was, in fact, my uncovered magenta nursing bra she was looking at. I buttoned my shirt and started to try again when Alexander took that moment to push Toby down and take the very truck that had started all this commotion.

Toby let out a wail like a scalded dog, and Alexander threw the truck with all his might into a nearby bush. 'No biting!' he said, pointing at Toby. 'Biting is rude!' Toby got up to run after the truck and soon they were both tangled in the bush, wrestling for it.

Here was a moment when I was truly outnumbered. With two kids, in moments like this, you at least have an arm for each. With three kids, you're just screwed.

'Stop it! Both of you!' I shouted, sounding just like my own mother had years ago when she had been outnumbered, too.

And then, I did the only thing I could think of. I set Baby Sam down on the sidewalk — at ten months, he wasn't crawling yet, or even thinking about it — stepped into the bush, took the truck, and wedged it high in the branch of a tree. Then I grabbed the two boys by the scruffs of their necks, dragged them to our blanket, sprinted back over to my now-almost-purple-with-hysteria Baby Sam, picked him up, put him on the boob, and then marched back to where the boys were.

'Anybody who moves off this blanket gets a spanking,' I said in my meanest mom voice, sounding for all the world like a 1930s gangster. It was an empty threat. Peter and I weren't spankers. And I wasn't about to spank anybody in front of the still-gaping crowd of Cambridge parents ten feet away. But, honestly, what else was I going to do? Send the boys to their room? I wasn't even entirely sure where our apartment was.

The bitee and his mother eventually gathered themselves up and limped out of the park, giving us the cold shoulder the whole way. It occurred to me that park etiquette probably dictated we should be the ones to leave. But, since we were waiting on Peter, we stayed. I tore open some cheese sticks. Alexander and Toby soon forgot about the whole thing — though not until after I'd given them the best talking-to I could muster about how we all had to work together in this time of transition — and they were back on the swings in no time. Alexander, sweetly, got down again and again to give Toby another push.

The old crop of parents trickled out, replaced by the after-work crowd. This batch was preppier and wealthier — pushing Bugaboos and carrying $200 diaper bags. One woman caught my eye as someone I might like to be friends with. She wore stylishly frayed khakis and clompy leather sandals. I kept an eye on her and willed her to come over and talk to me. The bitee's mother excepted, I hadn't talked to an adult since ten o'clock that morning, when we'd said good-bye to Peter.

And then she did come over. Her daughter toddled up to our blanket wanting to look at Baby Sam, who was now eating from a spilled constellation of Cheerios in front of him. The mom stood beside us, and I squinted up at her in the late-afternoon sun. I could tell she wanted to ask me a question. And from the way she was composing herself, I guessed it was a good one. I was hoping for 'You're new here, aren't you?' or something like it. Something that might lead to a real moment of exchange between the two of us, or, at the very least, a phone number from her and an invitation to call. I'd only been away from home six days, but already I was hungry for friends.

She did have a question for me, it turned out. And it was not about how long I'd been in town. Tucking her hair behind her ears, she squatted down next to her toddler — who was now picking up our Cheerios one by one, too — took a gander at me, sitting next to my ten-month-old, and said, 'When are you due?'

Here is my policy on that question: Don't ever ask it. Even if you're talking to a woman who is clearly about to have quintuplets. Just don't ask. Because if you're wrong, you've just said one of the most horrible things you can say to a woman. If you're wrong, you've ruined her week — possibly her month and even her year. If you're wrong, she will go home and cry, and not even be able to tell her husband what she's crying about. He'll ask over and over as she lies facedown on their bed, and she'll have no choice but to say, 'It's nothing,' and then, 'Please, just leave me alone.'

This woman in the khakis, she was wrong.

And I did go home and cry, but not until much later, because just at the moment she spoke, before I had even settled on a response, another woman approached us and leaned in to peer at me.

'Lanie?' she asked.

I met her eyes. I was pretty certain I didn't know a single person in Massachusetts, and so, given the circumstances, it was amazing, even to me, that I recognized her. It was Amanda Hayes from Houston, my high school's favorite cheerleader, and, even all these years later, she had not changed at all. If anything, she looked better. But still exactly as blond, lean, and smooth as she had been years ago. She might as well have been carrying pom-poms.

'Hi!' I shouted, too loudly. 'Hello!'

I might have been fueled by my fight-or-flight reaction to the woman in khaki pants, but I stood up and gave Amanda Hayes, a girl I'd barely known in high school, a hug. Then I threw myself into a kind of conversation-on-steroids with her, acting far more delighted to see her than I might have otherwise. I would have been friendly in any situation, just as we'd always been friendly to each other during assigned seating in Chorus, but I might not have been quite as riveted.

I was hoping that, witnessing a reunion of

two women who had a real connection to each other, the when-are-you-due girl might feel out of place and wander off. She didn't. Her child continued to eat my Cheerios, and she continued to stand there, smiling as if she were part of the conversation, as if the three of us moms were friends, drinking *mojitos* and whiling away another afternoon with the kiddos.

I asked Amanda every single question I could think of, trying to fill any conversational pauses before Khaki Pants started up again with her pregnancy topic. What was Amanda doing in town? How long had she lived here? What were her thoughts on Middle East peace? Where did she get those great sunglasses?

And Amanda, bless her, met my enthusiasm for our chat head-on. She answered all my questions, and volleyed several back at me, and just when I was starting to feel like we'd built a conversational wall that the woman in khakis couldn't scale, Amanda's daughter, Gracin — who was almost four and, it turned out, exactly one day older than Alexander — came running over to ask for a Band-Aid.

'Did you get an ouchie?' Amanda asked.

Gracin pointed at her arm. There was no ouchie.

'Oh.' Amanda peeled a Band-Aid from a stash in her pocket, then put it on Gracin, who ran off. Watching her go, I noticed she had Band-Aids all down her legs.

'She loves Band-Aids,' Amanda told us, with a what-are-you-gonna-do shrug.

And then, in that moment, Amanda paused to gaze at her daughter, now climbing up the ramp of the slide, and take one of those small moments that parents sometimes indulge in when their children are a little at a distance. She was admiring her, and possibly even wondering what stroke of insane luck had brought that exact child into her life, and feeling grateful for all her blessings. Amanda got caught up in watching her daughter, and I got caught up in watching Amanda, and so I was a split-second late cranking up the conversation again — and into that little gap, Khaki Pants leaned in, touched my sleeve, and said, 'So. When *are* you due?'

Amanda snapped around to look at me. 'You're pregnant?' she asked, ready to be delighted.

I couldn't decide what to say. Time got very slow. Baby Sam was chewing on a rock. Alexander had captured a bug and was building a little mud house for it. Toby had found a fallen branch and was dragging it around the park, showing it off. The sun had set and the light was fading from the sky. Peter still hadn't called. Finally, faced with the prospect of having to say, 'No, I'm just still fat from my last pregnancy. And it's possible I weigh even more now than I did when I was actually pregnant because it's been a tough year and my husband keeps bringing me tubes of frozen cookie dough,' I said, instead, in a voice that seemed to rise up without my permission: 'Yes.'

Amanda started to clap with enthusiasm. 'Four kids?' she said. 'Four kids!'

Khaki Pants, who'd been sure of it all along, said, 'It's so awful to be pregnant in the summer. Aren't you hot?'

A little woozy, now, from my sudden imaginary pregnancy, I just nodded and said, 'I sure am.'

I had the strangest moment of relief right then, in those seconds, as the impact of what I'd said washed over us. I let myself believe it just a little, and I let it explain a lot of things about why I just could not seem to pull myself together. I was pregnant again! Morning sickness, back pain. One baby still nursing. Three boys, a husband who obsessed over his work, no help. And no money at all. Of course I hadn't worn any lipstick since Toby ate my last tube in the checkout line at the grocery! I was too busy to look good!

11

Being pregnant is hard work!

Amanda sized up Baby Sam. Then she said, 'How old is this one?'

'Oh,' I said. 'He's a lot older than he looks.' I didn't have a lot of experience with lying, but it seemed like a good idea to be vague. I started packing up my diaper bag. It was time — past time — to move out. I shouted to the boys, 'Let's go see Daddy!'

While I folded our blanket, Khaki Pants said, 'I have a friend who got pregnant again on the night of her six-week checkup.'

Amanda chimed in, 'I have a friend with triplets.'

There was a pause, then, as all three of us stopped to pay silent tribute to the women we knew whose asses were being kicked even harder than our own were. Then we all seemed to realize at the same time that, with the addition of this fourth child, I would soon fit into that category. The category of people you make small talk about at the park: 'She has four kids and no help.' I didn't mind. It was better, certainly, than, 'Her baby is ten months old and she still looks pregnant.'

Amanda touched my shoulder. 'I am so throwing you a shower!' It seemed like a rash gesture. But we'd just had quite a conversation. And seeing someone from your hometown when you're far away can be a crazy thrill.

Besides, after our turbo-chat earlier, she knew all about me. She knew I could really use a shower, both literally and figuratively. She pulled a business-size card out of her wallet that read 'The Boatman Family' and had her phone number beneath. She said, 'Call me and we'll figure out the date.'

'I will,' I said, dropping the card into my big purse that housed everything I might ever need: wallet, keys, Q-tips, diapers, wipes, juice boxes, organic granola bars, pacis, and, down at the bottom, crushed cookies, stray raisins, and, this week, an old PB&J congealing inside its Ziploc bag.

Baby Sam loved to go through that purse and pull every single thing out, even separating the credit cards in the wallet from their nooks, beaming like a treasure hunter. He could dismantle and destroy the entire contents in under ten minutes. And even though I'd have much preferred a bag that was orderly, and even though I could've solved the problem so easily by just, simply, not handing him my bag, I let him have it time and again. It was such an easy response when he started fussing. I found, these days, I was so desperate for harmony that I gladly traded the contents of my bag — and all hopes for maintaining any level of organization — for even five minutes of everybody happy.

Taking Amanda's card, I knew that within twenty-four hours Baby Sam would find it in my purse, put it in his mouth, chew on it until it looked like a wad of gum, and then leave it on the floor where I'd step on it in bare feet many hours later on the way to the bathroom in the middle of the night. But it was okay. I wouldn't have called her anyway.

2

When we got back, Peter was sitting on the front steps with our new landlord, Josh — who didn't look a day over eighteen, though he was in his midtwenties. They were breathing hard when we found them, and were splayed out with their knees wide apart, downing gallon-size bottled waters.

We would later learn that Josh managed this and other properties for his elderly grandparents, that he had dropped out of Harvard in his senior year to deal with some 'substance issues,' and that his apartment, here on the ground floor of our building, was absolutely teeming with books — all of which he'd read. But on this night, he seemed almost like a high school kid: shaggy hair, baggy corduroys, lean muscles, and all. Peter seemed positively middle-aged next to him, and I tried to remember that when Peter and I met — in college — he had been younger than Josh was now.

Peter left to return the U-Haul and find the grocery. So it was up to me to do dinner and bath — our nightly naked-toddler calf scramble — alone.

Clomping up to the third floor with the boys was a challenge. I carried the baby with one arm, pulled Toby with the other hand, and uttered words of encouragement and focus to Alexander, who kept stopping to pick things up — a moth wing, a piece of Styrofoam. 'Up! Up! Let's go!'

Somewhere in one of our forty-two boxes, which I'd quit labeling at around 3 A.M. the night before we left, was a stash of canned ravioli and a set of Power Rangers plates. Baby Sam, not a late-afternoon guy — or morning, or midday, for that matter — fussed the entire time as I broke tape with my keys and popped boxes open. The older boys kept busy jumping on packing bubbles, and I remember thinking how great it must be to find fun so easily.

'Fun' was, in fact, a word that had stormed into my life since having children. I used it constantly these days. Somewhere early on I'd discovered that if you tell a child something is fun, for the most part, that child will believe you. As far as I could tell, this principle could not be overexploited, and none of the boys in my family ever seemed to catch on. And so, more times a day than I wished to count, I said things like, 'Don't forget to eat your fun broccoli,' 'Who wants to go start a load of fun laundry?' and 'Toby, go find your fun shoes.'

After opening eleven boxes, the entire living room completely in shambles, I made it into the kitchen to heat up that ravioli. It was bubbling at a good clip and probably past ready when I heard a very loud knock on the door. It wasn't Peter's knock, which was usually shave-and-a-haircut. This sounded more like a policeman's rap. I wondered, suddenly, if the mother of the bitee from the park had called the cops. I opened the door with a crazy feeling that I was about to get yelled at.

But it was no cop. It was a woman in a man's plaid bathrobe and leather slippers. Late forties, with blond hair in a straight bob. She had crisp green eyes with great smile crinkles at the edges. But she was not smiling now. Her mouth was a hard, straight line, and I knew for sure in that instant, I really was about to get yelled at. Or something equally bad.

'I live downstairs,' she said.

I decided to go with chipper: 'Hi! I'm Lanie!'

'Your children are jumping on my ceiling.'

I thought of them actually jumping on the ceiling, which made me smile. 'I'm sorry.'

'Please make them stop,' she said, and turned to shuffle down the stairs. Then she called over her shoulder, 'And you could crank down the volume on that screeching baby while you're at it.'

I was working on something I could say that would sound friendly, witty, and apologetic all at the same time, but before I'd even come up with 'Nice to meet you,' Alexander stepped out into the hall next to me and said, 'Mom? The *ravalowly* is on fire.'

Which it wasn't. I'd find out minutes later that it wasn't on fire at all: just burning. But the second after he said it, the smoke detector went off — which sent Baby Sam into a full-body fit of panic and inspired me to shout, 'Oh fuck! The pasta!' and had Josh-the-teenage-landlord up in our apartment in no time, disconnecting the batteries and saying, 'Yeah, these detectors are really sensitive to smoke.'

'That's a good thing, though, isn't it?' I said.

He grinned. 'Sure. Unless you're just burning your dinner.'

Josh left, and we ate the burned ravioli. I told the boys that it was exactly like the kind of food pirates used to eat, then gave it the proper name Pirate Stew — and they went for it. The baby, who had not really napped all day, nursed while we ate and then fell asleep in my lap — kind of a miracle, considering that Alexander and Toby spent the meal trying to imitate the sound of the smoke alarm. 'That's enough,' I kept saying to them limply, starting to buckle under the weight of it all. 'Inside noises, please.' Then, finally, 'We don't want to bother the mean witch downstairs.' And then I froze. Almost-four-year-olds, and the two-year-olds who adore them, never forget an insult — or a curse word. And I simply wasn't lucky enough to get away with saying something like that. It would come back to bite me in the ass. It just would.

'Mama?' Alexander asked then, stuffing a burned ravioli into his cheek with his fingers.

'What is it, cutie?'

'What does 'fuck the pasta' mean?'

★ ★ ★

Peter arrived home long after the boys were asleep. I had not cleaned up the boxes or the dinner dishes, and, in fact, the only thing I had done after the boys were quiet was set up the TV. Turns out, we had free cable.

As a parent, I was totally against TV. I did not let my kids watch it, ever. And, yes: I was aware that I was making parenting much harder on myself by not letting them watch. My mother had pointed it out countless

19

times, as had every single one of my mommy friends, all of whom depended on TV to help them get at least one crucial part of the day taken care of — the dishes, say, or a shower, or supper. My mother thought I was a real sanctimonious pain in the ass about it. 'An hour a day's not going to kill them,' she said. 'You're making yourself crazy.'

'It's a Pandora's box,' I told her.

And it was. I, myself, left to my own devices, would watch TV all day if I had the chance. I would forfeit real life for TV in a heartbeat. I loved TV. Loved it like an addict loves an addiction. I'd watch anything. I'd watch *Gilligan's Island*. I'd watch *The Price Is Right*. I'd watch the Food Network for hours and hours. Which is why, in Houston, we hadn't had cable. We hadn't even had our TV hooked up to any channels at all. I would have given the thing away entirely, but Peter, who did not understand the power TV had over me — and who could, in fact, watch TV and read a book at the same time — wanted to keep it.

'We can't not have a TV,' he said. 'Everybody has a TV.'

'If I were an alcoholic,' I asked, 'would you insist on keeping a liquor cabinet full of booze?'

'It's not really the same thing.'

'It's very similar,' I said, crossing my arms at him.

So we compromised. We had the TV and a DVD player — but no channels. We used to watch rented movies after the kids were asleep on weekends sometimes, though not as much since Baby Sam was born.

But here, when I'd pulled the TV out of the box, I found a cable at the bottom. Peter must have stumbled on it in the junk closet when we were packing, and put it in with the TV. When I went to plug the TV in, I found a cable hookup right next to the outlet. I stared at it for a good two or three minutes before, as decisively as a person falling off the wagon, I picked up the cable and attached it.

That was around 7:30. Now I'd been on the couch for almost three hours, flipping channels with delight, my eyes wide and glazed in a way that made our moving across the country and setting up an entirely new life seem uninteresting and unimportant. I felt a crazy kind of elation. I'd forgotten how much TV could pull you out of your own world. I'd forgotten how great it was. Books were a good distraction, but TV was like not even being there at all.

And then I stumbled on a documentary called *Living Large*, a week-in-the-life docu-mentary about an eight-hundred-plus-pound woman. Peter came home around eleven with groceries to find me hunched over on the sofa, face shiny with tears. He'd dropped off the sacks in the kitchen on his way in and taken a gander at the crispy brown raviolis congealed in the pot.

'What'd you guys have for supper? Roaches?'

I didn't answer. I'm not even sure I heard him.

Peter looked at the TV, then back at me. Then he came and sat down on the edge of the sofa, clearly not planning to stay. After a minute, he pulled two Hershey bars out of his pocket and gave one to me. 'Welcome to Massachusetts,' he said.

'I can't eat that,' I said.

'Why not?' he asked.

'Because,' I said, thinking for an answer. 'Because chocolate is a once-a-week thing, not a once-a-day thing.'

He shrugged and tore open his wrapping. 'Okay.'

Peter was thin. He was six feet tall with the metabolism of a greyhound. In fact, we were total opposites as far as looks. He was some kind of British-Scandinavian mutt, and I had inherited every single one of my mother's Colombian genes. He was blue-eyed and strawberry blond with freckles, and I had

22

black hair and black eyes — and, though I was much paler than my two younger brothers, I was much darker than Peter. Which wasn't saying much.

I had followed in my mother's footsteps and married a man who was my physical opposite — and, when we had kids, my recessive genes had teamed up with Peter's to produce three boys who were so blond and blue-eyed and freckled that people in Texas had routinely mistaken me for their nanny.

So Peter and I were different: He was bony and pointy and I was soft and round. He was, say, a celery stalk, and I was more of a pomegranate. I should add that he liked — and had always liked — my shape, and my complexion, and my softness.

And here is how Peter related to food: In addition to the basic three meals, he ate an extra breakfast every morning, snacked all day on anything he pleased, and, every night, had cinnamon toast smeared with butter and a tall glass of full-fat chocolate milk right before bed. Sometimes he'd down a box of cookies to boot. He could not comprehend what it might be like to view food as anything other than a source of unfettered pleasure. And he loved to bring me chocolate.

So, on that night, as we watched *Living Large*, he happily consumed both his chocolate bar and mine.

The star of the show was a lady named Mitzi, and she weighed 827 pounds. When she sat down on her bed, she could not get back up off of it. She literally got caught in her own body. The documentary was about her struggle to escape the prison of her own self — her stomach surgeries, her enrollment in a strictly monitored diet plan, the operation in which doctors carved off great hunks of her fat that thrashed in their hands like fish as they carried them to the medical waste garbage can.

'You have got to be kidding me,' Peter said.

I wiped my nose on my sleeve. 'What?'

'A thousand channels, and this is what you watch?'

I didn't answer. Mitzi was trying to get into a taxicab and was having some trouble.

Peter started laughing.

'It's not funny,' I said.

'Yes it is.'

'Peter — ' I said, but then I wasn't sure where to go next. I'd spent an hour and a half already with Mitzi. I'd seen childhood photos of her on the beach, wearing a kid's bikini and matching bandana. I'd seen her blowing out the candles on her fourth birthday. I'd seen her graduation photo, her prom dress, the day she gave birth to her twins. I'd always

24

been able to see beauty in women — except, of course, in myself — and I could see it in her: She had thick, wavy auburn hair. She had a wry tilt to her eyebrow. She had the longest black eyelashes I'd ever seen, and her eyes were so blue they were almost purple. Peter couldn't see her properly, and the documentary filmmakers couldn't, and even Mitzi herself couldn't. But I could.

The year after her husband had died of leukemia, Mitzi just didn't want to leave the house. And then her Pomeranian, LeRoy, got sick, too, and died. Her twins had moved away years earlier. She was all alone. And before she knew it, she had gained a hundred pounds.

'People don't just gain a hundred pounds,' Peter said. 'You have to work at it to get that fat.'

We were at an impasse, really. Because I was with her. I was right there with her. I knew exactly how your body could wander off like a toddler at the supermarket, leaving you racing through the aisles and shouting, 'Where are you? This isn't funny!'

'She didn't choose to be that way,' I told him.

Peter looked right at me and said, 'Nobody forced her to eat all those Ding Dongs.'

He walked over toward the TV and flipped

25

it off. Then he came back, pulled me off the sofa, and started leading me toward the bedroom.

'Peter,' I said, stopping to disconnect the TV cable. 'That's the meanest thing I've ever heard you say.'

When I stepped into our bedroom, I dropped the TV cable in the wastebasket. Peter looked at me like I was crazy, but I left it there. I knew I was better at resisting some temptations than others.

Our pre-children selves might have launched into a rousing discussion from there about women and body issues and our fast-food culture and the meaning of beauty. When we were dating, I had, in fact, given him *The Beauty Myth* to read. And he'd read it. 'Oh, God,' he'd said, when I brought it up once. 'I was so in love.'

'Was!' I said, hitting him on the shoulder.

'Yeah,' he said. 'Was.' Then he grabbed me and threw me down on the bed in a pretend-brutish way that made me laugh and hit him even more.

The selves we were now didn't do a lot of teasing, anymore — or reading, or throwing each other down on the bed. The selves we were now just tried to communicate basic information quickly to keep everything running along. The selves we were now just crawled into bed in our spaghetti-stained T-shirts, turned to opposite sides, and fell asleep.

Or, at least, Peter fell asleep. That night, I lay awake for a long time, watching the shadows on the wall, listening to the new noises, thinking, 'So this is home now.' When I closed my eyes, I pretended we were in our little rented house in Houston, a cottage with a laundry line out back and a brick patio where the kids pedaled around. We'd given our trikes and Big Wheels back to the Salvation Army before we left, since we didn't have room in the U-Haul. I couldn't believe now that we'd left it all behind. That we'd never drive up our little gravel driveway again, or eat dinner at the picnic table at sunset, or lie down under the mimosa tree.

Peter was not from Houston, but he liked it there. He'd moved there for me. We'd gone to college in Ohio and lived there for a few years after graduation. Then one day, out of nowhere, I'd said, 'I'd like to move home to Houston.'

Sweet, agreeable Peter had said, 'Okay.'

And it was as simple as that.

Now I told myself to try to think more like Peter. Any place could become a home if you put your mind to it.

My mind, of course, kept skipping back to

27

that woman in khaki pants in the park. The part of me that was kind to myself kept insisting that Khaki Pants had just seen my oversized shirt and assumed there was a pregnant belly underneath. But the louder part, the mean part, just had confirmation of what it had known all along. I was looking bad. This must have been how it started for Mitzi. She started feeling bad, and she started feeling ashamed, and before she knew it, she had snowballed. Literally.

In the dark, I ran my hands over my post-pregnancy belly, a warm, soft, gelatinous thing that had become a part of my life since having kids just as permanently as the kids themselves. I pressed on it and squeezed it. I had never anticipated how much pregnancy — and the parenting it led to — would age me. The stretch marks on my belly, the wrinkles on my face, the spider veins on my thighs. How had I changed so much so quickly?

Years ago, in college, I remember reading a statistic about women. Asked if they'd rather gain thirty pounds or be hit by a bus, 75 percent of women chose the bus. I was one of them, for sure. I remember thinking that, truly, if I gained thirty pounds, I might as well be run over anyway. Because I'd have no reason to live.

Now, at least thirty pounds later, lying next to my snoring Peter, my hands on my belly, I suddenly wanted to be my old self again so badly that I felt a physical ache in my chest. My pillow got wet with tears as I thought about it. And that was the moment when I knew, as clearly as a person can know anything, that it was time to change my life.

It's a moment that stands clear in my memory: in particular, the rush of excitement that came with the prospect of finding my lost self again. I did not even suspect that night that finding myself might also mean losing my husband.

3

The next morning, before I could even write 'change your life' on my to-do list, my mother called my cell phone to see how our move had gone. I closed my eyes when I heard her voice and tried, for a second, to pretend I was still home in Houston and she was calling to say she was dropping by with a pot of geraniums she'd found on sale.

My mom had the greatest voice — deep, and with an almost imperceptible Colombian accent that she'd worked hard to erase. She sounded almost entirely American with just a hint of something more exotic, and she could not believe that I had no ear for languages. She could do just about any accent — from Australian to Indian, and my brothers and I always used to beg her to show them off when we were kids. She rarely did, though. The only accent she cared to use was American.

This morning, she had several things to tell me — the most important of which, and the one she held back until after she told me that the hibiscus on the patio seemed to be dying, the toilet was backed up in the guest bath, and my youngest brother, Tommy, had just quit his job at the bank, was that she and my father had decided for certain last night that they were also going to be moving.

'What do you mean, 'moving'?' I asked.

'Moving,' she said.

I couldn't wrap my head around it. My parents had lived in the same house since before I was born. My mother started explaining it, but my head was still spinning. My father had been offered a new job — a better job — building a refinery overseas. It was something he had always wanted to do, and so now, suddenly, without even asking my opinion in the matter, they were doing it.

'Where?' I said. 'Where would you move to?'

My mother took a sip of her coffee, and then she said, 'Dubai.'

'I don't even know where that is,' I said.

'Don't be ridiculous, Elena,' my mother said. 'Of course you do.' She was the only person who called me 'Elena' instead of 'Lanie.' Except for Peter, sometimes — when he had something important to say.

I thought about Dubai. 'Middle East,' I said, finally.

'United Arab Emirates.'

'Right,' I said. 'Of course.'

'It's the Las Vegas of the Arab world,' she added, as if everybody knew that.

With a cranky edge in my voice, I said, 'Why can't you just move to the real Las Vegas?'

My mother was not going to let me pout. 'It doesn't matter,' she said, her accent just peeking through. 'Either we live in the same city or we don't.'

I was nursing Baby Sam, the boys were 'unpacking' one of the boxes for me, and Peter was in the spare room — the one that had doors into both our apartment and out to the landing of the stairwell — setting it up as a practice room so he could start giving piano lessons ASAP and earn some money.

We'd all been up since 4:45, when Baby Sam woke for the day. Usually he woke up cheerful and nursed in bed with me for a while before we got going, but this morning he woke up disoriented and cranky. He just fussed and fussed. I blamed the change of atmosphere. Real air was a very different thing from the air-conditioned air my boys had been raised on down in Texas. Real air was much more humid. We all felt like we'd gone underwater. That morning, Baby Sam didn't have to fuss too long before everybody was awake.

'Where did morning go?' Alexander had wanted to know when he shuffled into the living room. 'It's dark outside!'

32

'Where *did* morning go?' Peter said to me.

Peter showered while I watched the kids, then I showered while he made them jelly sandwiches for breakfast. By the time I was dressed, they were all sugared up and ready for action. And Baby Sam was by then inexplicably cheerful. Of course, so much about babies is inexplicable.

Peter was the breadwinner. In Houston, he'd worked as a music librarian and moonlighted as a piano teacher. Before kids, I'd worked as an art teacher at an elementary school and done a little painting of my own on the side. But when I was pregnant with Alexander, Peter had sat down with a calculator and figured out that it would be more expensive to put Alexander in day care than it would be for me to quit my job. That settled it. I would stay home until the kids started kindergarten and then go back to work part-time. It made a lot of sense in theory.

That same night, we'd also drawn up a budget to make sure we could survive on Peter's income. He was the visionary for the budget, but I became the enforcer. I was the one who paid the bills, clipped the coupons, and said no to the kids. 'No, we're not getting that plastic penguin.' 'No, you can't eat that chocolate robot.' 'No, we're not burying that

33

twenty-dollar bill for pirate treasure.'

It had taken us three years to get pregnant with Alexander. For the first year, we were casually trying. The second year, we were officially trying. And by the third year, we were desperately trying. We were gearing up to start all the fertility stuff when Alexander finally happened. The struggling gave us a sense of ourselves as not very fertile people, so it was a pleasant surprise when, just a month after I quit nursing Alexander, we were suddenly pregnant with Toby. He arrived just before Alexander's second birthday, and we thought of him as a lucky surprise.

But our biggest surprise was still waiting for us, because three months after I had Toby — when I was still breast-feeding around the clock; when sex was something Peter and I had just started having in a kind of obligatory way because it was 'good for the marriage'; and when we, just the weekend before, had decided definitively that Peter would get a vasectomy because neither one of us had the slightest interest in having another child — I got pregnant with Baby Sam.

I didn't even know I was pregnant at first. Why would I? I wasn't having periods yet. I wasn't even supposed to be ovulating. Mother Nature was supposed to be giving me a break. And, besides, even though we already had two kids, Peter and I were reproductively challenged. It was something we knew about ourselves the way people knew that they were fast readers or avid campers or lucky bingo players. We just weren't very fertile.

But when the morning sickness set in, I knew. Too nauseated to eat, but not nauseated enough to actually vomit. It's not the kind of feeling you forget. In my ob-gyn's office, Alexander ripping up a home-decorating magazine on the floor and a tiny little newborn-looking Toby nursing in my lap, I said, 'Please tell me this is the stomach flu.'

'You're pregnant!' the doctor said cheerfully, raising his hand for me to give him a high five.

I just looked at his hand, a few inches from my face. 'I can't be,' I said.

He shook his hand a little, trying to rouse me into meeting his enthusiasm. 'You can!' His smile got even brighter. 'You are!'

I let out a deep sigh.

The doctor lowered his hand to his side, realizing he wasn't going to find the delight he was looking for. 'It might not stick,' he then offered, writing something — perhaps, 'patient not embracing the miracle of life' — on his chart.

It wouldn't stick! It couldn't stick! I spent

the rest of that trimester expecting my body to come to its senses. And then, six months later, Baby Sam arrived.

And I will tell you the truth about it: I was a little shell-shocked at first. With my first two babies, it had been love at first sight. But with Baby Sam, for the first few weeks there, I couldn't shake the feeling that I was taking very good care of somebody else's baby. Until the morning he turned three weeks old. That morning, for some reason, I woke before he did and watched him sleeping, just inches from me in the bed. Then he opened his eyes and gazed at me with the most devoted, lovestruck look I'd ever seen. From that day on, he owned me. I was his.

So I was glad to have all these boys. And I was crazy with love for each one of them in ways I never imagined possible before they arrived. But I was also losing my mind a little. One baby with no help is tough. Two is even tougher. But three is just a recipe for insanity. The only thing that held me together had been my mother, who lived ten minutes away and stopped by at least once a day to help with supper or bring a potted hydrangea plant.

Which is why when Peter got into this graduate program in music composition at Brandeis, and when the committee that

36

reviewed his portfolio sent him a personal note of appreciation, and when they told him they were going to give him a free ride and a housing stipend, I burst into tears.

'I'm not going with you,' I said. 'We'll just have to text message.'

'It's only for three years,' he said.

'I'll be dead in three years.'

'No, you won't.'

'Yes, I really will.'

But I was going. This was his big chance. He'd applied before, to this and other schools, and had been turned down or not given enough money. This time around, either he had improved — which was possible (he was always practicing) — or the pool of applicants had shifted. They were throwing money and praise at him now, telling him that his composition portfolio was 'powerful' and 'compelling.' We were going. We just were.

My mother kept her chin up about us leaving town. Even though we saw her every single day, and these were her only grandchildren, and she was so integral to our lives that she could tell you which pair of underwear each boy was wearing on any given day, she didn't react when I told her. She said, with that way she's always had of stating things so firmly that she could almost make them true, 'Three years is nothing.' But in three years, Alexander would be seven, and Baby Sam wouldn't be anything even close to a baby anymore. In three years, she would be sixty-six. In three years, we'd have a new president, a new set of friends and — knock on wood — a new car. Three years was not exactly nothing. But I let it slide.

My mother, herself, had stayed put when raising her kids. She had wanted to stay in one place — the same house, the same schools, the same family friends. When my father, an engineer, got offers for assignments in places like Japan and Malaysia and Bahrain, she just said no.

'How did you pull that off?' I asked her once.

'It was easy,' she said. 'He wasn't going anywhere without us, and we weren't going anywhere.'

They stayed put, as she wanted. My parents were, on the morning she called me, still living in the house they'd bought in 1969. They'd paid $29,000 and had a $217-a-month mortgage payment for twenty-five years.

Now it was all paid off — I pointed out over the phone — and they were moving.

'We're not selling the house!' my mother said, as if I'd asked if she was going to burn all our photo albums. 'We'll just rent it out.'

38

'You're going to take every single thing in that house and wrap it up and put it in storage?' I asked.

'Yes,' she said, as if it were the simplest thing in the world.

We all knew my dad had always wanted to travel. Right from the beginning. And the thing about my mother is that she never planned to have kids. They had met in graduate school for engineering when there was barely even such a thing as a woman engineer. And, to boot, she was this sexy, black-haired girl from Colombia who was so smart she'd come all the way to the States to study. When my dad told the story, she was like Catwoman, purring around the campus, reducing all the male students to mice.

'You're so crazy,' she'd say to my dad, touching his hand. 'You were the cat, not me.' Then she'd stifle a smile. 'But I was no mouse.'

A month after their first kiss, they eloped. And here's the amazing part: Thirty-nine years later, they were still each other's best friends. Their marriage never should have worked. You can't date for a total of four weeks before getting hitched and have the marriage last. But, crazily, theirs had. Something between them was just right, and three grown children later, they were moving to Dubai like newlyweds on a honeymoon.

'It's the right thing to do,' my mother said now.

Whether or not she really wanted to stay home — whether or not she wanted to leave her friends, or her garden, or the country her grandchildren were in — she would never say. My mother was not a person to tolerate things being anything other than how they should be. She had quit her job when I was born, for example, and had never returned. But if it bothered her, you couldn't tell. And now, faced with the fact that my dad really wanted to go, and that my two younger brothers had both left home anyway, and that my father was rubbing shoulders with retirement age and not likely to see a chance like this again, she was not going to look back.

My mother said the neighbors, many of whom had raised their kids alongside us, were throwing my parents a farewell luau in two weeks, to which my father planned to wear a grass hula skirt over his swim trunks. The morning after the party, my parents would board a plane to go live in a country neither of them had ever been to.

'You must have known about this for a while,' I said.

'I wanted to wait until we knew for sure,' she said.

After we hung up, I went to look for Alexander and Toby. Baby Sam had been writhing on my lap during the conversation — nursing, then losing interest, then nursing some more — but the older boys had disappeared, wise to the fact that when I talked on the phone they could get up to all kinds of mischief. I found them in the bathroom with a can of shaving cream and a box of cereal Peter had bought the night before, making a 'sauce' in the tub. They were both soaking wet, and they looked so happy, and the room was such a mess already, that I just closed the bathroom door and let them empty out the can.

My parents. Moving. Alone in Cambridge was bad enough, but alone in Cambridge with my parents on the other side of the world seemed a hundred times worse. 'Don't be ridiculous,' my mother had said. 'We're no more useful to you in Texas than anywhere else.' But the idea of them in Texas was useful to me. The idea of things at our house in Houston moving at the steady comforting pace that they always had — my dad going out each morning at six for his three-mile walk with neighbors Jocelyn and Bill, my mom gardening in the backyard in the same style floral gloves she'd worn since I was an infant — had been more comforting for me than I'd realized.

'Just pretend we're still here, then,' she'd said.

'But you won't be,' I'd said.

'We won't be gone that long.'

'How long?'

'Three years.'

'Right,' I'd said, pouting again. 'Three years is nothing.'

4

I didn't tell Peter about my mother's call, though he was just in the next room. I had a rule for myself that I never went in his practice room when he was working. Otherwise, I'd have been in there constantly. Peter said, 'You don't have to stay out. Come in whenever you need me.' But since having kids, I was far too eager for company to leave something like a visit with Peter up to my own discretion. And there was some part of me that just didn't really respect 'practicing,' anyway. Those pieces he played over and over, they sounded fine to me. I wasn't quite sure what he was working so hard on.

In Houston, my parents had given us their old piano, and so I had heard Peter — or his students — playing just about constantly in the house. In Cambridge, all Peter had was a keyboard and headphones, so I hadn't heard a sound from him all morning. He was supposed to be unpacking and setting up, but I knew from the silence that he was practicing.

I fed some yogurt to Baby Sam and had some myself — standing at the counter, the way I always seemed to eat now — then went to hose down the bathroom and the other boys, who only got along this nicely when they were doing something slightly naughty. By the time I had cleaned up and had the boys rinsed, dried, and dressed, I had that frantic feeling that I needed to get out of the house right away. This apartment was already too small. It was the same square footage as our last house had been, but its towers of still-unpacked boxes and bowling alley layout and lack of a yard made it feel far tinier. Plus it was humid and hot without AC, and, up on the third floor, we collected everybody's heat from below.

But I still needed a shower in a big way. The shower I'd been wanting for two days, as with so many things in my life lately, had escaped me. I set the boys up at the kid table in the kitchen with some colors and paper, giving the important job of making sure Baby Sam didn't chew on the crayons to Alexander, who, as I slipped off to the bathroom, stretched his arms out like an emperor and said, 'Listen to my construc-tions!'

I'd just soaped up my hair when I heard Alexander, on the other side of the curtain, say, 'Mom? We need this towel.' By the time I peeked out, my towel, which had been resting on the back of the toilet, was gone.

'Bring it back, please,' I called.

Nothing.

'Mama needs that towel!' I shouted.

When I got nothing again, I started cajoling, then explaining, then threatening to try to get it back. Finally, I got mad. I got the kind of visceral, fist-shaking mad that only little children, with their particular brand of stubbornness and total disregard for the rules of society, can inspire. I stepped out of the tub dripping wet and started marching through our curtainless house buck naked. It occurred to me that our next-door neighbors might happen to glance out their windows and see me, but I decided it was unlikely. And, to some degree, I didn't care. All I wanted to do at that moment was find those boys, yell at them, and snatch my towel back.

I found Baby Sam alone, chewing on crayons, and the other two under the kitchen table, using the towel in a fort they were building. But before I could yell at them, I remembered — quite suddenly — that Josh the landlord had told me he'd be painting the exterior of our building this morning. I remembered that at the exact moment I found the kids, because just as I'd planted my naked self, hands on hips, in the kitchen, I looked up to see Josh standing outside the window with a paint roller in his hand.

He didn't see me. He was looking at the window trim. But I froze. Then I moved my arm in slow motion until my fingers touched the towel. I pulled it off the fort and wrapped it around myself, wishing like anything it were a giant beach towel — one the size of, say, a bedsheet. Or a circus tent. I don't think the boys even knew I was there. Except Baby Sam, who had seen my naked boobs, his favorite objects in the whole world, and then grunted to be picked up until I lifted him onto my hip and scurried back to my room.

It was a hell of a near miss. As I nursed the baby and then dressed, I realized that it wasn't the nakedness itself that was embarrassing. Giving birth three times and then breast-feeding everywhere from the sporting goods section at Target to the carousel at the zoo had really broadened my perspective on nudity. It wasn't being accidentally nude in front of Josh that had me still blushing twenty minutes later. It was being accidentally nude and *looking bad* in front of Josh that did. It was trying to picture what Josh would have seen if he'd seen anything — which I told myself over and over he hadn't.

There had been a time not too long ago when I had been a perfectly respectable-looking naked person. But since having kids,

I'd been going downhill fast. I was stretched out, I was baggy. I sagged and I bulged. After Alexander, I went up a size — and then, after Toby, at least another. After Baby Sam, I just didn't want to know. I hadn't gone shopping since he was born, and I lived in Peter's old button-down shirts and sweatpants. What did I need to dress up for, anyway? Putting on something nice seemed like begging to be spilled, sneezed, or thrown up on.

After Baby Sam was born, I'd gotten rid of my full-length mirror in what I'd meant as a gesture of kindness to myself, figuring I'd wait to get a new one until I was looking better. But then I never did start looking better. And now I didn't really have a sense of my body anymore. I was off in a kind of body wilderness, echolocating like a bat, eyes closed and sensing my way around. To be truthful, I didn't exactly know what I looked like anymore. But I had some hunches, which was why I'd become a lights-off kind of girl in bed. And why I was so very grateful to Peter's thickly bespectacled ancestors that he truly couldn't see a thing without his glasses.

Josh, though, didn't wear glasses. But I was 95 percent sure he hadn't seen me. Or maybe 85 percent. One thing was certain: It was time to get out of the house.

★　★　★

Fully clothed, I packed up some snacks, snapped Baby Sam into our baby backpack, and herded the other two out the door. We started working our way down the flights of stairs.

Near the bottom, we encountered the Mean Witch. She was in that same mannish bathrobe and looked just about as cranky as she had the night before, but today she was wearing, I must admit, some ultra-stylish Chanel glasses. She was headed back up with her newspaper and, as she squeezed by, said, by way of a greeting, 'Please tell me that baby doesn't wake up screaming every morning at four.'

I should have said, 'Only when we poke him with pins,' or something that would have shown at least a little chutzpah. But all I could come up with was — once again — 'Hi! I'm Lanie.' She paused a minute, I guess to see if I could do any better than that, then kept on her way up the stairs.

At which point Alexander, in a moment so predictable I should have put money on it in advance, turned to me in his loudest, most oblivious voice and said, 'Why does the Mean Witch wear such big shoes? Does she kick people?'

She paused on the steps, but then kept on walking.

I covered. In a voice as loud as Alexander's, I said, 'The Mean Witch from our bath-time story? She has magic feet!'

It was a pretty good save, given what I had to work with. But I could tell from the way the Mean Witch closed her apartment door that she had not been fooled.

I decided to look for a new park. I'd heard someone the day before say something about the park near Fresh Pond. I'd seen a street sign for Madison, and we were going to find that park. I strapped Alexander and Toby in, plied them with raisins and cheese bunnies, and decided we were going to need a better stroller. In Houston, we'd driven everywhere: to the park, to the grocery, sometimes even to the mail box at the end of our street. Everything was so spread out, there was really nowhere to walk to. Plus we'd had a backyard with a swing set. Leaving the house often seemed like asking for trouble.

But here, it was different. It was a walking town. At the end of our block, we had a bakery, a pizza shop, a grocery store, a book store, an antique shop, an ice cream stand, a bank, and a tattoo parlor. And there was no parking, anyway. And the roads in this town were so tangled up and crazy, they looked like they'd been laid out by ferrets. Not to mention those kamikaze roundabouts everywhere. I was happy not to drive. Strolling made much more sense.

I resolved to look on eBay for a cheap jogging stroller. Because we had no money. We'd had very little money back when Peter was working at the music library, and now, with him in school, we had even less. We had the opposite of money. Our only cash would come from his teaching assistantship and whatever piano lessons he managed to set up. Plus our little savings account, which was already destined for a speedy death. And it never even occurred to me to ask my parents for money. My brothers, David and Tommy, borrowed enough for all of us.

I had decided, years back when I quit working, to take a Mary Poppins approach to being broke and make a game out of it. I imagined myself like the thrifty main character of a movie, using my noggin to make being penniless hip. Everything we owned came from resale shops and garage sales. And though I always found great kids' clothes for absolutely nothing at thrift stores, great furniture was a little trickier. We had some very cool, retro-looking things in our house, like the Dick Van Dyke-style coffee table (seven dollars) and the wicker chaise longue with the broken back foot (twenty dollars). We also had a lot of bad, bland, office-y looking stuff. The Formica end table. The vinyl armchair. The polyester rug I'd found for thirty-five dollars at, of all places, the grocery store.

In the end, I decided it couldn't really be done. You can't really furnish a terrifically hip apartment for next to nothing. Especially not when that apartment is also ankle-deep with trucks, Legos, puzzles, balls, Play-Doh, and a million other unsightly kid things. I had just decided, instead of worrying about it, to turn off the part of my brain that cared about being stylish or impressing others with my decor. Given our circumstances these days, we just had to be frumpy.

I told myself it didn't matter. I wasn't defined by my furniture, for crying out loud. But Peter and I had a tendency to make friends with people who made far more money than we did. And had far better houses. And better furniture. It was hard not to feel some envy.

'They aren't happier,' Peter said once.

'They're a little bit happier,' I said.

'No,' he told me. 'I read an article about it. The more things people have, the more things they want. People who win the lottery wind up depressed and suicidal.'

I shook my head. 'I'd wind up happy.'

'No,' he said. 'You'd be miserable like everybody else.'

Somehow this prediction did not strike me as very supportive. 'Do you mean this is as happy as I will ever be?'

'Yep,' he said, pleased to have the inside scoop. 'Enjoy it.'

I'd been pushing the kids along the sidewalk up a long, gradual hill. Our double stroller had those wiggly front wheels that went sideways in every sidewalk crack. And, with Baby Sam in the backpack, by the time I got to the top of the hill, I was winded. I stopped for a minute in front of a hardware store to rest.

It was a very short rest. I couldn't have stood in that spot for longer than sixty seconds. But, in that time, amazingly, I managed to poke two straws into two juice boxes, hand a bread-stick back to Baby Sam in the backpack, and look up to see none other than Josh walking toward us. He hesitated midstride when he saw me. I raised my hand in a wave and gave myself this pep talk: *He did not just see you naked. There was surely a glare on the window. And he was concentrating on his work. Your luck is bad, but not that bad.*

'Hey, Lanie,' he said, bobbing his shaggy head a little.

'Hey,' I said.

'Out for a walk?' he said.

I clearly was. 'Yep.'

'Great day for it,' he said.

'Sure is,' I said.

'I needed some supplies,' he offered, holding up his bag as if he needed to explain himself.

Then we ran out of things to say. He made a couple of slow nods, and I did, too. And just as I was about to say, 'Well, see ya,' he leaned in a little bit and said, 'I didn't see anything, by the way.'

'Didn't see anything when?' I shouldn't have even asked. A half a second slow on the uptake and I'd dug myself a conversational grave.

'Before,' he said, gesturing toward our building with his head. 'When you were naked in your kitchen.'

5

The boys and I never did find the park. But between our house and the place where I thought a park ought to be, we found something else. A gym.

We were on our way home, the big boys getting restless in the stroller and Baby Sam drumming on my head with breadsticks, when I saw it. The place was called Fitness Express, with a train logo and the motto: 'We think you can.' It seemed to me like a gesture from the universe, and, without even pausing, I pushed our double stroller right toward the doors and wrestled it through.

Once in, I walked over to the beefy man at the entry kiosk, crumbs from Baby Sam's breadsticks all over my head, and said, 'How much is a membership?'

Now, it takes some guts, I think, to walk into a place like that when you are feeling as frumpy and self-conscious as I was on that day. I didn't know what the people on the other side of the lobby doors looked like, but I knew they didn't have yogurt stains on their shirts or raisins ground into their pants pockets. I had never been in a gym before, but it seemed like a pretty sure bet that I didn't belong in one.

But, at that moment, at least, I felt determined to become the kind of person who did belong. The faux-pregnancy debacle had catapulted me toward a frenzy of self-improvement, and I was damn sure going to make the most of it. I wanted a gym bag. I wanted a crisp, non-nursing sports bra. I wanted to pull my hair back into a no-nonsense ponytail and strut right through the lobby like I'd been there a thousand times.

The guy at the counter told me it was $149 to sign up, which was exactly half of everything we had in our savings account. On another day, I would have walked right back out. I never even splurged on toenail polish for myself. So it shocked even me when I threw our budget to the wind. Even though I had trained myself to ask before every purchase if I *needed* something or just *wanted* it, I didn't even hesitate on the membership fee. I said, 'Sounds good,' and handed over my only credit card.

I wasn't totally clear about what joining the gym would mean. Would everyone there feel a sense of camaraderie? Would we wear matching sweat suits? Would I come to think of these people here as some kind of very energetic extended family? The questions flittered past me, but I wasn't too worried about the answers. I was so rarely certain about anything, but I was certain about this. It was a good thing to do.

That night, before dinner, Peter gave me a chocolate bar.

'Dammit, Peter,' I said.

'What?'

'You aren't supposed to bring me chocolate anymore. We talked about this.'

'We did?'

'Yes!' I put my hands in my hair.

'What if I want to do something nice for you?'

'Then bring me something that is not chocolate.'

'Flowers?' he asked.

'Yes!' I said. 'Except they're expensive. And they just die in the vase and turn brown. So maybe something else.'

I could tell I'd stumped him. So I pushed on and told him about joining the gym.

'You did?' he said. 'Why?'

'It's only thirty dollars a month.'

And Peter said, 'Can we afford that?'

And I nodded with such an expression of certainty on my face that Peter didn't even really notice when I said, 'Sort of.'

'We can't afford flowers,' Peter said. 'But

we can afford a health club membership.'

'That's right,' I said. 'That's exactly right.'

There was still some negotiating to be done about time. Now that we had children, we were both operating at such a deficit of personal time that we had become a little bit Grinch-ish, negotiating our hours of freedom with peevishness and precision.

Here's what I wanted: for Peter to be 'in charge' of the kids after bedtime so that we could put them to bed at night, and I could head out to the gym to jog (or walk, or hide in the locker room) for an hour.

Here was the sticking point: If Peter was in charge, that meant he had to listen for wake-ups — whether it was the baby crying in the crib or Alexander wetting the bed. Which meant he couldn't wear his head-phones. Which meant he couldn't practice.

Peter tried to suggest just wearing one of his earphones — literally keeping an ear out for the kids — and it was so funny to me that he didn't know himself better by now. When Peter was practicing, or composing, or sometimes even just thinking about music, the outside world often ceased to exist for him. All other sounds fell away. His ears turned inward. And though it was sweet that he thought the sound of his children crying might penetrate his ears, he was wrong. When

57

Peter was in the zone, his ears were impenetrable.

Practicing put Peter in the zone. And since he practiced every night obsessively for hours and hours, losing an hour and a half of that time just really seemed to blow his mind.

'I don't understand,' he'd said after dinner. 'You're really joining a gym?'

'Yes,' I answered.

'But what are you going to do there?'

'I'm going to exercise, Peter. Like everybody else.'

'I've just never seen you go to a gym before.'

And here, I wanted to say, 'You've never seen me as a frumpy housewife before,' but I held back. There was, at least, an off chance that he hadn't noticed the ill effects of pregnancy, sleep deprivation, and stay-at-home parenting on my body, and I certainly wasn't going to be the one to bring these things to his attention. I figured Peter must have viewed me with gentler eyes than I viewed myself. If he saw me the way I saw myself, he'd have left me a long time ago.

Even after he was on board with the exercise concept, he was still struggling with the babysitting.

'What am I supposed to do with myself all that time?' he asked.

'You could clean the kitchen for me,' I offered. It didn't really answer his question, but it shut him right up.

And the next thing I knew, that very same night, the boys were all asleep, and I was walking up our long street toward the gym. No gym bag. No fancy sneakers. And, sadly, just an old nursing bra that had lost most of its hooks. But I had Peter's iPod (a gift from his folks), I'd downloaded some workout music from a site called PumpYourselfUp.com, and I was ready to rock.

At the swinging door from the lobby into the gym itself, I felt a tickle of nervousness in my chest, but I pushed through.

It was less Olivia Newton-John than I'd been expecting. I'd anticipated spiky hair, neon headbands, shimmery spandex leotards — and maybe a leg warmer or two. Instead, it was a gray office building with exposed brick walls and fluorescent lights. It was understated. A few ficus trees and some cubbies and it could have been an office in New Jersey. And the people seemed quiet and mild-mannered. Except for the sweat, the breathing, and the Beyoncé, these folks could have been surfing the Internet at work.

And with that quick evaluation, I scurried to a treadmill, eager to fade into the background as quickly as possible. I got on. I turned on the iPod. I started jogging. Just one foot in front of the other. I cranked up the speed until I was jogging in step with the music. And that was it! I was exercising!

I should mention that I was not a total stranger to exercise. Before we had kids, I had been a casual kind of three-or-four-times-a-week jogger. But I'd always been a little snooty about gyms. It just seemed strange to me to pay all that money for something like going on a jog. Jogging, I thought, should be done outdoors and — most important — for free. Why anybody would pay money to jog in place in a hot room with lots of other sweaty people, I could not fathom.

But, back then, I also used to jog during the morning hours. The sun was up, people were commuting to work, and I figured the scary men who might prey on joggers were fast asleep. Now I would be jogging at night. It was dark by the time the kids were asleep. Nighttime was a whole different thing. And so, the gym. Hot, sweaty, way too close to other exercising people, but safe. At least, safe enough. All I had to do was get the hang of the treadmill, where balance turned out to be tricky.

I had to keep my eyes in one place to keep from getting wobbly. Later, I'd observe that most everybody in the gym had the balance thing down. People read while jogging, or chatted with a friend on the next machine, or watched TV. One woman carried little hand weights. Another shook her finger like a band leader to the music on her headphones. A man in a T-shirt that said YOU ASKED FOR IT, YOU GOT IT turned around every few minutes and walked backward. Hardly anybody had to concentrate on it as hard as I did. But, that first night, it was okay. I was happy just to stay on.

And then I fell off.

My very first trip to my very first gym, and within twenty minutes of stepping onto the treadmill, I went flying off the back like skeet. I had thought I felt something under my foot and, like a person out on a real road might do, I stopped to look down. But, of course, I wasn't on a real road. I was George Jetson on a conveyor belt. The next thing I knew, I was on the floor with belt burns on my elbows.

The woman on the machine next to me turned without stopping and, as if shouting down a ravine, called out a horrified, 'Are you okay?'

'I'm good,' I said, waving her back to her workout. A few other people glanced back at me, but for the most part, they either didn't hear, or didn't want to acknowledge, my fall.

I stayed on the floor. The fall had deflated

me. I didn't belong here. What kind of a goober falls off a treadmill? I decided to go home. I was looking for a back exit and wondering if I could get my money back when someone came up behind me and lifted me to my feet. As it was happening, I assumed it was one of the chiseled, spiky-haired trainers, acting as a kind of lifeguard. And I felt so thankful to be rescued like that, for someone who belonged here to literally get me back on my feet. I felt a rush of gratitude for whoever had decided I should not have to pick myself up off the floor alone.

But when I turned, I did not find a buff trainer in workout gear. I found the opposite: the goofiest-looking person in the gym.

It wasn't his face or his body, which were handsome enough. It was his clothes and his hair. Midforties, he wore an untucked plaid button-down, jogging shorts, and flip-flops. He had wet blue eyes that looked a little like he'd been crying. He had a five o'clock shadow, I'd later come to know, at all hours of the day. And he had wavy, seventies-looking, overgrown, Ted Koppel hair that looked like he'd settled on a hairdo in high school and had never looked back. A room full of normal people in Nike and Adidas, and I had to be rescued by the weirdo.

I couldn't think of what to say.

He was a little sweaty from his workout. He pointed at me and said, 'Careful!'

I nodded, and said, 'Yes,' as if I were making a mental note not to fly off the treadmill again.

Then he asked, 'First time?'

I stared at him.

He said, 'I haven't seen you here before.'

'First time,' I nodded.

He crossed his arms over his chest. 'I can't imagine anything more humiliating than flying off the back of the treadmill.'

I nodded again.

'All these people,' he went on, looking around, 'looking at you like you're a total idiot.'

I drew in a breath to reply, but then wasn't quite sure what to say. I froze for a second, lungs full of air, and into that little pause stepped one of the trainers at the gym. To be precise: the sexiest, flirtiest of them all. The kind of man you almost dread talking to because you have to rise to his perfection, and the effort is exhausting. Though at this moment, his showing up was pure relief. He was saving me from Ted Koppel, and I felt a burst of gratitude.

'Saw you go flying,' the Sexy Trainer said. Then he put his hand on my shoulder. 'You are a lawsuit waiting to happen.'

And so I said, 'People are always telling me that.'

He tilted back and laughed much louder than I'd expected him to. Then he offered to show me how to use the treadmill, as if my little tumble had been, simply, the result of lack of training. I accepted his offer. I liked that notion. Of course I'd fallen off! Nobody had even shown me how to work the thing yet!

The Sexy Trainer took my hand and eased me back into place, and then I nodded earnestly as he showed me how to start, stop, speed up, slow down and, basically, put one foot in front of the other.

Then he cranked the machine up to a sprinter's pace, jerked his head toward the belt, and said, 'Hit it!'

What could I do? I straddled the belt, watching it rush under me like a river for a second. Then I stepped back on and ran my ass off.

'Attagirl!' the Sexy Trainer said. As he spoke, he looked away and stepped closer to my treadmill at the same time. And then, I swear, while glancing over at his next appointment across the room and seeming to forget me completely, he did something that I still wonder about to this day. He slapped my ass.

And then he was gone, loping across the gym toward a woman in velour sweatpants. And then I was alone — with my ass — suddenly noticing that Ted Koppel had staked out some territory on the treadmill next to mine and was sauntering along at a window-shopping pace. I kept on sprinting until the Sexy Trainer was out of sight, and then I slowed the belt down to a gentle jog. That was my rule for myself. I always had to stay on for an hour, even tonight. Even though my elbows were stinging and I had a total stranger's handprint on my ass.

How long had it been since I'd had anybody's hand on my ass? Peter's, even? I wasn't sure. With Peter, it could have been last week, or last month, or last year. There were so many people in my house all over my body at every waking hour, it was hard to separate out all the touching. But outside of my immediate family, my ass — my body in general — was pretty much on its own. I had been with Peter since we were in college. I was twenty when we met in an art class, and I fell for him so hard I might as well have been on fire. Now I was thirty-five. For fifteen solid years, my ass had belonged to Peter.

Who did this trainer think he was? Had I just been harassed? Maybe I really was a lawsuit waiting to happen. Maybe I could sue this gym and solve all our financial worries in one self-righteous swoop. Or had this guy been slapping my ass in the way that athletes do? Football players, for example, as they walk off the field. Maybe he was trying to welcome me into a community of treadmill-walking, StairMaster-climbing, elliptical-trainer-bouncing, ass-slapping gym enthusiasts. Maybe it was just a hello. Something he did as a matter of course. Something I was overreacting to. Something I should have felt flattered by.

That's when Ted Koppel leaned closer to tell me something. 'He does that a lot,' he said, and I couldn't tell if he was trying to make me feel better or worse. He went on, 'He never passes up a nice ass.'

And the only thing I could think of to say to that was, as strange as it felt, 'Thank you.'

I spent a good while that night fantasizing about what I'd do with the million dollars we could win in a lawsuit but, in the end, I decided to suck it up. Mostly because I wasn't going to let my ass get in the way of my self-improvement goals. But partly also, I must admit, to my own horror, because I loved, in a way that felt like an awakening, the fact that I had an ass, and that someone had noticed it, and that it had been nice enough to want to slap.

6

It was a great walk home from the gym that first night. My body was humming. My muscles were literally twitching. I was sweaty, and I took breaths in deep, gentle swoops. I knew myself too well to think anything in life was ever going to be easy. But despite my scraped elbows, damp hair, and muscles that were sure to be sore by morning, every single part of me felt just plain good.

And then I reached our door. And, like in a horror movie, before I even touched the knob, I knew from the eerie silence in the hallway that something during my brief absence had gone terribly, terribly wrong.

I stepped in. The apartment was quiet. Nobody was crying, which seemed like a good sign. I took off my shoes and tiptoed to find Peter and get the report. He wasn't in the kitchen, where I stopped for a glass of water. He wasn't in the living room, our bedroom, or the practice room. Had he gone out and left the boys alone? He wouldn't have done that. I checked the little back porch off the kitchen. I checked the balcony off the master bedroom bay window. And then I checked the bathroom. And that's when I knew, before I even turned on the light, that somebody had thrown up.

Flipping the switch confirmed it. The floor was piled with dirty towels. Judging from the height of the stack, somebody had thrown up a lot. I flipped the light back off and closed the door, and then turned, there in the hall, to find Peter coming out of the boys' room a few feet away.

He was — and I say this without exaggerating — covered in vomit. It was in his hair. It was on his T-shirt and his jeans. It caked his neck. His hands. His shoes. His belt buckle.

'Who was it?' I whispered, masking my grossed-out expression with a totally over-done look of sympathy.

He looked at me for a long time, his hand still on the bedroom knob. Then, at last, he said — in a tone that conveyed not only his exhaustion, his despair, his pride at having handled a catastrophe of such magnitude all on his own, and his solidifying opinion that none of this would have happened at all if I hadn't gone out for the night — 'All of them.'

'What?' I asked, in too loud of a voice.

He shushed me and steered me into the living room.

'All of them,' he confirmed, as soon as we were out of earshot. Then, without waiting for a reaction, he took off his shirt and headed toward our bedroom. Something in his posture as he walked told me exactly what he was thinking: that none of our children ever vomited when I was there to watch them.

'I'm sorry,' I said, following him.

He didn't answer. Just peeled off the rest of his clothes and dropped them on the rug. Right next to the hamper.

I couldn't help it. I said, 'Hamper?'

He turned to look at me.

I gestured at the clothes. 'Or do we want vomit chunks on the floor?'

He sighed a deep, slow sigh, like I was really kicking him when he was down. Looking back, keeping the floor chunk-free at that moment might not have been the most important thing.

'Never mind,' I said, wishing I hadn't spoken. But he was already bending, lifting the pile, and dropping it in the hamper like a dead thing.

'Now we'll have chunks in the hamper, too,' he said.

'Kind of a twofer,' I added, but he didn't smile.

I squatted on the floor and collected pieces of vomit with my fingers — noting in a casual way that I'd finally reached the stage in parenting where this did not turn my stomach — while he told me what had happened.

It started with Baby Sam, who Peter had heard crying on the monitor. He went in, checked his diaper, and was just about to put him back in the crib when he heard a rushing noise as the baby vomited directly into his ear. Peter cleaned most of it up, covered the rest with towels, and reoutfitted him — all without waking the two older boys. Baby Sam cried loudly during the whole thing, but once it was time to rock to sleep, he was ready, and he conked back out fast.

Peter hadn't been out of the room ten minutes when Alexander appeared in the bathroom where Peter was washing up, and, looking very sleepy and calm, said, 'Dad? I vomited in the hallway.'

'Okay,' Peter said, in the nonchalant tone parents use when the shit is hitting the fan. 'I'll clean that up. Why don't you crawl back into bed?'

'Well,' Alexander said, in his best bedtime stalling voice. 'I vomited in the bed, too.'

So back in Peter went. He changed the sheets, got new PJs for Alexander, tucked him in, and stroked his forehead until he dozed back off. Peter was just standing up to sneak out when Toby, on the top bunk, sat up and said, 'Dada?'

'Hey, Tobes,' Peter said. 'You feeling okay?'

In reply, Toby threw up on his head. Peter said it was like standing under a downspout. 'It was,' he told me, as he tried to scoop out his ear with a Q-tip, 'a tsunami of barf.'

Peter was putting Toby back to bed, on new sheets and in new PJs, when he heard me open the door.

'I thought it smelled kind of funky in here,' I said.

He said, 'Wait till you smell the vomit-orium.'

'The clean-up towels are on the bathroom floor — ' I started.

'And all the sheets are in the tub,' he finished.

I gathered every vomit-soaked linen I could wrap my arms around to take down to the basement to wash, as Peter waited — buck naked in the hallway — for me to clear out so he could take a shower.

'Peter?' I said, peeking over the fuming sheets in my arms as we passed each other.

'What?' His eyes were tired. There's nothing like a parenting crisis after bedtime to knock the wind out of you.

I held his gaze for a minute, trying to think of something I could say at that moment to

71

thank him for his help, to acknowledge that looking after young children was truly exhausting, and to remind him that it would all be worth it in the end. Finally, I settled on: 'You've got a great ass.'

★ ★ ★

Here's what I need to confess about Peter and me: We were not exactly in love anymore. After fifteen years and three children together, we were often other places besides *in* it. We were under it, sometimes. Or above it. Or against it. Or in arm's reach of it. Or in shouting distance of it. Or rubbing shoulders with it. But not in it. Not lately. Not since Baby Sam was born. Baby Sam was, you might say, the straw that broke the Love Camel's back. And now that camel was lying in the desert in the baking sun. All alone and very thirsty.

I hate to say it, but I will. Children, despite their infinite charms, are an absolute assault on a marriage. They don't mean to be, but they are. We'd held up pretty well under the siege, and there was certainly still a lot of love, but it was nothing like the crazy, tingly, I-can't-breathe-without-you love we'd kicked things off with. Those early years, those college years, those pre-children years — they were a good, good time.

I'd had one of those totally irrational, teen-idol crushes on Peter long before I knew anything about him. Junior year, he lived in the dorm next door, and I'd see him around a lot — on the path to the library, at the bike rack, in line for bagels in the cafeteria. Every time I saw him, I swear to you, my hands started shaking. I had to stare at the ground just to keep my balance.

Crushes like that don't even make sense. All I knew about Peter was what he looked like, and the curve of his long fingers as he held his charcoal pencil in our Life Drawing class, and the flip of his shaggy hair, and the robin's egg blue T-shirt he wore sometimes that said I'M NOT LISTENING. I had never even spoken to him, except for one time, at the library, when he had been walking out the door with his girlfriend just as I was walking in, and we bumped shoulders. We both said, 'Sorry,' at the same time, and our eyes caught each other's.

That was it for me. That one brush against his wool sweater, and I couldn't get through even one page of *The Marx-Engels Reader* all day. One look from Peter, and I forgot how to read.

My friend Connor thought crushes like that were the truth of two souls recognizing each other. But I didn't believe in souls. Not, at least, when it came to infatuation.

'That's ridiculous,' I said. I was sure I was just being shallow. That I just liked him because he was cute.

'He's not that cute,' she said. And then, 'He's about on par with Rob Garrison or Steven McFarland. Why aren't you on fire for them?'

'I don't know,' I said. Then I shrugged, knowing how lame my answer sounded: 'His eyes?'

But it was just what she wanted. 'His eyes!' she said, pointing at me. 'And what do you see in those eyes?'

She wanted me to say 'soul.' She thought she had me cornered. 'Oh, you know,' I said. 'Standard stuff. Pupils. Irises. A little sleep in the corner.'

Peter was friends with Connor a little bit because they lived on the same floor. When Peter broke up with his girlfriend, Connor called me with the news, and she and I drank champagne in her room to celebrate and then walked out to the frozen pond near the field house. There, my breath making steam against the blue night air, I confessed everything to her: the way I woke up an hour early on the days I had Life Drawing to shave my legs in the shower.

The way he'd stood in front of me in line at the post office and I'd gotten so breathless I'd had to leave. The way he'd brushed against me in the stairwell of Biological Sciences and, in response, I had felt so lovesick I'd had to rest my head against the cool window glass to keep from throwing up. It couldn't be love, I told Connor. It was too horrible.

'That's exactly love!' she said. 'Love is exactly that horrible!'

She wanted to match-make, now that he was free. But I choked with fear at the idea of it, and I suddenly couldn't believe that I'd mapped out my entire obsession for her. What had I been thinking? How well did I even know Connor, anyway? I made her swear secrecy about everything I'd ever said to her.

'Even on unrelated topics?' she asked. 'Place of birth? Favorite foods?'

'On everything,' I said. 'As far as you're concerned, I don't even exist.'

On the walk back, I insisted we change topics. But then Connor said, 'Can I just tell you one other thing?'

'Make it quick.'

She told me that she'd heard Peter broke up with his girlfriend because he liked somebody else.

'Why didn't you tell me this earlier?' I asked.

'I was saving it for last,' she said. Then she started poking me in the ribs through my coat. 'Maybe it's you!' she said. 'I think it might be you.'

'It can't be me,' I said. 'That never happens. Crushes are never reciprocated. That's the definition of crush.'

'I'm going to ask him who it is,' she said.

'Please don't.'

'Why not?'

'Because once I know it's not me, then I'll know it's not me.'

'But you just said it couldn't possibly be you.'

'It can't,' I said. 'But it's one thing to think that, and another thing to know it for sure.'

'You're a crazy girl,' she said.

'Promise me you won't ask him.'

'I promise,' she said.

But then she asked him. She came up to me at breakfast the next morning. She was on her way out, and I was on my way in. We stood near the coffee urn, tray to tray, and she said in a stage-whisper, 'I know who it is.'

I'm pretty sure I actually gasped. 'Who is it?'

'I thought you didn't want to know.'

I gave her a look.

She gave a quick sigh, and then said, 'Well, I can't tell you.'

'You have got to be joking.'

She shrugged and then said, 'I promised I wouldn't tell.'

'You promised me you wouldn't ask!'

'But this is kind of a deal breaker, he-won't-be-my-friend-anymore-if-I-don't-keep-my-word kind of thing.'

'I won't be your friend anymore if you don't tell me.'

She sized me up for a minute. Then she said, 'Yes, you will.'

I set my tray down on the metal rack with a little too much force. My coffee spilled and ran across it. 'I can't believe this!' I said.

'I can't tell you,' she insisted again. 'But I can do something else.'

I eyed her.

'Come to my room at four o'clock.'

I shook my head. 'I have a class at four.'

'Skip it. Come anyway.'

I watched her face.

'Do it,' she urged, and then kissed my cheek good-bye.

In the end, I skipped my class. The Art and Architecture of Ancient Egypt and Mesopotamia was no match for information about Peter. I had a C in that class, anyway. And even though after breakfast I had decided that Connor was a sadist and a bad friend, at four o'clock that afternoon I was sitting on her Laura Ashley comforter, drinking a cup of Lemon Zinger she'd brewed in her hot pot.

When there was a knock at the door, Connor said, 'Come in,' and winked at me. The door opened, and it was Peter. Even though I'd suspected she was up to something, I had not imagined it would involve Peter in the flesh. My hands started shaking as soon as I saw his face. I almost dropped my mug.

And what followed was, in truth, one of the greatest moments of my entire romantic life. What followed was a moment that I have replayed in my head so many times, the memory is now like a scratched and flickering old movie clip. Peter stepped into the room, clearly expecting to see only Connor, saying something like, 'So, what did you — '

And then, just then, he looked up and saw me there, trembling mug in hand, and as his eyes met mine, he totally and completely forgot what he was talking about. He froze with his mouth open. He was speechless. For ten seconds, he stood with his hand on the doorknob. Ten terrifying, euphoric, deeply satisfying seconds.

And then it was too much. I had to do something. I lifted my hand and waved. It broke the moment. He regrouped. He raised his hand, too, and then turned to Connor. 'I've got a — ' He gestured to the door and stepped back. 'I've got a thing now. But I'll be sure — ' He moved his foot over the threshold into the hallway. 'To catch you later.' The door clunked closed. He did not say good-bye.

We waited, utterly still, a good two minutes, mouthing 'Oh, my God!' at each other without making a sound. Then Connor tiptoed over to the door and peeked into the hallway to make sure he was gone, turned with her arms in a victory sign, and we both started to jump around and scream. We were so loud that the girl next door, a senior with a single, had to bang on the wall.

Connor was louder than I was. 'It's you!' she kept saying. 'It's you that he likes!'

'Yeah, but you already knew that,' I said, as we settled back onto her bed.

'Actually,' she said, with a flirty smile. 'I never asked him.'

I was too happy to react. Who cared?

She went on. 'I just knew you'd never skip that class unless I had something good.'

'Well,' I said, looking back at the place where Peter had just been standing. 'That was something good.'

'It sure was,' she said.

We stayed in Connor's room a long time after that. I kept wanting to relive the moment. I kept saying, 'He totally forgot what he was going to say!' And then, 'What do you think that means?' I knew exactly what she thought it meant, because she thought it meant what I thought it meant, but I loved to hear her say, over and over, 'I think it means he likes you!'

7

There was no more vomiting that first night I'd gone to the gym. I startled awake at every sound on the monitor, but nothing. The next morning, everybody was fine. No fevers, no discernible nausea. We gave everybody Pedialyte in sippy cups for breakfast and waited for round two, but nothing came. By the time we were all dressed, Peter had decided that the whole thing had been a mass protest against my going out.

'Right,' I said.

Later in the morning, as I was heating up a second breakfast of chicken broth for the boys, Peter, who had already 'left' to go work in his office and who had a piano student from the university arriving at nine, popped his head back in the kitchen.

'I've lost a stack of papers,' he said, and I pointed to a pile on the counter, semi-obscured by a plastic truck and a box of cereal.

'Right,' he said, and picked the pile up quickly, trying to get back out of the kitchen before the boys really registered that he was there. He swung back around to dash out the door, and an envelope fell to the floor. I'd seen this envelope before, in other years. It was the application for the Hamilton Fellowship. Peter had been trying for it since college.

'You're not applying for that thing this year, are you?' I asked, as he bent to pick it up. It was a three-week residency that took place over Christmas. People who won it got to spend the holidays writing in seclusion at UCLA, and then the week after the new year playing their compositions for crowds of adoring musicians. It was the most prestigious fellowship out there.

He didn't understand why I was asking. 'Sure. Sure, I am.'

Sometimes Peter teased me with a straight face. He'd tell me the movie was sold out when it wasn't, or that he'd eaten the last cookie when he hadn't. He was good, but I was better, and after all these years I'd learned to spot the place near his nostril that dimpled whenever he was faking. I looked at his nose. No dimple.

'You're not serious,' I said, shifting into spelling-words-out mode as I geared up to disagree. I did not want the boys to think it was being with them I objected to. 'You're not leaving me a-l-o-n-e with three b-o-y-s at C-h-r-i-s-t-m-a-s time.' I wanted it to be all statement, but it was also part question.

'No,' he said.

'Because you wouldn't do that.'

'No,' he said, shaking his head slowly. Then he added, 'Unless I got the fellowship.'

I put my hands on my hips. Baby Sam, who looked very Flock of Seagulls that day with his hair going everywhere, was shaking his sippy cup so violently that broth was spurting out the top like an automatic sprinkler. The other two had taken the straws from their juice cups and were blowing bubbles in their bowls.

'I'll never actually win,' Peter said.

'Good,' I said, 'because you're not l-e-a-v-i-n-g me at Christmas. Not with no family and no help in a strange city.'

'Right,' he said, now antsy to get moving.

'So why even apply?' I pressed.

'I have to apply,' he said.

'Why?'

'In case I win.'

'But you just said you weren't going to.'

'I'm not. Do I ever win?'

'So why apply?'

'Because if I won, it would make my career.'

'Haven't we done enough for your career lately?'

I didn't want to feel so angry. I wanted to

be good enough at parenting, self-sufficient enough, that I could just say 'Go,' and mean it. I wanted for Peter and me to be able to pursue our dreams without having to worry about details like family and Christmas. But that wasn't how it was anymore.

He paused. 'It's for three weeks. It's not that big a deal.'

'It's for three weeks, and that's a huge f-u-c-k-i-n-g deal.'

Now he was getting mad. 'Are you saying you'd stop me from doing the most important thing that could ever happen to my career?'

'I'm saying you promised not to l-e-a-v-e me at Christmas.'

'But that was before.'

'Before what?'

'Before I won the fellowship.'

There was a knock on the office door. His student. It was time for Peter to escape.

I pointed out, 'You haven't won the fellowship.'

'Believe me,' Peter said. 'I know that.' Then he kissed each boy on the head and was off to greet his student and think about other things. I, of course, stayed right there, the conversation echoing in my ears. I took the soup pot and dropped it into the sink with a great clatter.

Then Alexander said, 'Mama?'

'What is it, handsome?' I said, trying to shift my voice from shrill housewife to soothing mother.

'Can I have some more soup?'

'Let's see how your tummy does with that,' I said. 'We'll have some more a little later.'

Alexander relinquished his empty bowl, and as I reached out to take it, he said, again, 'Mama?'

'Yes, cutie?'

'You won't be alone at Christmas. I'll keep you company.'

★ ★ ★

That was our first week in Cambridge. After that, we settled in. We unpacked and unpacked and unpacked — and still barely made a dent in the tower of boxes in the living room. We found the discount grocery store and the Salvation Army. We put away dishes and bath towels and books. We painted lots of pictures to hang on the walls. We found another park — a bit more of a walk, but with an apple red slide and two bouncy sheep to ride on. We found a double jogging stroller, by a great stroke of luck, at a garage sale, and then sold our other one online to help make up the cost.

I'd had the grand idea that we could tape newspaper pages on our windows and make custom shades — leaving spaces near the top so we could see the sky — and then fingerpaint them. But, in the end, the prospect of all that paint all over the floor and the boys and the furniture tuckered me out, and we never painted the pages. The newspapers stayed up, though, and over the coming months my eyes would scan the headlines over and over: 'Man Steals Birthday Cake,' 'Daycare Goes Broke,' and 'Lab Rats Eat Selves to Death.'

The boys and I tromped around the city — big boys in the new jogger and Baby Sam up in the backpack — exploring for as long as they'd tolerate being still. The new stroller was easy to push and impossible to turn, which kept me on my toes. I stashed a pile of flyers for Peter's music lessons in its pouch, and whenever I could, I stopped at telephone poles to put them up with packing tape.

I had convinced Peter to put his photo on the flyers, insisting that he had far more sex appeal than the woodcut image of piano keys he'd started with, and within a few days, we'd decorated almost every pole in the neighborhood with Peter's handsome face. I had taken that photo in our old backyard in Houston, and his blue eyes, even in black and white on a photocopied flyer, were incandescent. It made me happy to see the flyers around the neighborhood. It made me feel a little bit less alone.

Though, of course, I wasn't alone. I was, in fact, never alone. I couldn't even sit on the toilet without holding the baby on one leg and one of the boys and a book on the other. I talked to them all day, played with them, joked around. Truly, from the moment the first one woke up until the moment the last one fell asleep, I was the eye of a hurricane of boys.

In Houston, I'd had friends. The boys and I had amassed park friends and library friends and Children's Museum friends. But here, I didn't have anybody. I'd see moms in the grocery store with their kids and it was all I could do not to walk up and ask where they were going next to see if we could come with them. Peter was the only adult in my life, which is never a good dynamic for a marriage.

Peter, in contrast, was meeting people right and left. He was training to be a teaching assistant, and there were all kinds of parties and concerts and events scheduled. He had professors to meet, and fellow students, and, eventually, the undergraduates he'd be teaching.

Plus, his lessons were filling up. Beginners met him at our house in the practice room, and they worked on basics on his keyboard. More advanced students met him in one of the practice rooms at school to work on a real piano. He was doing things. He was out in the world. He was acting instead of reacting.

Every night at dinner, Peter had stories. Granted, he could barely work them in without Alexander shouting things like, 'Daddy! I have a sweet tooth! Do you want to see it?' But when Peter did get to speak, he had great tales to tell. About the professor with the walrus mustache who had tripped down the stairs, or the music hall that had once been a stable, or the woman from admissions who had recognized his name from his application and gasped — literally gasped! — before saying, 'I love your work.'

For my part of the conversation, I'd say things like, 'I found these canned beans for seventy-nine cents at Market Basket,' or 'Toby put a worm in his mouth today.' I started, more than ever, to feel like the weakest conversational link.

But I kept going to the gym. I went night after night, no matter how tired I was, or how feverishly I just wanted to crawl into bed, or how many times I'd been up with the kids the night before. I went and continued to learn the lay of the land and get familiar with the people there. I saw Ted Koppel again every few days, riding the stationary bike in flip-flops, reading a beat-up paperback, and drinking from what looked like a flask. Once, he saw me eyeing him and held it up to me in a toast.

And I started to believe in the gym. I told myself that one hour of jogging-slash-walking every night was something that I could really hold on to in this new city — this new life — where I felt so adrift, and that committing to something as simple as an exercise routine would help me stay steady.

To tell the truth, even after the first week, I was feeling different. I found that I was less upset about things. Something was taking the edge off for me. I was homesick, but not quite as painfully. I felt lonesome, but not quite as intensely. I got frustrated when the boys poured honey all over the kitchen floor, but not quite as bitterly.

It was nice to be doing something that was only for me. I had been longing for something that was just mine for years now. I had tried to explain to Peter once, and he had been obtuse about it. 'The kids are yours,' he'd said.

'They're mine, but they aren't me.'

'But you're doing a great job of raising them.'

'Sometimes,' I said. 'And sometimes they are unraveling every roll of toilet paper in the house while I sit on the sofa with my head in my hands.'

'You can't tell me they aren't great kids.'

'No,' I said. 'And I wouldn't want to.'

Peter had a gleam as if he'd won.

'But,' I pushed on, 'when Toby picks his nose and wipes it on the couch, I don't exactly beam with pride and say, 'I did that! That's all me!''

Peter shook his head.

That was the tricky part. You poured inordinate amounts of time and attention and affection into your kids, but the result was indirect. You didn't point out a cat to your one-year-old and then watch him, minutes later, say 'Cat.' Instead, you pointed out a hundred cats to your one-year-old and then, one day, watched him point to a cat and say 'Mama.'

That was what I wanted Peter to understand — that everything you did for your children was filtered and refracted through their personalities. There was nothing you could take credit for. You just tried to hold yourself together, give them lots of hugs, get them in the tub at least once a day, and hope for the best.

What I needed so desperately, and did not

have in my life, was something I could point to and say, 'I did that.' Something that was a direct reflection of me.

When I first started going to the gym, I thought the gym could be that for me — something I felt proud of. If nothing else, I could feel proud of the fact that I hadn't missed a workout all week, or that I could stay on that treadmill for an hour straight without — knock on wood — flying off the back. If nothing else, I'd be able to point to my discipline for and commitment to living a healthier lifestyle. That seemed like something.

Later, I'd discover that I actually wanted to do something that only I could do. And an obsessive adherence to my exercise regime didn't entirely fill that order. But it was, without question, a good start.

Two weeks in, I was feeling good. I was feeling spry. I was having crazy moments of total elation and wondering if they were runner's highs. I'd be putting trucks back in the toy bin, say, and I'd suddenly feel overcome with euphoria about my life. Nothing had actually changed in those moments, but it was like sun rays cutting through an overcast day: Everything suddenly felt brighter. It had to be chemical.

I was also starting, more and more, even

though I knew it was premature, to feel like a gym person. I had these great moments when I felt strong and fierce and in charge. I was a person who went to the gym! I'd bought a sports bra and some athletic socks! I had a pair of nylon shorts! I was an improved version of myself. Ten days of exercise was enough to get the ball rolling on a whole new self-concept.

I was having one of those good moments one morning when Alexander, sitting on my lap after breakfast, said to me, trying out a new word: 'Mama, are you 'plump'?'

I wasn't quite sure how to field that one, but it seemed like the wrong choice to burst into tears or run out of the room. I decided to play it cool. 'I'm a little bit plump these days,' I said.

Alexander nodded and took that in.

'But you know what?' I asked.

He looked up at me.

'Plump mommies are very good to have, because they are supersoft to cuddle with.'

At that, he squeezed his little self against me, and I felt like I'd given the best answer to such a question a little-bit-plump mother could possibly give.

Of course, then, within a week, Alexander had told two women at the park, in his most earnest and complimentary manner, that they were also 'plump mommies.' Not too long after he called it out to a woman behind us in the checkout line, I explained to him that only a plump mama's own children could tell her how plump she was.

'Why?' Alexander had asked.

'I don't know,' I said. 'That's just the rule.'

8

I was very alone in those early weeks in Cambridge. And so I was surprised and, at the same time, grateful to the universe when Peter came out of the practice room on the morning of our Cambridge two-weekiversary, holding his cell phone out to me and saying, 'You've got a call.'

It was Amanda Hayes.

'I figure you lost my number,' she said. 'But it's okay, because your husband's flyers are all over town. He's cute!'

'Thanks,' I said.

'How's the pregnancy going?'

'Good,' I said, glancing Peter's way to make sure he was gone.

'How far along are you, again?'

It was, I knew, the perfect moment to confess. But then a shriek came from the kitchen, and I had a genuine diversion. 'Hold on,' I said to Amanda, and followed the sound to find Alexander pulling Toby around by his feet on a dish towel.

'We're sledding,' Alexander explained when I got in there.

'Alexander, he doesn't like it,' I said,

picking up a crying Toby and patting his back. 'No more sledding. No more.'

I put the phone back to my ear. 'Sorry.'

She had moved on from chitchat. 'We're headed to the park, if you want to meet us.'

I did not hesitate. Before I'd even had time to start weighing the awkwardness of maintaining my faux pregnancy against the pleasure of having another adult to talk to, I had already heard myself say, 'Yes.'

At the park, Amanda had spread out a file folder of shower ideas on a picnic table and worked through it piece by piece as the kids pretended to be lions in the sandbox. She was really planning a big to-do. She had clipped photos of flower arrangements. She had printed shower games off the Internet. She had sample menus. She was choosing between a cowgirl theme and a south-of-the-border theme with a margarita machine and a mariachi band.

And, looking at a page with a recipe for mini-empanadas that Amanda had high-lighted in yellow, I realized three very important things: One, she had more money than she knew what to do with. Two, she was bored. And three, I was going to have to come clean about this pregnancy situation.

'What does your husband do, again?' I asked.

95

'Oh,' she waved her hand. 'Business.'

'Financial stuff?'

'Yeah.' She was busy looking for the photo of the *tres leches* cake. 'Portfolios.'

I waited for more.

She paused and looked up at me. 'It's too boring to talk about.'

I wasn't really sure where to go from there, so I just said, 'He sounds nice,' though she had not described him at all.

That got her attention. She looked up. 'He's not always nice. But he's handsome.'

It took her a minute to get back to planning after that. But when she did, she cut to the chase.

'I'm going to invite everybody I know to this thing,' she said. 'It's going to be huge. I was going to do it at our place, but now I'm thinking we won't have the space. We're going to need a venue.'

It was too much. It really was. And before she started reserving rooms and putting down payments on things, I had to stop her. I took a deep breath to begin my confession just as Alexander walked up and said, 'Mama? I need to go potty.'

I had asked him ten times before we left. 'You have got to be kidding me,' I said.

He pointed at his butt and turned it toward me for illustration. 'I need to poop.'

'Alexander, why didn't you go at home five minutes ago?'

He shrugged.

I looked around, double-checking that there was, in fact, no bathroom at the park. It looked like we were about to have to pack up and go home.

And then Amanda, without looking up from her file folder, said, 'Use a Ziploc bag.'

We both turned to look at her.

'Just have him squat down over it,' she explained.

I had a Ziploc bag in my big purse. It had an old turkey sandwich in it, but I could toss that out. Still, the idea seemed too gross. So much about living with children, of course, was gross. The way they stuck their fingers in my cereal, the way they backwashed into my water bottles, the way they wiped their extra sunscreen or dirty hands or runny noses on my clothes without any hesitation. Of course, I barely noticed anymore. Parenting had lowered my standards in lots of ways.

'It's no grosser than dog poop,' Amanda said, marking a big X on one of the pages in her file.

In the end, we did it. Baby Sam sat beside us in the grass while Alexander and I squatted behind a tree. It was actually not too bad. Less gross, in some ways, than the public restroom experience. At least we were out in the fresh air. The moment was over fast, but I figured something out, down behind that pine tree: I really liked Amanda. And in minutes — after I'd scrubbed both of us down with every remaining wipe in my bag — Alexander was back on the swings, the plastic bag was in the trash can, and I was turning my attention back to the shower.

At the picnic table, I hooked Baby Sam up to nurse. Then I took a deep breath and said, 'Amanda?' I felt a little woozy.

'What?' she asked, still not looking up.

'I have to talk to you about something,' I said. I waited until she met my eyes, set the flan recipe down, and gave me her full attention.

'Amanda,' I said again, trying to gather momentum. I couldn't watch her face. 'Amanda, I'm not pregnant.'

I expected her to throw her file folder at me, maybe. Or shove it back into her purse to save for a more deserving friend. I certainly expected her face and her voice to harden in anger. I thought she might even grab Gracin and leave the park in a huff.

But none of those things happened. By some great stroke of luck, even though I had told the truth plainly, she had misunderstood me. She thought I was telling her that I'd had a miscarriage.

She took a breath. She covered her mouth with her hands. 'Oh,' she said, after a minute. It even looked like her eyes got teary as the words sank in. 'Oh, I'm sorry,' she said, and leaned in over Baby Sam to hug me.

I'd really like to be able to report that I was mature and upstanding enough to have corrected her. I could see myself putting a hand on hers and saying, 'No, no — ' and explaining the whole thing. I could have done that. I should have. But you know what? I didn't. I made a loophole out of the fact that I had miscarried — twice — years ago, before Alexander. I told myself she was close enough, and I let her believe that I wasn't pregnant *anymore*.

Amanda pulled back from her hug, her face soft with sympathy. She ran her pointer finger under her eyes to make sure her mascara wasn't smearing. Then she spoke the words I can still hear to this day. Because I'd never been sure just exactly what it was about me that made Khaki Pants assume I was pregnant that day. My great fear was that I actually looked nine months pregnant, and I just hadn't noticed.

So when Amanda said, 'Those early miscarriages are for the best, anyway. What were you? Six weeks? Seven?' I hugged her again, decided I was devoted to her for life, and gave myself permission to drop the subject forever. It really seemed unlikely to ever come up again. But later, of course, it would.

9

The next morning my parents were flying to Dubai. I woke up imagining the two of them boarding their plane: my mother polite and reserved in the aisle with her prim carry-on, and my father, in his golf shirt, helping other people squeeze their bags into the overhead bins.

I tried to call them to wish them a good trip, but our phone number — the one I had known as the number to home my entire life — had already been disconnected. Neither of them answered their cell phones, either.

My mother returned my call when the boys and I were in the produce section of the market. I had put off going to the market all week, and we'd gotten down to canned peaches and Chex Mix.

'Can you talk?' my mother asked.

I fed each of the boys a free sample of watermelon. 'Sure,' I said. 'We're grocery shopping.'

'Your dad and I have made a decision that you aren't going to like,' she began. 'And it's already done, and it's not up for discussion.'

'That's a heck of an opener,' I said.

'I just want to help you accept the news and move on,' she said.

'Okay. Accept what news?'

'I don't want to have to go through a whole thing with you about it,' she went on.

'A whole thing with me about what?'

There was a little pause, and then she said, 'We sold the house.'

I couldn't imagine what house she was talking about. 'What house?'

'Our house.'

I stopped walking. 'Our house? You sold our house?'

'Sweetheart — ' she started.

'You were going to rent it! You were going to box everything up! You were going to be back in three years!'

'Well, sweetheart,' she started again, her voice working overtime to soothe me. 'We got an offer we just couldn't refuse.'

'What kind of offer?'

'A big, generous offer for lots and lots of money.'

I had moved out of produce into the seafood section, where a little sample tray had crackers with tuna salad. I handed one to each of the boys while trying to keep my voice down. Still, I was practically shouting. 'What amount of money could possibly seduce you into selling the only home our family has ever lived in?'

She paused. And then she said, 'They offered us a million dollars.'

That got me. 'A million dollars for the house?'

'A million dollars for the lot.'

I didn't know what to say.

'The neighborhood's really taken off,' she said.

'I'll say.'

And then I thought about the word 'lot.' 'The lot?' I asked. 'Don't they want the house?'

'It's a developer. He's going to build a big mansion.'

I couldn't help it. I shrieked, 'They're tearing it down?'

She didn't have to answer.

'What does Dad think about this?' I asked.

'He thinks a million dollars is a lot of money.'

The boys were starting to fuss. They'd lost interest in the healthy snacks, and it was time to hit the hard stuff. I steered us to the cookie aisle and popped open a box of Nilla Wafers.

'What do David and Tommy say?'

'We haven't told them,' she said. 'But you know men,' she added. 'They don't hang on to things the way women do.'

My parents' cab had just pulled up in the driveway and honked. 'I know it's a lot to take in,' my mother said. I could hear her zipping her bag in the background. 'I'll call you after we get there, and I'll answer all your questions.'

I was now getting teary in the grocery store. The boys were occupied with cookies, I was standing still with one hand holding the phone and the other pressing against my forehead. Throwing sugar at the boys had bought me a few minutes to concentrate, but it was clear that a few minutes wasn't nearly enough.

I'd been so busy with my brood of boys and my cacophonous parenting life that I'd left my parents to do any crazy thing they wanted. I hadn't been paying attention, and now they were bulldozing my childhood and leaving the country. I felt a rising panic in my chest, a feeling like I had to stop them from getting in that cab. Right now, they were there, as they had always been, standing in the front hall near the squeaky front door with beveled glass panes. The house was empty, sure. But it was still there. As soon as they left, everything would disappear. I started talking fast.

'Don't go,' I said. 'Just wave the cab away.'

'We have to go, Elena,' my mother said, her voice distracted, like maybe she was checking

104

for her passport at the same time.

'No!' I shouted, there in the cookie aisle, suddenly wishing I had time for an emergency consult with my brothers. I felt sure we could stop it if we set up a united front. But we couldn't set up anything. There wasn't time. There was only a taxicab in our family driveway.

'This is crazy!' I went on. 'Think about what you're doing! What about your rose garden? What about the gate you and Beverly put in between our backyards? What about the dent in Tommy's door from when I threw that shoe at him? What about the growth-chart lines on the kitchen doorway? What about the crape myrtle you planted in the spot where we buried Bailey?' My voice had ratcheted up a bit. The tears started to spill over. 'Mom!' I was pleading now. 'You can't do this! You will always regret it.'

I heard the taxi honk again in the background. Then I heard my mother tell my dad she was coming. She had to get off the phone. She wasn't going to discuss this in front of my dad. It was time to say good-bye. Things were already in motion. And it occurred to me, as she hesitated, that she wasn't necessarily calling all the shots. I don't know if she could have stopped things if she'd wanted to. But as far as she was going to let me know, she didn't want to. She wasn't really a person to share her vulnerable moments. When people lost it in my mother's presence, she became all business. 'Finish your grocery shopping, Elena,' she said in her most determined voice. 'I will talk to you about all this at a better time.'

★ ★ ★

When we got home, I carried the boys upstairs and then went back down for the grocery sacks and the mail. Baby Sam had wailed for me on the living room floor as I left, and I took the stairs two at a time, feeling guilty, worrying that he thought I was never coming back.

I put the groceries away one-handed, with Baby Sam on my hip, and then I opened the only interesting piece of mail in the stack: a box from my mother.

Inside was a stack of four DVDs and a letter on my mom's gardenia stationery. The letter said,

Dear Elena,
Your father and I thought you might like to have these. I am missing you and your little ones very much today.
Love, Mom

106

I opened up our TV cabinet, which was always closed when the boys were awake, and put the first DVD in. The DVDs were, as I suspected, home movies from when I was a baby, transferred from film reels. The first images were of my mom, big as a house — pregnant with me — waving at the camera. She had her long hair pulled back in a kerchief, and she was standing in front of the very place she and my dad had just driven away from.

I was mesmerized by the movies, there in the living room. Baby Sam was still on my hip, and the big boys were still in the kitchen. I suspected they'd found the boxes of maxi-pads and panty liners that I'd bought at the store and were now sticking them to every surface. But it was okay. Wasteful, but okay. Sometimes I was willing to shell out a box of maxi-pads for a few minutes to myself.

I watched the DVDs for almost fifteen minutes. I saw my parents bringing me home from the hospital, my mother cradling me in a yellow blanket, my father holding me on his lap and reading the paper. I watched our first cat, Liberace — a pet I only remembered from pictures. I hadn't seen these movies in years. When we were younger, back before the Super 8 projector broke, we used to make popcorn and watch them on the wall of my parents' bedroom. I don't remember once ever feeling sad or melancholy or lost during those movie nights. Back then, it was just fun. We'd tease one another and throw popcorn at our old selves.

Now the movies had me in tears. The timing wasn't great. And the company that had transferred the reels to the DVDs had added a wistful musical score that really emphasized the passage of time and how all things fade and die. And the flickering, ethereal quality of the images made my childhood seem so dated, so *vintage* — it was as if it existed in a past so distant that I'd never be able to reach it again. Which, of course, was true.

The past in general — I found myself thinking, as Baby Sam sucked on my shoulder — was something that was already gone. Of course. But, until this moment, some things had felt more like the past than others. Some things had felt more lost than others. At this moment, I really understood that I would never live with my parents again.

We would never sit, all three kids at the big table in the kitchen, eating pancakes faster than my mother could cook them and sneaking sips of maple syrup. We would never build another fort on the green sofa. We would never hunt Easter eggs together, or pile into the station wagon, or go trick-or-treating. I would never be a child again. I would never fall asleep to the sound of my mother washing dishes in the kitchen outside my room. I would never crawl in next to her after I'd had a bad dream. I would never eat a Popsicle on the back steps, or do a flip on the trapeze, or crank a Matchbox car up to the top of the plastic garage.

It had not occurred to me to mourn losing those things until now. I had done each of those things, somewhere along the way, for a last time — without realizing it was the last time. And even after I knew that I was no longer a child, somehow I'd assumed those things could have come back to me. Or that I could have gone back to them. But watching the movies on this day, I became aware of infinite losses. Before I knew it, I had sunk to my knees.

That's when the boys walked in. They were both completely nude, except for maxi-pads stuck all over their bodies — butts, knees, hair, tummies, and, yes, even penises. Alexander was marching, raising his knees up high and then stomping the floor, and Toby was copying. The two were all ready to do a parade for me when they noticed the movies.

They had seen TV before. TV was everywhere. They'd seen it at the dentist's office and in the doctor's waiting room. They'd seen it at the diner where we used to go for breakfast back in Houston. They'd even seen it on, from time to time, at my parents' house. But they'd never seen anything like it in our living room. They stopped cold.

'What's that?' Toby asked.

'Well,' I said. 'That's baby Mommy.' The maxi-pad parade was totally forgotten. They stood slack-faced in front of the TV, and just when I was starting to think I'd better turn the thing off before their brains were erased, someone knocked at the door.

It was the Mean Witch. She was dressed today — in a pair of linen slacks and a blue-gray silk T-shirt. I had never seen her out of pajamas, and I was struck by how elegant she was. Mean, but elegant.

She, in turn, was struck by what she saw: me at the door, my face puffy and eyes red from crying. Baby Sam on my hip with his hand inside my blouse, and in fact inside my bra, feeling its way across the topography of my boob as if discovering it for the first time. And the Maxi-Pad Brigade flaunting their naked stuff in the living room, unable to decide which deserved their attention more: the flickering screen or the live visitor in the doorway.

It crossed my mind that seeing me so vulnerable might soften her a bit.

But she said, 'I see the lunatics are running the asylum.'

I smiled at her, but only with my mouth.

Then she seemed to remember why she was there, and started up, a bit more friendly this time: 'Josh is going to install a new shower at my place, and I'm wondering if — when he does — if I can borrow yours.'

She wanted something from me! 'When?'

'Next week.'

I paused a minute, just to draw out her discomfort. Finally, I said, 'Sure. Of course.' What else could I say?

She could have left right then, but instead she lingered a little. 'Josh wants me to use his. But I'd really prefer yours. If you don't mind.'

'As long as it's not Straitjacket Week.'

She didn't know what to say to that, but she did take a minute to look at my face for what might have been the first real time.

And then, knowing I had her pinned down at last, I said, 'I'm Lanie, by the way.'

'I'm Nora.'

I stuck out my hand, and she shook it just as Alexander called to me with enough urgency that I leaned into the living room to answer him.

'What is it, Alex?' I asked.

'Mama!' he said. 'Look!' He pointed at the TV screen, at some footage of me as a roly-poly baby in nothing but a diaper. 'You were plump then, too!'

★　★　★

Later, Josh explained the whole thing to me while he replaced a light fixture on our landing.

We had never mentioned the naked-in-the-kitchen incident again, though my heart still clenched in embarrassment every time I saw him. But he was easy and casual with me, in that Generation Y way. And even though I wanted that naked me sighting to be no big deal, I couldn't help but feel just a tiny bit offended as I came to realize that I'd had no impact on Josh at all. Until, at least, I started to suspect that another person in our building had enough impact for both of us.

Josh talked about Nora nonstop while he worked on that fixture. All I had asked was, 'What's up with Nora's shower?' and thirty minutes later, Josh was concluding his remarks on the state of her apartment with, 'What can I tell you? She's got the worst shower in the building.'

'That's quite a distinction,' I said.

'It's a big job,' he told me. 'One I'm not exactly qualified for.'

I watched his forearm flex and relax as he turned the screwdriver. 'So much of life is that way,' I said.

'It may take a while,' he went on. 'Nora's just going to have to shower at my place until I can get it done.'

'Actually, she's going to shower up here,' I said.

He looked at me and lowered his arms. He looked dismayed. 'She is?'

'She asked me about it this morning,' I said.

'She doesn't even like you guys,' he said, looking down at his screwdriver.

'What's the deal with her, anyway?'

He looked up, his expression lit with admiration. 'She's mean, isn't she?'

I looked at him. 'She sure is.'

He nodded. 'Well, she's brilliant, for one. She and her husband used to teach these packed psych classes at Harvard on grief. I took one the semester before I dropped out.'

'How was it?' I asked.

'Fuckin' amazing,' he said.

'Okay,' I said. 'So: brilliant and grumpy.'

'No,' he said. 'Not grumpy. Not always.' Then Josh climbed down off his ladder and peered over the railing to check the landing below. The coast was clear. 'Her husband died last year.'

'Died of what?'

'Lung cancer. And he didn't even smoke.'

I nodded.

'She took care of him the whole way through.'

'Okay,' I said.

'And then she quit teaching,' he added. 'Which is ironic. Since she was the author of *Grief Is a Way of Life*.'

'She wrote that book?'

Josh nodded. 'And others.'

There was a pause. Then Josh added, 'So I think she's a little — ' He shrugged, and I realized that was the end of his statement.

And so I nodded. She certainly was.

Nora was fifteen years younger than my mother, and I tried to imagine my mother a widow at forty-eight — what her life would have been like without my father, what it would have done to her to devote all her energy to a project as hopeless as saving a dying husband.

Nora and her husband had been building a country house when he got sick. Josh wound up coming inside and telling me all about it while I let the kids fling Play-Doh all over the kitchen. I was riveted by the information about Nora, but Josh used the word 'fucking' so many times that I started kicking him under the table. 'Spell it if you really have to,' I told him.

Nora and her husband had sold their row house in Boston to buy an undeveloped lot near Rockport overlooking the ocean — which was, by the way, how they came to rent cheap student housing from Josh. It was close to campus, and it was meant to be temporary. They'd teach during the week and then camp at their place on the weekends to inspect what the construction crew had been up to in their absence.

Josh had visited with them one weekend after they'd poured the slab and Nora's husband, Viktor, who was Swedish with heavy black glasses and spiky yellow hair, had walked Josh around, describing each nook so vividly that Josh felt like he'd already seen it.

Nora and Viktor had picked out every doorknob and bathroom fixture together over several years, as they saved and planned and talked about their project. Those pieces were in storage in labeled boxes and the house frame was up when Viktor started coughing one night and couldn't stop. Josh had helped Nora drive him to the hospital, and the next time he saw her, she was a woman who knew, in some deep place in her body, that her life's love was dying — even though they were embarking on treatments, and even though they were staying positive.

When Josh had first met Nora, she'd been direct and friendly, with a big laugh that showed all her straight teeth. But the year Viktor was sick had quieted her.

'No kids?' I asked.

'No kids,' he shrugged. 'She says she doesn't like them.'

'What about the husband?' I asked Josh. 'Did you like him?'

'Sure,' Josh said. 'But I liked her more.'

Nora went out to the property a few times after that. The construction crew had finished out the shell and all the stonework, but the inside was completely raw: no floors, no walls, no plumbing or kitchen fixtures. When they got to a stopping place, Nora had just locked the house and hadn't gone back.

'It's still there?' I said.

Josh nodded.

'She needs to get back out there and finish it,' I said.

'I don't think she'll ever go back out there,' he said. 'I'm surprised she hasn't burned it to the ground.'

10

The next morning, my mother called me on her new international cell phone. I had barely heard from her since she'd moved away — except by e-mail. To my mom, e-mail was the postcard of the telecommunications world. All of her e-mails read something like this: 'Got the new espresso maker today. Hot and sunny here. Hope the boys are doing well. Love you!' I got at least two of these a day — and often a group e-mail to me and my brothers. Hardly satisfying.

My whole life, my mother had been the most dependable person I knew. She was always on time — or a little early. She always sent birthday cards to everyone in her book — and she bought all the cards at the first of the year so she'd be ready when the time came. She woke up at the same time every day, ate dinner between 6:00 and 6:15, and, every Friday night, read a mystery novel in the bubble bath.

I knew, of course — everybody knew — that she hated cell phones. And that she practiced a kind of civil disobedience with them. She lost all her phones. She forgot to change their batteries. She refused to remember how to check her voice mail. For my mom, talking on the phone meant, specifically, talking on the white push-button with the fifty-foot curly cord that had been in our kitchen since 1969. Anything outside that paradigm just couldn't compare. If she couldn't cradle a phone between her ear and her shoulder, she did not want to use it. I couldn't fault her for liking things the way they used to be. But it was time to adapt.

Where was my gardening mother? My organizing-the-cookbook-shelf mother? My just-thought-I'd-call-and-tell-you-about-the-time-you-took-your-first-steps mother? My let-me-take-those-boys-for-you-so-you-can-have-a-nap mother? She'd been replaced by a having-lunch-at-the-club, taking-ballroom-dancing, sorry-I-missed-your-call mother.

The house sale had closed weeks ago. It was gone. I'd expected a phone call on that day, but instead I got an e-mail: 'House closed this morning. Don't stew about it. Move on with your life! Love you!'

But on the morning my mother called — at suppertime in Dubai — she took up the conversation as if we'd just been chatting five minutes before. I had barely finished 'Hello?' before she said, 'I just put something in the mail for you.'

'What?' I asked. I was mopping apple juice up off the floor with a wipe.

'My cameras,' she said.

'What cameras?'

She let out a little sigh, realizing, I suppose, that she was going to have to start from the beginning.

She had found all her old cameras in the storage closet when they were packing up. She'd dabbled in photography — something I didn't know — when she was younger, and she thought their trip to Dubai might be a great time to get back to it.

'But last night I had a dream,' she said. 'And it was you. You had all the cameras around your neck.' My mom believed in dreams. And not in a Jungian, all-the-characters-are-you kind of way. She believed in them literally.

'So I packed them up this morning and mailed them to you.'

'Mom!' I said. 'That's crazy!'

'I've lost interest in them, anyway,' she said. 'I'm riding horses now. And making jewelry. And needlepointing Christmas stockings for the boys. And learning tai chi.'

'What am I going to do with your old cameras, Mom?'

And then my mother gave me a little miniature version of her signature ass-kicking.

'You're going to fish your artistic dreams out of the toilet and start taking some pictures.'

There was nothing to say to that. She wasn't wrong. My artistic dreams were in the toilet. My plan had been to paint. Not to be famous, exactly, but at least respected by my peers. While my brothers had floundered around, dabbling in business schools or bicycling around Europe, I had been tunnel-visioned. I knew what I wanted. I wanted to be an artist.

Now I had an MFA in painting, a totally useless degree, and I had not done anything with it. My vocational life had been a chain of disappointments — galleries who almost wanted to show my work, projects that fell through. A few years after graduate school, after I'd spent several years working on paintings that wound up stacked in my parents' garage — and were now, post-move, stacked in their climate-controlled storage unit — I took a job at a school, teaching art to little kids. And before I knew it, I was up to my elbows in paste and construction paper and glitter.

I quit painting altogether. I just quit. It was a relief, actually, not to be failing as a painter anymore. I became an art teacher instead. I was good! The kids loved me! The parents loved me! We did clay snakes and papier-mâché puppets and decoupage treasure boxes!

Many years and three kids later, I'd almost forgotten that I'd ever painted at all. It seemed like a lifetime since I'd touched a brush. But my mother had always maintained that I'd come back to it — that it would pull me back. She remembered who I was, she told me. Even when I didn't. And so the cameras were on their way.

'I don't have time to take up photography, Mom,' I said. 'I can barely get the dishes done. I haven't changed our bedsheets since we got here.'

'You'll have to figure it out,' she said — adding, 'It's time,' as if she knew everything there was to know. Which she kind of did. Then she threw out a suggestion off the top of her head, as if answers were that easy to come by: 'Take pictures at the park while the boys play.'

'I'm busy when I'm at the park with them. I am mothering!'

'They don't need you nearly as much as you think they do.'

'Okay,' I said, feeling a sudden, sharp irritation at her bossy proclamations about parenting. 'I'll just drop Baby Sam in the grass and run around shouting, 'Cheese!' to everyone in the park.'

My mother ignored the sarcasm. 'Oh, I don't think you want to pose them,' she said.

I sighed a noisy sigh. 'What should I do, then?'

'Document motherhood,' she said. 'Capture the world around you.'

'Tell you what,' I said. 'You come back to the States and babysit, and I'll take all the pictures you want.'

And then my mother, who had a knack for getting the last word, said, 'It's not about what I want, sweetheart. It's about what you want.'

11

Peter started classes on a one-hundred-degree scorcher in mid-August, and that night I won a coupon for a free personal training session at the gym.

I'd become a regular at the gym by then, and I was starting to get the lay of the land. I always went to the back row of the treadmills because I didn't want anyone staring at my ass. I wanted to be the starer, not the staree.

It was so strange to be in this playground of adults. Since Alexander had come along, I really hadn't been in kid-free places very often. I liked the way it felt to be there. No one stealing anyone else's stuff. No one asking to be pushed on the swing. No one flicking his tongue at me like a lizard because he wanted to nurse. And my arms — with no one to carry and no diaper bag stuffed full of gear and no stroller to push — felt so light I sometimes feared they might float upward by themselves.

The gym honed my focus. During the day, I was totally scattered. It was complete chaos at all times. Alexander would 'wash dishes' in the kitchen sink, while Toby flung pieces of the train set all over the living room, while Baby Sam cried miserably to be picked up as I Spray 'n Washed mountains of banana-encrusted laundry. On some level, I was just a voice shouting directions and a pair of child-repositioning arms.

And, when you have children, you assume a certain persona. You are the mom, the voice of authority, the boss. Sometimes, back in Houston, when I'd gone out to the dentist, say, and my mom had watched the kids for an hour or two, I'd realize as I was driving back home that I felt like I was getting back into character.

But here, inside the white noise of all the machines, it was just me. Me out of breath on a treadmill. Me, acutely self-conscious. Me, shaking my groove thing. But me nonetheless. And the place had turned out to be pretty funny — and not nearly as intimidating as I'd assumed. There were all the middle-aged men who ran on the treadmill so fast they looked like they might get swept underneath and pop out the other side. There were the Gen Y girls in pink short shorts with words like 'princess' or 'tease' written across the butt in rhinestones. There was the woman on the machine right in front of me whose black thong rode up over her hipster sweatpants, and the woman on the StairMaster who wore no shirt over her leopard-print sports bra. There was the man who smelled like a wet dog, the bald guy with the do-rag, and a young doctor in his scrubs who found a reason to talk to every good-looking woman in the room. There was the girl who sang out loud to her head-phones. The guy who was reading *The Odyssey* in Greek. The man who grunted like a wild boar every time he lifted anything, including his gym bag.

My favorite people by far were a couple who came together every night. She was tall and pear-shaped with wild, red, curly hair, and he was shorter and Asian with a smile full of straight white teeth. They had matching iPods. They wore coordinating T-shirts. They shared a locker, and they did the same exercises at the same time: twenty minutes on the elliptical trainer, twenty minutes on the treadmill, then sit-ups — in sync — push-ups, curls, the row machine, squats, and on and on. That routine varied, but it never varied that they did it together. He was always chivalrous and polite, getting her mat for her, fetching her water bottle. And she was always making him laugh.

I decided they were married, but had no kids. I decided they had a spare, slightly funky, modern apartment somewhere near Harvard Square. That they'd go home from the gym every night and shower, maybe even together, then chop up a healthy meal full of vegetables and lean protein, climb into a queen bed with a smooth down comforter, watch a little TV, maybe fool around, and then drift off to sleep. The life I imagined for them seemed so clean and uncluttered, so sensible and safe, so loving. I couldn't help but ogle them every time they came in. I wondered if they noticed me doing it.

Because I certainly noticed Ted Koppel ogling me. He came to the gym a night or two a week, usually in baggy shorts with a baseball cap and a Harlan Coben novel tucked under his arm. He'd move from machine to machine and act very busy, but I could feel his eyes on me. For some reason, it wasn't creepy or threatening. Just really more of a puzzle. There were many attractive women in spandex at the gym. And though I could not for the life of me imagine why Ted Koppel would pick me to ogle, it was fun to try.

★ ★ ★

The Sexy Trainer told me about my free session while I was jogging on the treadmill. He stepped up on the nose of the machine so we were face-to-face. The sight of him so close threw me off balance and I had to put my feet on the running boards for a minute.

'You won!' he said a couple of times, until I caught up with him.

'I didn't know I had entered,' I said, stepping back on.

'Everyone was entered automatically,' he said, reaching over to press the incline button. The machine tilted up a bit.

'What do I need to do?' I asked.

'Just get ready to have your ass kicked,' he said.

I wasn't particularly certain that I wanted to have my ass kicked. Getting up at six and going all day with the boys and then dragging myself to the gym after they were asleep to spend my only free time all day jogging in a steamy room to fitness remixes of 'I'm Too Sexy' seemed like ass kicking enough. I was relieved when he told me they didn't have an opening for me for a couple of weeks.

'Okay,' I said.

But the gym thing seemed to be working. I still felt lumpy and jiggly and uncomfortable at the gym, but the truth was, in the month since we'd moved, my jeans had gotten looser and my bra straps had started falling off my shoulders. Life in Cambridge had turned out to be great for my health. I walked everywhere. I was constantly in motion in a way that I'd never been in Houston, where I lived in my car, ate drive-thru too many times a week, and sat most afternoons on a blanket in the backyard. In Cambridge, I pushed a stroller as heavy as a bulldozer with Baby Sam on my back everywhere I went, made multiple trips to the park and back, and lugged three kids up and down three flights of stairs more times a day than I could quantify.

Even things like doing the laundry were aerobic in Cambridge: I'd haul the basket down to the basement, baby on my hip. Then I'd realize I needed the detergent, dash back up for it — Baby Sam in tow — then back down, start the load, then back to the apartment to make the boys alphabet soup, then back down to move everything to the dryer, then another trip up and then down later to retrieve all the clean clothes. And most of it taking the stairs two at a time so the big boys didn't burn the place down in my absence.

It was hot here, too, with no air-conditioning. Not Texas hot, but, since there was no way to escape it, even more draining. So I sweated all day and drank tons of water to compensate. It was too hot to cook anything or use the oven, so we munched on cold things like carrots and hummus and grapes all day.

It's true that right after we moved here I'd made a pledge to change my life. But I hadn't changed it that much. I hadn't stopped eating or even bought a scale. But so much had changed by accident — just by adapting to my new city — that the few things I was doing had a big impact. And so in what seemed like record time, and with very little effort, I was tasting the honey of what it felt like to be the old me.

Though the old me, actually, had no place in my current life. If I'd stopped to think about it, I'd have known that. But I didn't stop to think about it. I was moving too fast.

★　★　★

As I became aware of my body again, I marveled at my boys, who were all about their bodies. They loved nothing more than to run around naked holding their noodles. Such things are so easy when you are too little to be self-conscious. It's fun to be naked! It's fun to hold your noodle! Simple as that.

There really is something about boys and their penises. Alexander spent his whole second year with his hand down the front of his pants. He didn't know exactly what that thing was down there, but he knew for sure he wanted to hold it. I remember saying to him one time, as he fought me while I tried to fasten his diaper, 'Buddy, you have got to develop other interests.'

And I don't know how we started calling our boys' penises 'noodles.' The books say to call private parts by their proper names like any other body part. You wouldn't give a foot a silly, totally unrelated name like 'foo-foo.' A foot is a foot, and it's not a big deal. But 'penis' is kind of a particularly daunting word, one that sounds so out of place when you're talking to a baby — and the girls' equivalent is even worse. Somehow, despite the experts' advice, we just started saying 'noodle.'

Toby was the one who shortened 'noodle' to 'noo-noo.' If Alexander could hold it, he didn't have to talk about it. But Toby — always verbal — talked about little else. He'd sit in the bathtub with the thing in his hand, saying over and over, 'Noo-noo! Noo-noo!' If he resisted getting out of the bath, I'd point out, 'You can bring your noo-noo with you,' and he'd suddenly consent.

Toby's noo-noo, in this way, became a kind of character in our lives. If I needed to finish a diaper change in a hurry, I would tell Toby that Noo-Noo was sleeping, and we'd tuck him into his diaper bed together while I fastened up the diaper with ease. If Toby was fussy, I could distract him by inquiring about Noo-Noo. 'Tobes,' I'd say, 'how is Noo-Noo doing?'

And he'd pause from his tantrum for a minute to really consider the question. Then he'd answer, 'Happy.'

And after three boys, I understood Freud for the first time. Not just the penis envy thing — though I did get that now, too: Who wouldn't want one of those great things? — but the whole concept of the civilizing force of the superego. A whole semester of college psychology had come into clear relief for me, all these years later. Freud was saying that humans slowly learned to value things other than their penises. Not the most accurate theory for girls, but, now that I'd had a glimpse into the infant lives of boys, pretty spot-on for them.

Girls, of course, were a different story. We, as a gender, were a whole other kettle of sexual fish. I asked Amanda about it one time, to see if Gracin ever noticed all the fun stuff she had down there, eager to affirm that female sexuality was just as big a deal as male.

'Sure,' Amanda said. 'I've seen her feel around a couple of times.'

I hooted with laughter. I didn't even know how to count the number of times my boys had gone for the gold. It would have been like trying to count the stars.

'Infinite?' Amanda asked.

'And then some.'

So boys — our boys, at least — were noodle guys. But Baby Sam really took the whole thing to the next level when he said his first word — 'noo-noo.' He was not alone, of course, in wanting to talk about his penis. Peter pointed this out. Men talked about penises their whole lives. 'I bet there are a thousand slang words for penis.'

'I don't know that many,' I said.

Peter looked at me and raised one eyebrow very slightly, then rattled off a partial list: willie, winkie, knob, Johnson, John Thomas, bishop, Oscar Mayer, love rocket, meat, beef, man-handle, cock, dick, doink, sausage, frankfurter, and Tall Texan. 'Give me ten minutes,' he added, 'and I'll come up with fifty more.'

I tried to think of an equivalent list for girls — not names that guys had made up for girls, but names that girls used for themselves. I couldn't think of any at all that girls had invented. The truth of it was, girls really just didn't chat too often about such things.

'Maybe you should start,' Peter suggested.

'Clearly, we're way behind,' I said.

I asked Amanda at the park later. 'Do you know any slang words for clitoris?'

'Sure,' Amanda said, and ticked off a bunch of them off while she set up a snack for the kids at the picnic table. 'Clam, candy, pearl, doorbell, love button — '

'Those are guy words,' I said, stopping her. 'Can you think of any words that women use for themselves?'

She thought about it, but she couldn't.

I was still impressed with her list, though. 'Were you this raunchy when you were a cheerleader?'

'Oh, honey,' she said. 'You have no idea.'

We walked a little. Then I asked, 'What do you guys call Gracin's — ' I didn't even have a word for it — 'stuff?'

'We don't,' she said.

'Exactly.'

All this noodle talk eventually brought Amanda and me to the question of what it all said about men. Amanda was pleased to be able to contribute that she had just seen an article about how often men thought about sex — a study done at Johns Hopkins and summarized in *Glamour*.

'How often?' I asked.

'Guess,' Amanda dared. 'What percentage of the day do you think men are thinking about sex?'

'We're talking about the waking hours?'

She nodded.

I thought about it. I tried to think about how often I thought about sex — which, in recent years, was not nearly often enough. I figured I'd start there and then add twenty-five percentage points. Or maybe thirty.

But I couldn't seem to figure out how often I thought about sex. If I was thinking about it, I wasn't thinking about it very hard. And usually, if I did think about it, it was because Peter was thinking about it. But I didn't know how to assign a daily score. There were far too many days that passed when I didn't think about it at all.

In my defense, I certainly had streaks when I thought about it daily, at least. But like it or not, I had to give myself negative points for the days I forgot to think about it. The truth is, I wanted sex to be an expression of passion. But, spending my days up to my knees in fire trucks and playground sand, listening endlessly to Alexander's stories about big dinosaurs that ate candy and ripped people's heads off, I wasn't exactly in touch with my passion. Mom-life lacked a certain dignity that, for me at least, seemed essential for something like desire to ignite.

Which is not to say I couldn't be talked

into it. I could. But I was coming more and more to believe that women's desire was different from men's. Women's desire seemed to come from their feelings — a physical ache in the heart that ravaged the body. And I confess it had been awhile since I'd felt anything like that.

All figured together, I probably should have given myself a zero percent. But that was so depressing, I just couldn't. I fudged a five, then added twenty-five for a guy total of thirty. But somehow that seemed too low. I added ten more. Forty percent of the day. It seemed impossibly high and, at the same time, not high enough.

'Forty,' I finally guessed.

'Nope,' Amanda said, delighted to have the answer.

'What is it then?'

She pointed at me. 'Fifty. Fifty percent of the day. Fifty percent of the day men are thinking about sex. On average.'

'That's truly amazing,' I said.

Amanda nodded, as I paused to take it in. And just at that exact moment, I glanced over to catch Toby — who had just recently started offering snacks to Noo-Noo from time to time, telling me it was hungry — bend the straw of his juice box, poke it into the top of his diaper, and squeeze in some refreshments.

When Toby looked up and saw the two of us staring at him, he just announced, 'Thirsty,' and continued on.

Amanda nodded again. 'Just another reason,' she said after a minute, 'why women should be running the country.'

12

Back in college, I had not seen Peter again for days after he'd fallen speechless in Connor's room. I had looked for him in the cafeteria and on the bike path. I had hoped to run into him near the mailboxes, and I had visited Connor every day in the hopes of bumping into him. Finally, on the day of our art class together, I knew I'd see him. I got up an hour and a half early and not only shaved, but tried on three different outfits. I stood in front of the mirror for so long, and changed back and forth so many times, that my sleeping roommate finally shouted, 'Just pick one!' through her comforter.

I was the first person to class, but Peter was late. I watched the door as each person came in and sat down. Fifteen minutes into class, he still wasn't there, and I felt anxious, like I wanted to go out and look for him. It made me worry that Connor and I had celebrated for no reason. If he felt about me the way I felt about him, he'd have come to class early, too.

And then, just as I was deciding that he never liked me to begin with, he appeared in the doorway — on crutches, with his leg in a cast. My face got hot when I saw him. I ducked my head. I tried to pretend that I was very busy drawing the nude art major posing in the middle of the room. A girl from Peter's dorm had helped him carry his sketchpad and portfolio to class — and I could tell by the way she carried his art supplies that she had a crush on him, too.

Everybody but me stopped drawing when they saw him. Even the nude shifted out of position to get a better look. He made his way across the room, careful not to knock over any easels, and perched on a stool right across from me. The class crowded around and asked what had happened. Peter just shrugged and said, 'I fell off a roof.' That seemed to satisfy everyone, and a guy from the rugby team grabbed a box of Sharpies so we could all sign the cast. By the time I had a turn, there was barely any room left, and so I just drew a little heart near his big toe. His smooth, pink, neatly trimmed big toe. I was tempted to try to touch it — just brush my fingers past it somehow — but I couldn't figure out how to pull it off.

I did not look at him once after that for the rest of class. I gazed at the nude model and worked on my charcoal drawing as if nothing else were in my head. Of course, the only thoughts actually in my head were about Peter, and how he was feeling, and what kind of a stupid boy falls off a roof. And if my lipstick was still shiny, and if he was looking at me — because it kind of felt like he was, but I didn't dare lift my eyes to check.

Near the end of class, with fifteen minutes left, we tacked our drawings up on the critique wall, as we always did. Twelve nudes went up. And then Peter made his way over — his drawing dangling from his fingers and flapping against his crutch as he moved. And when he lifted it, I saw — wc all saw — that it was a drawing of me, at my easel. We'd all been sketching the nude, and Peter had been sketching me. The sight of it made me bite my lip. I couldn't imagine at that moment that anything better could ever happen to me.

Peter came over to stand side by side. 'What do you think?' he asked, keeping his eyes on the drawing, as if we were at a museum. Our instructor was just stepping up to examine the drawings.

'I think you're about to get in trouble,' I said.

As the critique started, our teacher, Shane, a wild bohemian missing a front tooth who was famous for ripping up drawings he didn't like, lingered in front of Peter's for a long time. I was sure he was going to rip it down, crumple it, and make an example of Peter about following directions. But instead, he turned around with a delighted, snaggle-toothed smile. 'This is the best one of the bunch,' he said. Then he narrowed his eyes at us. 'Why?'

'Because it's not like the others?' the rugby player volunteered.

'In what way?'

'It's not a picture of the model.'

'Wrong!' Shane shouted. 'Wrong!' Then he looked around at all of us. 'What makes this drawing beautiful? What makes it strong? What makes it work?' The rugby player raised his hand to try again, and Shane pointed at him as he walked over, leaned in, and said, 'Get it right this time.'

'Passion,' the rugby player shouted, as if Shane were a drill sergeant.

Shane reached over, grabbed the rugby player by the face with both hands, kissed him on the cheek with a big smack, and then shouted, 'Passion! Goddamn right.'

I have never in my life, not even for five minutes, looked as good as I did in that drawing. As I stood in the art room during the critique, I wondered if Peter really thought I looked like that, or if he just lacked the skills to draw the real me. Or if, impossibly, he thought the person he'd drawn on that paper actually was the real me. Or even if, by some miracle, that beautiful girl was the real me — and I'd just never noticed.

13

On the day my mother's cameras arrived in Cambridge, I did not open the box. As soon as the tape was off, the boys would want to touch, carry, drop, and dismantle everything inside. As much as I found myself wanting to see the cameras, I put the box on top of the fridge for after bedtime.

When I finally got to it — after the gym that night, while Peter shelved all our books alphabetically — I found three cameras. They were like no cameras I had ever seen. They were, I'd later learn, 'twin lens reflex' cameras — little boxes that hung at your belly as you peered down through the top. One was very nice and heavy, a Rollei, and the other two were plastic — toy cameras from the sixties that my mom had picked up for fun. I had no idea what to do with them.

'Take a photography class,' Amanda said at the park, as she leafed through a copy of *Vanity Fair*. 'They have them at Harvard Extension.'

'I can't afford to,' I said, knowing full well that Amanda would not understand that limitation.

'They have scholarships,' she said. 'Didn't you do art in college?'

'I did,' I said. 'But that doesn't mean they'll give me any money.'

'We should tell them your grandfather was Ansel Adams,' she said.

I laughed.

Amanda didn't laugh. She said, 'People go crazy for fame. Famous people get whatever they want.'

'But I'm not famous,' I said.

'But your grandfather is.'

'Amanda,' I said. 'You can't just make things up like that.' This should have been obvious, of course.

'Sure you can.'

I looked at her with new eyes. 'Is this how you get what you want?'

'Honey,' she said, putting on her sunglasses, 'I have everything I want.'

She insisted that we pack up the kids that very moment and stroll over to the Extension office to fill out an application on the spot, though I made her promise to keep quiet about my famous grandfather when we got there. She promised she would, but from that point on, she talked to me as if my grandfather had in fact been Ansel Adams.

'I won't tell,' she said, winking at me. 'But I think your grandfather would be very disappointed for you not to use him to your advantage.'

As we got closer to Harvard Square the sidewalks were covered in shade. We were deep in that part of Cambridge where the trees that edged the road felt ancient and wise. The sidewalk was warm, but the shade was cool, and my sandals flapped against the pavement. I'd been outside this summer more than any other since I was a kid. I found myself suddenly glad to be exactly where I was.

Within fifteen minutes, we arrived at the office to find that the signup period and financial aid deadline had already passed — and that, in fact, notifications were set to go out the very next week.

'Look at her,' Amanda said to the freshman manning the desk for his work-study job. Then she squeezed my cheeks. 'She's going to make this place famous.' She leaned way over the desk to give the freshman a little peek down her shirt.

Then things got flirty. 'Harvard,' the freshman pointed out, 'is already famous.'

Amanda was ready for that. She reached out and touched the tip of his nose. 'But not the extension school.' She looked over at me. 'Not yet.'

In the end, he wound up taking my forms,

changing the date stamp, putting them at the top of the stack, and inviting Amanda to a keg party at his dorm.

'I'm married, babe,' Amanda had told him, tucking his number into her pocket. 'But I'll think about it.'

On the walk home, I wanted to clarify: 'You're not really going to think about it.'

'Hell, no,' Amanda said. Then, after a second: 'Or maybe I will.'

I looked over at her then, as, in a pleasant voice, without meeting my eyes, she added, 'I think my husband is having an a-f-f-a-i-r.'

I stopped walking. 'What?'

Amanda did not even slow her pace, and I had to scramble to catch back up.

'I'm just getting a weird vibe,' she said.

'What kind of vibe?'

'A perfume-on-the-clothes vibe,' she said.

'That could be anything,' I insisted. 'Women in the elevator. A coat in the coat closet. A department store sample.'

'I guess,' she said, still not looking in my direction. 'But it's the same perfume every time.'

'Maybe it's not perfume. Maybe he changed deodorant.'

She nodded. 'I hadn't thought of that.'

'Or shaving cream. Or shampoo. Or aftershave.'

She was still nodding. 'I'll have to do an inventory of his products,' she said. 'That's a good idea.'

'Have you asked him about it?' I asked.

'Hell, no!' She checked to see if the kids had caught the curse word.

'Do you think he would lie?'

'That's what I would do,' she said. 'If I were c-h-e-a-t-i-n-g and he asked me about it. I'd lie and say I wasn't, and then I'd take it even further underground.'

I almost spoke, but she wasn't finished: 'Or try to cut things off, but then accidentally ratchet up the passion because I couldn't have the person I really wanted.' She'd given this some thought. She shook her head like she'd decided something. 'Nope,' she said. 'He can't know I'm onto him.'

I wasn't sure how Amanda felt about all this. Most women would be absolutely hysterical at the prospect of being cheated on. But Amanda was not most women. She was particularly poised. She was particularly strong. And she was particularly beautiful. Even though most beautiful women I knew didn't feel beautiful or understand how beautiful they were or feel secure in their beauty, Amanda had more social capital than your average girl. After all, not long before, she'd been leafing through a magazine. Granted, I had never been in her situation, but I couldn't help thinking I wouldn't be reading about fashion and style if I were. Though who knows what I'd do if I'd actually been in Amanda's shoes. And thank God I wasn't.

Without intending to, I started asking questions designed to provoke some emotions from her. Because I suddenly needed to know not just what she thought, but how she felt.

'Who do you think he's c-h-e-a-t-i-n-g with?' I asked.

'Oh, I don't know. Somebody at the office.'

'What will you do if it turns out he is?'

'I've been thinking about that. Do I have to leave him?'

'Probably,' I said.

'Because we actually have a great life together. At first, I thought, 'Well, I'll just leave.' Which seems like the self-respecting thing to do. But I really don't want to.'

'You probably don't want him to be c-h-e-a-t-i-n-g on you, either.'

We walked a little until I heard her sniff — and that's when I realized she'd started crying. She wiped her cheeks with her palms, and said, 'No.'

'Are you okay?' I asked.

She nodded, and then put her finger to her lips and pointed at her daughter, down in the stroller.

Then Amanda shook her head as if to shake herself out of it, and said, 'This kind of stuff happens every day.'

'But not to you,' I said.

'No,' she said. 'Not until recently.'

There was a little pause, while we pushed the strollers along. The sky was starting to look gray, like it might rain.

'He'd have to be insane to c-h-e-a-t on you,' I finally pronounced.

'He would. He really would. And I'm great in b-e-d, too. I have these c-r-o-t-c-h-l-e-s-s panties that he loves.'

'You do?' I was shocked. Not so much at the crotchless panties — or the fact that she could spell 'crotchless' so effortlessly out loud, as if it were one of those parenting words you had to spell all the time, like 'cookie,' or 'bedtime,' or 'shots' — as at the idea of a person with children having a sex life that allowed for props. My sex life with Peter — and if I'd been talking out loud instead of thinking, I would have made little quotations around the words with my fingers — was far more like improv.

'Sure,' she said. 'We've got all kinds of stuff. The panties, some s-p-i-k-e heels, a little w-h-i-p.'

'You do?' I stopped walking. I was very impressed.

'Surely you have some s-e-x toys,' she called over her shoulder.

'No!' I said, catching up.

'Not even things from the kitchen? Spatula? Champagne flutes?

'No.' I suddenly felt like I hadn't been applying myself.

'You've been together how long?'

'Fifteen years.'

She let out a low whistle of disbelief. 'That,' she said, 'is a miracle.'

★　★　★

Later that night, as I got dressed for the gym, I told Peter all about the conversation. I felt a twinge of guilt about spilling the beans, but I couldn't seem to help it. And I told myself that all married couples tell each other every secret they know, anyway. And I so rarely had anything interesting to say. (Though that night, at dinner, I had been able to contribute, 'Toby poked his penis with a screwdriver today,' to which Peter had replied, totally deadpan, 'Flat-head or Phillips?')

And I got his attention. I told him about the crotchless panties. I told him about the heels and the whip and the champagne flutes. I might even have thrown in an eggbeater, just to up the ante.

Peter said, 'What do they do with the champagne flutes?'

'I don't know,' I said, 'but it's gotta be good.'

Peter nodded, taking it all in.

'Do you wish we were having sex with champagne flutes?' I asked.

Peter shrugged. So easy to please. 'I just wish we were having sex at all.'

It was a good point. Our issue with fertility had really taken some of the fun out of it for me. It was hard to get into the whole sex thing nowadays because I knew, in vivid detail, what it could lead to. I did not want to get pregnant again. And we had never quite found a good birth control: I was still waiting for Peter to do the right thing and get a vasectomy, and he was still procrastinating. So at the moment, we were not using anything, hoping that luck and infrequency would protect us.

I changed the subject back to Amanda. 'What do you think about the affair?' I asked, eager for the guy perspective. 'Do you think he's cheating?'

'We're talking about two people I've never met.'

'But what do you think?'

'I don't know,' he said.

'Would you cheat on a wife who was beautiful and used kitchen appliances as sex toys?'

'No.'

'Because of the 'beautiful' part or because of the 'kitchen appliances' part?'

He caught my eyes. He thought I should already know this answer. Then he said, 'Because of the 'wife' part.'

★   ★   ★

The next week, I got a letter saying I'd been accepted into the photography class — and had a scholarship, as well. But the scholarship was for only half of the tuition, and we didn't have $175 for a class any more than we had $350.

I read the letter and dropped it right in the trash can. What use was it? Then, a couple of minutes later, I fished it back out. And the next thing I knew, I was down at the Extension office, in front of the receptionist's desk with all of my boys and a bag of Oreos in my hand to keep them quiet.

'I'm just wondering if there's someone I could talk to about financial aid,' I asked.

The receptionist was young. She had on a T-shirt that was so tight I could see the seams on her bra. 'You have to fill out a form,' she said, pulling out a form I'd already submitted. 'What do you need to talk about?'

And then I got kind of tongue-tied. I'd been ready to make my case to a financial administrator, but I hadn't figured on having to make my case to this teenager first.

'I just want to see about the possibility of applying for more aid than I received.' I sounded greedy. I felt greedy.

'I don't think they do that.'

'I'm just wondering if I could talk to someone about it.'

And then, with an almost imperceptible sigh of irritation, she stood and said, 'Let me check.'

I watched her strut down the hallway while I replenished the boys' Oreos. Her panties were riding up over the edge of her low hipster jeans, and I suddenly felt irate. That wasn't office attire! What was she thinking! And who was she to make me grovel in the office of the Extension School?

A few minutes later, things were going better. I was awkwardly trying to wheel our crazy stroller into the office of an administrator named Vida King. She was a tall, beautiful African American woman with buttery brown eyes and cheekbones that could win a prize. She had her hair in cornrows pulled into a thick ponytail at the nape of her neck. She had slender fingers and a French manicure. And when she looked at me, she didn't tilt her head down — just looked with her eyes. Something about that posture made her seem like a queen.

I tried to get the stroller into her office, but after ramming her doorway three times, I gave up, and we just talked in the hallway.

'We gave you financial aid already,' she said, after I explained why I was there.

'Yes,' I said. 'But it isn't enough.'

She stepped over to her file cabinet to look me up, and I waited for her in the hall. I had a quick urge right then to mention Ansel Adams, but I decided against it, because: one, it was morally wrong; two, I was a terrible liar; and three, Vida King did not strike me as the type of woman to swoon in the face of fame.

I kept talking, raising my voice a little so she could hear me. 'I don't have a hundred and seventy-five extra dollars. I don't even have fifty extra dollars. So, really, unless I get a full scholarship, I can't take the class. But something in me just feels desperate to take the class. So I figured that I'd at least ask if there might be any extra financial aid. It really is the difference between taking the class and not taking it. And, though I didn't even know it until just now, it feels like the difference between breathing and not breathing.' I didn't hear anything, so I added, 'As crazy as that sounds.'

She was paging through my file. 'Photography is an expensive hobby,' she said. 'Even if we waived the entire tuition, you'd still have film and paper to buy as well as a fee for your share of chemicals.'

'Oh,' I said. I hadn't thought about that. The boys were starting to fidget, and I'd run out of cookies. It seemed like my visit here was coming to a close.

'Why did you say this class is so important to you?' she asked.

I was being evaluated. She was forming an opinion of me. I needed a good answer, but I didn't have one. I didn't know why I wanted to take the class. All I knew was that ever since I'd applied, I'd thought about it every night. I was about to say that. I was on the verge of rambling on about how painting hadn't worked out for me, but now I was thinking maybe I'd been meant to do something else all along, when a sentence came into my head, and I just said it:

'I'd like to do a series of portraits of beautiful women,' I said. And then, without even considering that it might sound like sucking up, I added, 'And I'd like it to include a portrait of you.'

I suppose if I really sat down and dissected my motivations for asking to take her portrait, I'd find some flattery in there. But mostly I was just being honest. I saw women all the time who I thought were beautiful. In the checkout line, at the DMV, in the elevator, at the bank. Women who didn't look exactly like models, but who were knockouts just the same. Women who probably looked in the mirror and saw crows'-feet or too many freckles or crooked teeth. I had often thought about how great it would be to have a coffee-table book with photo after photo of real, beautiful women. It had just never occurred to me until that moment that I could be the person who put that book together.

Vida King had barely reacted to what I said. But after a minute, she looked up from my file and said, 'We do have some discretionary funds we can use for supplies in situations like yours.' And then she pulled back her beautiful lips and gave me a beautiful smile that showed every single one of her beautiful teeth.

'Beautiful,' I said, and smiled right back.

14

Going to the gym was addictive. It was thrilling. I felt like I was coming up for air. It felt great to be in motion. And my looser jeans gave me jolts of delight all throughout the day. It felt, in a way I couldn't deny, like I had found something very important that had been lost. The feeling was so good, all I wanted was more.

And so when Amanda told me about a diet sweeping the nation that was 'all protein all the time' — except for lunches on the weekends, when you got to feast on white bread and potatoes — I decided to do it with her.

Now, I'd tried my fair share of diets, as most girls have. I'd done enough of them to know that I didn't like them. And even at my lowest moment, on the walk back from the park after the pregnancy debacle, I had not even considered dieting. Because going on a diet seemed to lead inevitably to going back off of it. I didn't want to yo-yo or do anything extreme. I just wanted to make some changes I could live with.

So it is hard to explain why, suddenly, after

one chat with Amanda, I was willing — even eager — to throw out all my fruits, breads, cereals, juices, and frozen cookie dough. Partly, I loved the feeling of getting my body back, and I wanted to hurry things up. And partly, Amanda was just a persuasive speaker.

'It cleanses your body,' she explained at the park that day, after a rain, while the kids splashed in shallow puddles. 'It flushes all the bad stuff out and restores you to a state of purity.'

Purity sounded good.

'My mom did it,' Amanda said, 'and she felt absolutely reborn.' Amanda could have been an infomercial. She was, herself, in a fugue state of preparations. She'd spent the morning throwing out every grain of sugar or crumb of bread in her house. People who did this diet suddenly shed unwanted pounds effortlessly, slept better, became more articulate, had better sex — and more of it — grew thicker hair, lost their wrinkles, developed whiter teeth, improved their eyesight, read faster, made more money, gained IQ points, and were able to realize their dreams.

'Realize their dreams?' I asked.

'Oh, you know,' she said. 'Because of increased confidence.'

I nodded my head. 'Right.'

'It's like my nose job,' she said. 'I don't look that different, but I feel different.'

'You had a nose job?' I asked. I couldn't tell.

'It's very subtle,' she said.

'But you look exactly the same.'

'Exactly the same,' she said, pointing at me, 'but better.'

The diet couldn't, of course, do all the things it claimed to. I knew that. But if even a part of it were true, I found myself thinking, it would be pretty great.

'It's no carbs at all for the first six weeks,' she explained, pulling out a little booklet she had in her back pocket. 'And then you phase a few back in. But none of the nasty ones.' She had me. She really had me. And even when she added, 'You have to eat beets, hard-boiled eggs, and kalamata olives every single day,' I was on board.

Before I knew it, I was home and tossing every carb I could spot into garbage bags. Though I couldn't bring myself to throw all that food away: I must have bagged up at least seventy dollars' worth. Instead, I put the bags in the back of Peter's closet, under a pile of winter coats.

That night, we had wieners, cottage cheese, cheese sticks, water, and beets for dinner. Peter came out of the practice room a little later and found us eating. 'What's this?' he asked, eyeing the food.

'We're eating healthy,' I said.

'Hot dogs are healthy?' he asked.

And I said, 'Meat is the new salad.'

He went to the cereal cabinet, but it was empty.

'Where's all the food?' he asked.

I wanted to tell him what I was doing, but I didn't want to call it a diet. I just didn't ever want him to even suspect all the mean things I was thinking about myself. Or the crazy things I was willing to do to change my thinking.

'It's a strength-training regime,' I said. 'It maximizes your muscle benefits.' Peter had already lost interest. He was poking Baby Sam in the belly. 'Kind of an all-protein thing,' I said.

'You're going to be eating this way?' he asked.

I nodded.

'All meat all the time?'

I nodded.

'It's good for you?' he asked.

'Yes,' I said. 'It gives you thicker hair, whiter teeth, stronger bones, longevity to die for, and a better s-e-x life.'

He surveyed the table for a minute, assessing the situation. Then he said, 'I'll do it with you,' and grabbed a hot dog off the lazy Susan.

I found this gesture indescribably touching. 'Thank you, Peter,' I said.

★ ★ ★

Peter didn't make it three hours on the diet. He was doomed from the beginning. In his whole slender, ectomorphic life, he had never, not even once, restricted what he'd put into his mouth. The idea was as foreign to him as, say, restricting showers, or restricting clothes, or restricting air. He could not wrap his head around it.

When I got back from the gym that night, he was eating a chocolate bar.

'Hey!' I said, pointing at it. 'You can't eat that.'

He didn't follow. 'Why not?'

'It's not on our healthy eating plan,' I said.

'But I'm hungry,' he said.

'Then you must eat a hot dog or a piece of cheese,' I said, as if I were talking to Alexander.

'Or a beet,' Peter added.

'Or a beet,' I confirmed.

Peter held the chocolate bar in his hand for a minute. Then he set it on the counter. Then he picked it back up. Finally, he said, 'I'm having the chocolate bar.'

'You're really terrible at this,' I said.

I felt a little smug that night, a little superior about my powers of self-deprivation. I could really control myself! I knew how to say no.

But I fell off the wagon the next day, too. I was pouring the boys' apple juice. And I wanted some. I really wanted some. I wanted some so badly that my mouth started to water. But I resisted. I set their sippy cups in front of them and put the bottle back in the fridge.

But then later, as the boys were watching home movies of my childhood trip to Disneyland, I snuck back into the kitchen and glugged half the bottle down, standing at the open fridge.

And there, with that bottle to my mouth and a gullet full of juice, I had a little epiphany: I did not want to live that way. As eager as I was to feel anything other than frumpy again, I wasn't going to do it like that. I didn't want the sight of apple juice to send me into a frenzy. I didn't want my life to be circumscribed by all the pleasures I couldn't taste.

The next time I saw Amanda, she said, 'I've lost four pounds! And my teeth are definitely whiter.' She gave me a big smile for proof.

And not until she said it did I realize, suddenly, that she had not needed to lose any weight to begin with.

'Why are you dieting, anyway?' I asked. 'You're already perfect.'

The question didn't interest her. 'Perfect is in the eye of the beholder,' she said. She moved on, but I found myself thinking about her husband — about what it must be like to crawl into bed next to someone every night who might or might not have been cheating on you that day, whose hands might or might not have been in someone else's hair, whose skin might or might not have been touching someone else's skin. I guess all marriages exist with that kind of uncertainty, though most people try not to think about it. Amanda was thinking about it, and dieting as if it were the only way to hold her life together. Of course, what neither of us realized then is that sometimes there is no way to hold your life together. Sometimes things just have to fall apart.

★　★　★

Not long after our attempt at healthy eating, I strolled with the boys past a dessert shop that I'd never seen before with an elegant sign that

162

read LIFE IS SWEET. It had a black-and-white-striped awning, and the sidewalk out in front was painted confection pink. I slowed my pace way down, gazed through the window as we passed, and ogled the desserts in the pastry display. They were enormous: the kind of desserts you could get lost in. Plate-size pieces of cake with inches of icing swirled all over them. Everything seemed overflowing with richness and chocolate and decadence.

I did not want to live a life without dessert. I did not want to live a life without those kinds of pleasures. I wished to be my old self again, but I did not wish to suffer to get there.

And so, as the boys and I continued on our walk, I set out a little list for myself of rules to live by: I was going to stop eating my meals standing at the kitchen counter — I was going to sit to eat like everybody else. I was going to go to the gym five times a week. I was going to drink water instead of juice and try to eat more vegetables. I was going to look through my old CDs, the ones that had been entirely replaced by nursery rhyme albums and counting songs, and boogie around with the kids to at least one 1970s funk song every day. I was going to keep an ongoing list of pleasures in life that were almost as good as food, things like back rubs and pedicures and going to the movies. And finally, come hell or high water, every single Saturday, I was going to go down to that insanely seductive little bakery at the corner of Huron and Archer — by myself with no distractions — and eat a giant piece of chocolate cake, bite by bite.

That didn't seem so hard.

* * *

Later that same night, Peter came up with a plan of his own. He decided that he wanted to go to the gym, too. He brought it up with me one night as I was heading out the front door. He had just seen a banner in the gym window that we could add a second membership for $19.95.

'We can afford that,' he said.

'No,' I said. 'You can't go.'

Nora was using our shower that night, and, at that moment, was not too many feet away. It had been two weeks since I'd agreed to let her use it. Apparently Josh had lost some of his gumption for the project after finding out that she'd be using our shower instead of his. He had only started work downstairs that morning. When I'd asked her if she thought we'd be getting a new shower, too, she'd

164

shrugged and said, 'I pay a lot more rent than you do.'

I had heard Nora's water turn off just before Peter stopped me. I didn't want her to hear us talking, so I kept my voice close to a whisper.

'It would be fun for me,' Peter said.

'No!' I said. 'The gym is my thing.'

'I'm sure there's more than one treadmill.'

'The gym is my one thing,' I said again. 'My only thing.'

'I just sit around all day,' he said. 'It's not healthy.'

'Here's what I have,' I went on: 'The gym.'

'And the kids,' he added.

'Sure, the kids,' I said. 'We both have the kids. But that cancels itself out.'

'Here's what you have,' I said, counting on my fingers: 'Classes, professors, practice time, students who worship you, time to write — '

'Papers to grade,' he went on, 'kids who don't practice, pressure to be the best, a giant piece due in January, carpal tunnel from practicing on that little keyboard, and writer's block.'

'You have writer's block?' I asked.

He nodded.

It was an opportunity for me to feel sympathy for him, to offer him comfort. But instead of sympathy, I just felt irritated. 'Well, what are you doing all day, then?'

He looked a little irritated himself. 'I am trying to write. And failing.'

And then Peter played his trump card. 'I can't seem to write,' he said, giving me a little glimpse of how distraught he was. 'And I read online that working out frees up trapped creativity.'

Now, suddenly, he'd raised the stakes. Now my not sharing the gym was putting his livelihood in jeopardy. In that moment, I lost the argument. I heard Nora knock something over in the bathroom. I rubbed my forehead with my palm and lowered my voice. 'When would you even go?'

'I'll just go after you do.'

'That's not going to work,' I said. 'They close at nine.'

That stumped him. 'Maybe we could take turns,' he suggested.

And then I had my dander up again. Because I was going to the gym every weeknight. I was in a groove. I liked going. I did not want to give up any nights. I did not want to take turns. I did not want to change anything at all. Writer's block or no, he wasn't taking my nights.

But he really wanted them.

'Two. Just give me two.'

The gym closed at five on the weekends.

Giving him two left me with only three, and I told him so.

He said, 'That's still more than I have!'

'But it's not nearly enough!' My voice had gone up. I glanced over at the bathroom door, then moved Peter a little deeper into the living room.

'Peter,' I said. 'You're really asking me for something I can't give you.'

He studied me then, trying to decide if I was really serious. He didn't understand, and I wasn't about to explain it. It wasn't that I wouldn't. I couldn't.

'Maybe,' Peter suggested in a louder voice than either of us realized, 'we could ask the woman downstairs to babysit.'

'No,' I said.

'Why not?'

'Because she's a b-i-t-c-h. That's why.'

It's funny to me now, looking back, that I was so used to spelling things with Peter when I wanted to communicate something private, I spelled something like that to him so loudly with Nora only a few feet away — forgetting that she, too, like most adults, could spell.

Before Peter could respond, I heard her voice in the bathroom. She said, 'I can h-e-a-r you!'

Peter looked at me like I'd really blown it.

The door opened. Nora, in her pajamas and bathrobe, with her wet hair combed neatly, was holding her refolded towel and a little shower basket.

'I'd be happy to babysit two nights a week,' she said.

We both stared at her.

Then I started to say, 'No thank you, we're fine' — which, in retrospect, would have sounded ridiculous, given that she had clearly just heard our whole fight — but Peter beat me to the punch. He said, 'Great!' and swooped his arms around Nora and gave a big enough hug to lift her off the floor.

The hug caught her by surprise, and she let out a little laugh as he lifted her. I had never seen her do anything other than scowl — and as soon as her feet touched the floor, the smile was gone. She smoothed her hair.

'Peter,' I said. 'Can I talk to you in private?'

We moved into our bedroom, and I shut the door.

'She's not babysitting our kids,' I whispered.

He looked at me like I was crazy. 'Because?'

'Because she's mean.'

'Offering to babysit doesn't seem so mean,' he said. 'Maybe now she wants to be nice.'

'Or maybe she wants to light the place on

fire while we're away.'

'I guess that's possible,' Peter said, in a give-me-a-break tone.

And I was acting crazy. Here Nora had just offered to solve this whole problem. What did it matter if I liked her or not? But I resented Peter for the whole situation. Didn't he have enough good things in his life? Did he really have to siphon off mine?

'Fine,' I said. What else was I going to say? Then I pointed right at Peter. 'But she's up to something.'

15

That night, Peter went to the gym to sign up and I stayed home to keep an eye on Nora. She'd set her shower things in a neat pile by the door and was now getting the tour of our house. I had a pot of tea brewing for us on the stove in hopes that it might make us feel like people who would have tea together.

'This apartment looks like hell,' she said, as I walked her through the living room. 'The plaster is cracking, that light fixture looks like it's going to explode, and that oven's got to be forty years old.'

I cocked my ears. Was she going to criticize me? Did she possibly think she could point out one flaw in my apartment or my life that I hadn't already examined from fifty different angles? She had no idea who she was messing with. 'It's not the plaster,' I said. 'It's the toys everywhere, the fact that we can't afford curtains, the shitty furniture, the bad paint colors left over from the last tenant, the crayon drawings on the walls, the ground-in raisins in the rug, the pee stain on the couch, and the general sense of desperation.'

That got her. She followed me into the

kitchen. 'I just meant you should call Josh. Make him fix that stuff.'

'I *have* called him,' I said.

'Oh.' Then, 'He has several other buildings,' she said, by way of excusing him.

'His grandparents do,' I pointed out.

'Right,' she said. 'They sure keep him busy.'

I poured the tea and we sat across from each other. There were so many things I would rather have been doing at that moment. Me in my sad little exercise togs and her in her husband's bathrobe. After a pause, I finally said, 'I'm just not sure why you're doing this.'

'I'm trying to be n-i-c-e,' she said.

'Right,' I said.

We each took a sip of tea. Then she squinted a little and said, 'Too little too late?'

I shrugged. It wasn't quite enough of an answer for me. Not for a person who seemed so decidedly to enjoy being mean.

Nora was watching me with a look on her face like she could read my thoughts. She raised her shoulders in defeat. 'And,' she added, 'I really need a reason to get out of my apartment.'

The kitchen was very quiet after that. I could hear the neighbor's TV going, the hum of the refrigerator, and the faucet dripping. After a while, I figured I'd better say

171

something. So I threw a good one at her, just to stir things up. I said, 'Josh saw me naked in here once.'

Her eyes snapped open as if I had screamed.

'He did?' And there it was again, that smile from before, but now just at the eyes. She thought it was funny. Which it was.

I gave a little eye-smile back. 'He was painting outside. And my kids had taken my bath towel.'

'Unbelievable!' she said.

'He was very polite about it,' I said.

'What did he say?'

'He told me he hadn't seen anything.'

'But had he?'

I made a little grimace and nodded.

She tilted her head at me. 'I can count on one finger the men who have seen me naked.'

'Well,' I said, 'my number seems to be growing.' There it was again: the eye-smile. The more I saw it, the more I wanted to see it. 'We should go streaking one night and get your number up.' Then, a real smile, which she covered with her free hand.

'He really was very nice about it,' I said again.

'He's a sweet kid,' she said.

'He kind of adores you,' I said, following a hunch.

She looked up in a thoughtful way, and then started nodding. 'Does he? Huh.'

After another little silence, Nora insisted that I go ahead and go to the gym. She pointed out that Peter would be home soon, anyway. If I left now, I could get my jog in before they closed.

It seemed crazy to leave the three most precious people in my life in the care of a person who had never said a nice thing to me until tonight. And yet, it also seemed crazy to stay home when I could so easily go. I hadn't seen it before, but now that she was here in my kitchen, her soft PJ collar too large around her neck, I saw something in her: a decency that had been hidden before. Suddenly I felt as certain of her as anyone ever is with the people they entrust their children to. For no tangible reason, I felt she would take good care of them.

She thought it was ridiculous for me to miss my nightly ritual when she was sitting right there in the kitchen. 'You can't possibly need more than one person to look after your kids when they are asleep.'

I decided to level with her. 'I'm nervous they might wake up.'

'Do they wake up a lot?'

'No,' I said. Then, 'Sometimes. It goes in waves.'

She sized me up a little, and then said, 'What's the problem?'

I took a breath, and then with a jolt of fear that I might be about to kill this new babysitting arrangement that really seemed to have some potential and destroy any possibility of seeing another smile from Nora, I said, 'We all call you the Mean Witch.'

She was unfazed. 'So?'

'So if Alexander were to, say, wake up and find you here with no parents anywhere to be seen — '

'He might think I had eaten you?'

I nodded. 'Or turned us into mice. Or sold us to a troll. Or put us to sleep for a hundred years.'

'I see,' she said.

'He's been concerned about some of these things,' I said.

'You mean, living so close to a witch.'

I nodded.

'And why does he think I'm a witch?' She already knew the answer to this question. Maybe she wanted to see what I'd say.

'I'm not sure,' I said.

She knew I was lying, of course. Alexander thought she was a witch because I had told him she was a witch. Not thinking that he would take it literally. Not thinking that the fact of a witch in the apartment downstairs would become one of those truths that he hung on to that could never be disputed.

'Here's what I'll tell him,' she said, 'if he wakes up. I'll say that you and his daddy caught me when I was flying on my broom and caged me up here and took away all my magic powers. Then you fed me whipped cream and magic strawberries that turned me into a good witch. Now you've gone to fetch the Golden Tiara from city hall, and when you get back, I'll put it on and can never be bad again.'

I blinked a little. She was good. 'We'll have to get you a tiara,' I said.

'Oh, I have a bunch downstairs.'

I wasn't sure if she was kidding or not, but I didn't really care. This time, when she said, 'Get going,' I went.

As I approached the gym it occurred to me that Peter did not know I was coming. He thought I was staying home the whole time with Nora. Something about surprising him at the gym made me anxious. What if he was flirting with someone? What if he acted differently when I wasn't with him, and I was only now going to glimpse it?

It was one thing to see him in his pajamas, padding around our house. It was another thing entirely to see him across a crowded gym of strangers.

Nora had solved our basic problem: I did not have to give up my nights. But she hadn't changed the fact that I still didn't want him to be there. It wasn't, as I might have led Peter to believe, that I was possessive of the gym. I was just self-conscious. I didn't want him to see me sweaty and red-faced in my limp T-shirt, panting for breath. I might not have looked like a supermodel when I first woke up in the morning, or ever, but I never looked as bad in everyday life as I did at the gym. And I knew this for a fact because there were mirrors everywhere. I couldn't miss myself.

I just felt that there were enough strains on the romance of our relationship — from Peter's work schedule, to general parental exhaustion, to crying children, to never having time alone together, to not even being able to get a sentence uttered without Alexander shouting, 'Daddy! Don't talk to Mama! Talk to me!' — for me to want to add even one thing that might work against it. Like a fresh, nightly image in Peter's head of me looking terrible.

So when I stepped into the room that had all the cardio machines in it and I spotted Peter across the way jogging on a treadmill, I did not go over and say hello. I slunk to the back row at the opposite corner near the water fountain and, busily, as if I were any stranger, set about doing my own workout.

But I watched him the whole time. I watched his calf muscles flexing and releasing with each step. I watched the way he brought his right arm back a little farther than his left. I watched his floppy yellow hair — so much blonder under the fluorescent lights — and noticed how dark it was down near his neck, where it was wet with sweat. It was bizarre to see him from a distance. I was used to him close up.

It was also bizarre to compare him to the other people in the room — something I definitely didn't want him doing to me. Peter did well by comparison. Most of the guys there were just plain unattractive. Perhaps, during the day, in their business clothes, they were okay. But here, in their workout shorts, with their furry legs and their red faces, they looked like warthogs. Pink, sweaty, cardiovascularly challenged warthogs.

It was fun to note that Peter was cuter than every single guy in the gym — including Ted Koppel, who was lifting weights in his flip-flops and a Hawaiian shirt, and who was watching me watch Peter. Ted Koppel knew I was ogling Peter but couldn't have known that Peter was my husband. I wondered if Ted Koppel thought I had a crush on a total stranger at the gym. At some point, of course, Peter was going to notice me watching him. And then he'd come up and give me a kiss. But for now, Peter was as far away from me as anybody else in the room.

The vast majority of the women at the gym looked super-sexy, by the way, in contrast to the men. The women had their black spandex workout gear, their hair up in perky ponytails. They didn't seem to sweat so much as glow. They moved on their machines like little forest nymphs. Not all of the women were small, of course, but all of them, with the possible exception of me, seemed clean and put-together and fragrant.

I tried to think of what I'd say to Peter when he'd finished his jog. He couldn't walk out the door without passing right in front of me. And by this point in the workout, I was starting to feel a little like a sweaty warthog myself. I thought about going to get a sip of water from the fountain just as he was about to go by and hiding my face until he was gone.

As he slowed his machine to cool down with a few minutes of walking, I actually felt a tingle of fear in my fingertips. I hadn't felt nervous about Peter in years, but something about not wanting him to see me, and, at the same time, really wanting to talk to him, made things kind of intense in a way I hadn't anticipated. Something about the fact that he was right there, but I couldn't talk to him. Something about how handsome he was. I felt like a middle-school girl hiding by her locker as her crush walked by.

When he stepped off his machine, I forced myself to keep walking. He was my husband! He had watched me give birth — three times! I was not going to hide at the water fountain like a thirteen-year-old girl. My heart was absolutely pounding as he started walking in my direction. I couldn't look. I may even have held my breath.

But something happened as he left the gym that I never would have expected — something that left me wondering if we had let ourselves float so far apart during these baby-raising years that we had, on some level, truly become strangers. Because Peter walked right past my treadmill to head out of the gym. Just walked right on by, three feet away, and didn't even notice I was there.

16

The very first time I ever heard Peter play piano was in college — a few days after he'd sketched my picture in Life Drawing. That day in class, I had thought he might give me the drawing. But he didn't. He just took it down after the critique, made his way back over to his easel, and slipped it into his portfolio. I was too shy to ask him for it. I was too shy to even try to talk to him again. Instead, I just messed around with my supplies, acting very busy and preoccupied, until he left.

Once he was gone, I went to the window to look at the side-walk down below, and when he appeared on the path, I watched him work his way toward the cafeteria. My stomach was in a fist. I had blown it. He had drawn my picture in art class, and I hadn't even thanked him. I had barely even spoken.

If I were a smart girl, if I were the girl I wanted to be, I'd have walked right over to him after class, brought my body up next to him, and put my mouth to his in a great passionate kiss there in front of everybody. If I had risen to the moment, I would have done something as brave as he had. At the very least, I could have carried his drawing supplies to lunch.

But now he was limping down the path to the cafeteria alone. A guy on a bike waved at him, then hopped off to walk alongside and carry his things. I stood at the window until they had rounded the arts building, and then I slowly packed up my stuff, dropping my own uninspired drawing of our class nude in the trash can on the way out.

After that, I was sure I'd lost him. He had put himself out there in the most exceptional public way, and all I had said to him was, 'I think you're going to get in trouble.' What I should have offered was encouragement, some kind of gesture to bring him closer. But I'd been too scared. I revised the moment over and over in my mind, making myself braver each time. But what had happened had happened. I had missed my chance.

I kept an eye out for him everywhere after that. With those crutches, he should have been easy to spot. But as the days went by and I didn't see him, I started to worry that I'd been wrong to see his drawing as a gesture of love.

'Don't be stupid,' Connor said. 'Of course he likes you.'

'Maybe he was just uninspired by the model,' I said.

'No,' Connor said.

'Maybe his final project will be to draw every person in the class, and he just started with me.'

Connor thought about that one. 'That's more plausible,' she said.

Peter and I were, in fact, the two students that Shane liked best in that class. In any given critique, Shane pointed out our drawings as examples to everybody else. I was an art major, so I was hungry for the praise and encouragement. Peter, of course, was a music major, so he didn't really care.

It was conceivable that Peter had worked out some kind of funky, real-people final project with Shane. I was still stewing over what mine would be, and we didn't have to decide for a month yet. But Peter had a kind of enviable, easy brilliance like that. The more I thought about it, the more convinced I became that I was just a drawing project.

'But what about the other day in my room?' Connor demanded.

'Maybe we misread it,' I said. 'Maybe we wanted to believe so much I was the person he liked, that's what we saw.'

Suddenly, we could think of a hundred

reasons Peter might have seemed nervous in Connor's room.

'Maybe he suddenly remembered he'd forgotten to turn in a paper,' she offered.

'Maybe it was an instant headache,' I said, building momentum. 'Or a stomach cramp. Or a wave of nausea.' What had we been thinking? We were stupid girls. We could so easily have conjured the whole thing. In seconds, we had come up with more alternate reasons for his behavior than I cared to count, including a forgotten tutorial, a previously unrevealed shy streak, a panic attack, a toe cramp, and — Connor's suggestion — a sudden bout of diarrhea. But when I thought about his eyes that night at the moment he saw me there in her room, I wanted it to be love so badly that I had to rest my head in my hands.

Now I was desperate to see him. I needed new interactions to help me judge his feelings. But I was also discouraged. Connor and I had talked up a love and then talked it away. And that's why, on the night I found him playing piano in the lobby of their dorm, I could not bring myself to say hello.

It was late. I had missed dinner working in the printmaking studio, and on the phone, Connor had offered me some of the apple strudel her mother had just sent. I had bundled up and walked over to her dorm, anticipating, as I always did, the detour I would take to walk past Peter's door and the tingle of fear I'd feel at the possibility that I might see him — but also at the idea that he could be in his room, just feet away from me, only a door between us. He had a bumper sticker on his door that said SAVE THE SKEET, a photo of him as a child in a cowboy hat, a photo of Bob Dylan, a quail feather, and a number of *New Yorker* cartoons that mocked classical musicians.

But Peter wasn't in his room. He was in the lobby. I heard the music before I'd even walked into the building.

The sound seemed to fill up the dorm. I knew it had to be him. I'd never heard him play, but I just knew. I stopped walking just inside the dorm doors and froze. I couldn't decide if I should walk past the common room or sneak up the back stairs and avoid the issue altogether. In the end, of course, I had to see him playing. I had to peek for myself.

Peter was alone at the grand piano in the corner. His back was to me, and his crutches leaned against a nearby chair. I stood behind the doorway, just edging around. I was even afraid to look. I didn't want him to feel my eyes on him and turn around.

184

But I didn't have to worry. The longer I watched him, the more I realized he was barely even in the room. His whole body was moving — his fingers and hands and arms, his good leg as he pumped the pedals, his shoulders. There was something so athletic about it. It was as if he were trying to climb into the keys somehow. As if he were more inside the music, pushed around by its currents, than he was making it. It was like nothing I'd ever seen.

And the music itself. These days, in Cambridge, he played classical music, but back then, he played a lot of jazz, too. Even though almost everyone else in the music department played classical, Peter loved ragtime. Other music majors called him Joplin. He was a little bit famous.

Right then, he was obsessed with a thing I'd never even heard of called stride piano, which was a way of jumping back and forth between octaves. He'd hit a chord down at one end, in the high notes, and the next second, he'd hit a corresponding chord in the middle with the same hand. His hands leapt out to the ends of the keyboard and then back together as if he were conducting an orchestra. I could not for the life of me imagine how he could move his hands that fast and hit the right keys every time. I knew next to nothing about music. But after that night I knew one thing for sure: He was incredible.

And it turns out, he was incredible. At the end of the year, I wound up with one of the art awards, but he wound up with every music award there was.

Watching him that night made everything worse, because now I knew what I was dealing with. He wasn't just a cute guy from the library. He was something special. There was a reason that I wasn't on fire for Rob Garrison and Steven McFarland or the other comparable boys in his dorm. It was because they weren't Peter. It was because Peter Coates, I knew, in that clear-headed way that only twenty-one-year-olds can know things, was the only person I would ever love.

I felt sick to my stomach after that. I couldn't even eat my apple strudel. I poked at it with a plastic fork while Connor talked about her anthropology paper on Australopithecus. I fidgeted to get back downstairs. I listened to determine if he was still down there playing.

'These early hominids,' Connor was going on. 'They're just really a mystery.'

'Sure,' I nodded.

'Don't you like the strudel?' Connor pointed at it.

'Um,' I said. 'I just walked past Peter.'

She raised her eyebrows. A much better topic than hominids. 'Did you say hi?'

I shook my head.

'Dammit!' she said, swatting at me. She resolved to send me back downstairs — I could see it in her face as she got up and moved to her dresser. She pulled out some hairspray and a comb and started to mess with my hair. I closed my eyes and wrinkled my nose. 'Don't make me look like a drag queen,' I said.

'I'm just freshening you up,' she said. 'You look a little limp.'

After hair, we did lipstick and eyeliner. Then she made me switch out my sweater for one of hers that was slightly tighter.

When she sent me back downstairs, she had to push me out the door like a baby bird. She said, 'Be brave!'

'Come with me,' I begged.

'Nope,' she said. Though I could tell she wanted to. 'It would ruin the effect.'

Peter was still playing. I could hear it, even up on the third floor. I steered myself down the stairs. I'd just tell him I loved his drawing. Easy. And then we'd either start chatting, or we wouldn't. He'd either reel me into conversation, or he wouldn't. We'd either have a spark, or we wouldn't. But all I had to do was say that one sentence to him, now with slightly better hair. 'I loved your drawing.' Or maybe 'loved' sounded too desperate. But 'liked' seemed lukewarm. I settled on 'really liked.' Then, judging from his reaction, I could convey extra passion by adding, 'Really. A lot.' If that seemed appropriate.

My hands felt clammy, and I shook them a little as I made it to the bottom of the stairs. The music was all around me now. I moved toward the common room — and it was suddenly full of people. Two guys — friends of Peter's — were tossing a Frisbee back and forth across the room, and a gaggle of girls were standing around the piano, talking to Peter and bobbing to the music.

I froze, then turned and walked out of the dorm. Out on the sidewalk in the cold night, I could see Peter through the windows. The room was lit warm and yellow, and for the first time all night, I could see his face. He seemed cheerful and happy, and he was chatting a little with the girls. But he also seemed far away, like his mind was elsewhere, like the music was a louder voice to him than any person's in the room.

17

On the night I had my free personal training session, I lost my wedding ring.

It was a plain gold band, half of a his-and-hers matched pair that we'd bought from an estate jeweler for two hundred dollars. My ring was inscribed with the name 'Herbert' and Peter's was inscribed with 'Geneva.' I had insisted to Peter that I didn't mind having a pre-owned ring, that I liked the idea of its history, which was true. We'd had our own initials engraved in the rings to put our own stamp on them, but sometimes we called each other by those other names when we were feeling ornery.

'Herb,' I'd say to Peter, 'can you bring me a glass of water?'

I'd squeezed my training session into the last hour before the gym closed. Only a few other people were there, including the couple I loved so much and Ted Koppel. I was a little embarrassed to have my ass kicked in front of Ted Koppel for some reason, and I kept wishing he would go home. The last thing I needed was someone taking note of how out of shape I was. Though that's exactly what the trainer was doing — on a clipboard. And not just any trainer. The ass-slapping trainer.

He had turned out to be just as much of a flirt as Ted Koppel had promised that first night. I'd kept an eye on him. He flirted with absolutely everybody. His hand had been on every single ass in the room. His flirtatiousness was so broad, it was meaningless.

But not when he was working. Now we were in training mode. Now he was a hard-ass turning me into a hard-body — in fifty-five minutes or less. He put me through a series of tests — how many push-ups I could do (five), how many times I could go up and down the stairs in two minutes (three), and how many times I could jump rope without tripping (forty-six) — marking everything off on a clipboard. It was deeply humiliating. I knew I was out of shape, but I had never quantified it in this manner. If I'd known he was going to be measuring me like this, I'd probably have declined the session. After a while, he put me back on the treadmill, tilted it as high as it would go, and had me walk on it until I thought my lungs might collapse.

The next test was sit-ups. The trainer pulled out a mat and said, 'Let's see how many you can do. Three minutes. Go.'

First, let me say that I know how to do a

sit-up. Everybody knows how to do a sit-up. It's a simple motion. But even though I knew exactly what to do, and even though I commanded my body to do it, I couldn't. It was a strange kind of paralysis. My brain was giving the command it always gave, but my body just didn't follow.

'Go,' the trainer said again.

'I can't,' I said.

I'm sure the trainer, by virtue of his job, had met many people in his work who told him that they 'couldn't' do something that he told them to do. I am equally sure that he thought those people were wimps. I did not know how to explain to him that I wasn't exaggerating. It wasn't that I didn't want to sit up. It was that I couldn't. Whatever muscles I had called on in the past to make that very same motion just weren't there.

'They're there,' he said. 'You just have to find them.'

I lay flat. I told my body to move. Nothing happened. I thought about the dark brown stretch marks that had crisscrossed my belly like brambles each time I'd been pregnant. I imagined the muscles underneath looked just about as bad. Maybe I'd broken them. Or ruined them. Maybe my abdomen had just said, 'Enough!' and thrown in the towel.

Whatever was going on, I had to lie there

for five excruciating minutes while he tried to pep-talk me into the five sit-up minimum.

In the end, I got one — if we rounded up.

So by the time we made it to the pull-up bar, I was ready to try extra hard, to show this perky fitness enthusiast that I didn't have a bad attitude. I gathered every ounce of gumption I had and pulled my chin up to the bar. But somehow, as I squeezed the bar, I managed to pinch the skin between the bar and my wedding ring. I dropped to the ground to look at my hand.

'We're not even close to done,' the trainer started to say, but I turned my hand, now pooling a dark blood blister under my ring, toward him. 'Damn,' he said, a little impressed. I wasn't making this one up.

He made me take off the ring and offered to hold it for me. He wasn't sure how big that blood blister was going to get, and it was clear that my jewelry was getting in the way of my personal best. But I wasn't going to hand off my wedding ring to a total stranger. In nine years of marriage, I had never taken it off. Instead, I tied the ring to the drawstring of my pants in a carefully tightened triple knot.

At the end of the evaluation, we had learned many things about me: I had a strong back, biceps, and calves. My 'areas for improvement' included my triceps, hamstrings, nonexistent stomach muscles, and pretty much everything else. We had also learned that I had a tendency to become sarcastic in the face of intimidating physical challenges, and that my positive attitude was questionable.

I walked home, deciding that the whole point of 'one free session' was to humiliate people into taking out loans to finance personal training. I hadn't expected such a graphic depiction of my state of disrepair. I'd just thought we were going to mess around on some of those machines for a while and wrap things up.

It wasn't until I was almost home that I remembered to put my ring back on. I reached down and found the drawstring on my pants. Then I found that, despite my three very tight knots, it had come untied. My ring was gone.

I turned and sprinted back up the hill to the gym doors, my muscles, which had already been quivering, screaming in protest the entire way. I couldn't remember the last time I'd run so fast. I didn't know then that the next day, and the day after it, and the day after that, I was going to be so sore I could barely make it up the steps or lift the baby. I didn't know then that my muscles were about to hurt so badly I wouldn't want to touch, much less use, them. All I knew was that I had to find my ring. Right away.

The gym doors were locked when I got there, and everybody seemed to be gone. The lights were off inside. I knocked, and then banged, hoping maybe the trainer was in the back, wondering what Peter would say when I arrived home with no wedding ring — wondering if he would even notice, in fact. Or if he would just assume it to be there and fail to notice its absence the way I always failed to notice he'd gotten a haircut: I knew what his hair looked like. My eyes knew what to see without even looking.

After a few minutes, I bent over to catch my breath and regroup. It was September now, and starting to get chilly. My T-shirt was wet with sweat, and I noticed suddenly that I was cold. And that's when Ted Koppel pulled over to the curb in his Jeep and rolled down the window.

'Can't stay away?' he teased.

I could not disguise the panic in my voice. I said, 'I lost my wedding ring!' and then I turned to bang on the door some more.

He made a sharp whistle like you might make to a dog.

I turned around and he was holding it up

to me. 'I was just on my way to hock it,' he said.

He leaned out the window and then, to my absolute disbelief, tossed the ring to me. I watched it fly up and then curve back down, and I had the sinking feeling I used to have in soft-ball that, despite the importance of rising to the moment, I would drop it. I raised my hands, even as I imagined the ring flying past them, hitting the ground, rolling into the gutter — even as I wondered out loud what kind of a person would toss another person's wedding ring through the air like that.

As the ring came closer, I clasped both hands together and, by some luck that had never been with me before, caught it. I clutched it tight for a minute as Ted Koppel explained that he'd found it on the floor next to the water fountain. He'd stepped on it, actually.

'I didn't know you were married,' he said.

'Yep,' I said, popping my ring back into the little groove it had worn into my finger as proof.

Ted Koppel offered me a ride home, which I refused, and then he seemed to linger a little, as if he were trying to come up with a new topic of conversation. But I was going home. I had my ring, and I was done. I thanked him for finding it, but he shook his head. 'Just good luck,' he said.

On the walk home, I thought about Ted Koppel. He appeared to be a fashion-challenged, authority-bucking, iconoclastic loner with no regard for the meaning of marriage. But part of me liked the fact that he was always checking me out: Even when he wasn't watching me, he was watching me. He was not, on any level, a threat to Peter. I didn't even like him. But I will confess, if you really want to know, that I did like being liked.

18

The next night, Thursday, I skipped the gym (as I would do all semester) to go to my first photography class. Peter did not seem to notice my willingness to give up the gym on those nights, or contrast it with my flat refusal to sacrifice even five minutes of gym time for him. Or maybe he was just giving me a little breathing room. Either way, I felt grateful to him for letting it lie.

That night, I raced over to the Extension School lab and was totally out of breath when I walked in late, ready to apologize to the instructor. I had planned it all out: how I would sneak in the back and take notes on everything he or she said and how, at the appropriate moment, I would pull him or her aside to explain my bedtime predicament: that with three little squirmy kids, bedtime took two adults minimum, and I wouldn't be able to leave the house until the bedtime routine was over. I'd be late to every class, and that was that — but my lateness did not reflect my level of enthusiasm. It was an important speech, since I was already desperate to win the approval of my instructor, sight unseen.

I'd been planning what I'd say all week.

But instead, when I walked in, I had to revise my plan. Because the instructor of this class, the person standing at the front of the room, wasn't just a 'him' or a 'her.' The instructor was, of all possible people in the world, Ted Koppel.

I froze as soon as I saw him. And he froze, mid-sentence, too. People waited for him to start talking again, which he didn't, and then they started looking back and forth between us. One guy even cleared his throat.

Finally, Ted Koppel spoke. He said, 'Are you going to be late to every class?'

And I said, 'Yes. I am.'

He'd been introducing himself to the group when I walked in, and it took him a few seconds to pull himself together. But once he revved up again, he really got going. For weeks, all I'd really known about this man at the gym was his penchant for flip-flops and tropical apparel. Now I got specifics — countless details about his life in an avalanche of personal history, starting with his name, which was not, of course, Ted Koppel. It was Nelson Frank. And he was, among other things, a divorcé and former magazine photographer. 'I'm ex-paparazzi, too,' he told us on that first night. 'I just didn't have the balls for it.'

'Who did you stalk?' a guy in plaid shorts wanted to know.

'I was strictly D-list,' Nelson answered. 'They had me on the Danny Bonaduce beat.'

He was recently divorced. Very recently. As in two-weeks-ago recently. Or at least, that's when he'd signed the final papers. In class, he wore rumpled corduroy pants and rumpled oxford shirts — and his flip-flops. He told us his wife had ironed for him when they were married, but that he hadn't wanted her to. She had done it because she couldn't stand to see a grown man walking around in wrinkled clothes. But she resented it. Now he was free to wear his clothes the way he liked, but she'd ruined it for him. He couldn't even be himself anymore.

This was the bulk of his welcome talk.

'I'm forty-five years old,' he told us, 'and I have nothing.'

Some of the grandmotherly types in the class argued this point, offering encouragement and trying to help him find a bright side.

'No,' he cut them all off. 'I have nothing. But let's talk about photography.'

We were expected to develop our own film and make our own prints in the darkroom. It was black-and-white photography, and if we wanted lessons on taking pictures of our grandchildren with digital cameras we weren't going to get them with Nelson. Real photography was about finding the extraordinary — in the ordinary or anyplace else. He showed us around the facility. It had a big light table to look at negatives on, some totally dark closets for handling exposed film, and a large darkroom with long sinks in the middle for developing pictures. It was a clean, busy place, and I loved it right away.

The darkroom had a black cylindrical door to keep the light out. When I stepped in, Nelson stepped in after me. As the door spun around us, he said, 'You're the one on scholarship?'

'Yes.'

'I saw your application. Those were some great paintings.'

'I don't know,' I said. 'Maybe.'

We walked into the darkroom.

'You don't think they were great?' he asked.

'I think they never amounted to much,' I said.

The class was assembling behind us for a lesson on enlargers. He leaned over to me and said in a whisper, 'It's nice to see you in something other than workout gear.'

And I couldn't think of anything to say then, other than, 'Thanks.'

In the darkroom, he talked to us about

chemicals and timers and the basics of how to print, and then he told us that his ex-wife had taken his dog when she left. 'I found that damn dog,' he said, as we all looked on. 'I'm the one who named her.'

'What's her name?' a bald guy with a thick beard asked.

'Her name is Babette,' he said. 'And she can balance a bottle of San Pellegrino on her nose.'

Nelson had worked for a variety of local papers before landing this teaching job. He was still freelancing, but this job gave him some security — something his wife had always wanted. Now he had the security, but not the wife. He also had a portrait business, he added, if we knew anybody who needed pictures. Weddings, kids, pets. He did it all.

We had been instructed to shoot a roll of film before the first class, so I had brought my mom's camera to a photography store on Mass Ave. the week before to ask them how to use it. I bribed my children with lollipops to sit still, while the sales guy, who had numbers tattooed all over his forearms, walked me through the steps. It wasn't too hard. I just had to crank a spool of film about as wide as a lasagna noodle into the body of the camera. Then I had to focus and check the light meter. And then snap.

Later, at the park, Baby Sam had gnawed on a granola bar while the other two boys built a giant volcano of pebbles and I walked all around taking photos. I discovered a couple of things during that trip to the park: One, I loved taking those photographs. I loved looking through the eye of the lens, scanning for a perfect shape or moment to capture. I loved the idea that the art was already there, and all I had to do was find it. And two, because this camera hung at my belly, because it was so old-timey that people didn't get how it worked — or even know it was a camera — and because the click it made when I snapped the picture was almost imperceptible, I could take pictures without anybody realizing what I was doing. Folks thought I was fiddling with my camera — or possibly my purse — when, in fact, I was focusing, snapping, and moving on to the next target.

I loved the anonymity of it. I loved moving through all the crazy personal moments happening all around me and recording the most vivid — the baby reaching to be picked up, the mother rubbing her tired eyes, the boy in the plaid shirt with the toy plane. We were supposed to shoot one roll of film for class, but I had shot seven.

Nelson showed us how to develop film that

first night, and I developed all my rolls. I felt a crazy urgency about being there. I was not going to waste a single second.

'I assume you're all here because you're missing something in your lives,' Nelson said to us, as he brought the first class to its close. We were gathered around the light table. 'You're hoping I might be able to help you find what you're looking for. Well, let me tell you something. Photography will break your heart. You'll either have no talent for it, which will be awkward and make you feel worthless, or you'll be great at it, which will be worse.' He was moving around us as a group, seeming to think out loud. 'But whatever you're looking for,' he continued, 'I can guarantee you're not going to find it. Not for three hundred bucks at an extension school. That's not how life works.'

He started handing out the syllabus and some coupons for his favorite camera shop. Then he pointed at me. 'This one here was a painter. But she never made it. If she had, she wouldn't be here.'

He scratched his forehead. 'Here's my advice: Go whole hog. You want to change your life? You want to do something that matters? Something that makes you feel proud? Something that nobody else can do? Then I better not see just two pictures a week, I better see twenty.' He looked around to see that we all had our handouts, which we did. 'Now,' he said, heading for the exit, 'I'm going home to get drunk.' His flip-flops squeaked on the way out. The door slammed behind him. And we were dismissed.

'What a jackass,' the bald guy said, as we stood blinking at one another like a herd of cattle. 'That guy's a dick.'

We all nodded, me included. Of course. Of course he was. But I, for one, was going to do whatever he said.

The second class, I spent the entire time in the darkroom. I cannot describe how thrilling it was to watch the images of the photos appear on the paper as it floated in the chemical baths. And from the very first picture I printed — an image of a little kid about to drop from the monkey bars, taken from below, his arms on either side of his frightened face at one angle and his mother's arms reaching for him at another — I knew that I wanted to be in that darkroom every breathing minute that I could.

Perhaps it was just the timing. Maybe I was just ready to be consumed by a pursuit of my own. It's possible that if I'd gone back to painting at this exact moment instead of photography, it might have hit me the same way. But that's not the way it happened. I started this class, and before I knew it, I was spending every evening minute that I wasn't at the gym in the darkroom.

At the park, I took a lot of pictures of Amanda. She loved it when she could pose: She'd kiss at the camera and lean in like Marilyn Monroe. She liked it less well when I followed her for candids. 'Now you're being a nuisance,' she'd say, as I snapped pictures of her holding Gracin up to the water fountain.

'I'm not interested in taking your picture when you're acting beautiful,' I said. 'I want to take your picture when you're being beautiful by accident.'

'Nothing beautiful is an accident,' she said.

And when I took pictures of Gracin with her legs covered in Band-Aids, Amanda said, 'Let me take the Band-Aids off.'

'It's the Band-Aids that make the picture,' I told her.

I took photos everywhere. That camera was around my neck at the grocery, around the neighborhood, at the drugstore, and, of course, at the park. The boys wanted to play with it, but I was uncharacteristically stern. I protected it in a way that I had never protected my wallet, or my makeup, or my toothbrush. I told the older boys it was 'dangerous' and they must never touch it, and I told Baby Sam that it was 'hot.' He was good at hot. We ate hot peas and hot carrots and hot broccoli all the time. He knew what to do with hot, and whenever he was near the camera, he'd blow on it.

At the darkroom, Nelson developed a tendency to hover behind me while I was printing. 'You're the only one in here doing anything interesting,' he whispered over my shoulder while I was working.

'Okay,' I whispered back.

And then he started talking to me about the gym. He had joined to get fit and make his ex-wife sorry she left him. His plan was to buff up, and then swing by her new apartment in a tight T-shirt and jeans. 'That'll kill her,' he said. 'That'll really kill her.'

★ ★ ★

On the night of our first critique, three weeks into the class, I had fifteen photographs. Everybody else had two each.

'Should I put them all up?' I asked Nelson.

'Hell, yes!' he said, loudly, gesturing at the class. 'Show these bozos how it's done.'

Some things take a long time to learn. Some things, you have to study and work on and tweak and strive for. Most things have been that way for me. Very few things have come easily. Even my paintings had required hours and hours of angst and labor and revision and touch-up. And even when I finished them, I wasn't satisfied.

But photos came easily. I seemed to have a knack. As fall blew in, I got a library card and started checking out photography books — falling asleep at night with their big spines pressing against my belly. Walker Evans, André Kertész, Diane Arbus. And I fell asleep hard. Because we were up by six with Baby Sam, I was squeezing everything about me into the hours between the boys' bedtime and mine: the gym, the photography class, my weekly plate of chocolate cake. Lots of afternoons with the kids, I'd just lie on the sofa while they sprayed entire cans of whipped cream into the bathtub or colored on the walls in their rooms with markers. *What the hell*, I figured. *Josh could always repaint*.

It was not a perfect situation. I didn't really have the space in my life to cram in a new hobby. But there it was.

Nelson didn't let us crop our pictures, so, really, there wasn't much to be done with each image. Either it worked or it didn't. I found I got about one picture on each roll of film that was worth printing. And I knew it as soon as I saw the contact sheet. I'd print it, and then move on to the next one in an all-consuming rhythm.

I wasn't much interested in the technology, or the chemicals, or the math. Some people loved to talk about equipment and lenses and types of film. Guys in the class could stand around the light table for hours, comparing cameras in their collections. I didn't care at all. I just loved the images. I just wanted to see them appear on the paper.

But maybe that was the difference. The photographs I was taking were like accidents. I wasn't setting up a portrait studio and arranging the lighting just so and tilting people's heads. The pictures I was taking just caught little moments. They were almost like snapshots. And so there was very little to criticize after I developed the film. I hadn't been trying for any particular effect, so every picture that worked was a delightful surprise.

At home, I started tacking the photos up on the wall in our bedroom.

'These are better than your paintings,' Peter said.

'How is that possible?' I demanded. 'I've been doing this for three weeks.'

Peter shrugged. 'You've found your thing.' He loved it when answers were simple.

After that first critique, when my fifteen photographs had taken up half the wall, Nelson handed me a key to the darkroom. He said I was the real thing. 'Work as late as you want,' he said. 'Just lock up when you go.'

So I started staying late — sometimes until midnight, or after.

Nelson would often hang around with me a little after everyone else left, complaining about his ex-wife, who had stolen all his money, and asking me if he should grow a mustache.

'Nelson,' I said, 'I'm working here.'

'I have her name tattooed on my ass,' he said in response. 'Did you know that?'

But I barely heard him. I was busy. I was in the midst of an artistic awakening that I did not want to waste one second of. I was so consumed by my new hobby, in fact, that I hardly even blinked when Peter told me he won the Hamilton Fellowship. 'You're sure you don't mind?' Peter asked again, before he mailed back his acceptance letter. 'Three weeks at Christmas is a very long time.'

I waved the notion away. 'We'll be fine,' I insisted. 'You just show those geniuses out in California how it's done.'

Peter didn't know what to think. 'Last summer, you were totally against it.'

'Last summer, I was less happy.'

Nora still babysat two nights a week for Peter, and I still went to the gym four — every night that I didn't have class. Peter went to the gym himself and, sweetly, came home and did the dishes before he showered. Things continued much as before. But something had shifted for me.

For four years, my mind had been entirely on our family — how much everyone had or had not eaten that day, who needed laundry done, who needed a haircut or a diaper change or a Band-Aid. I did all those things that moms do. And I still did them after I started taking photography. But — and this was the difference — I'd added something new to think about. Something just short of thrilling.

I wanted to take pictures all the time. And the buzz of that desire inside my body woke me up a little. Not just to life, and to art, and to my old sense of self as a person who had things to say about and contribute to the world — but also to Peter. I'd been so jealous of his practicing for so long. I'd felt like I was in competition with his piano for his time. But now, suddenly, I understood how Peter felt. I understood what it was like to be on fire like that. And how that fire lit up everything around you.

There was a shift between us. I stopped resenting Peter's work. And Peter, suddenly, started missing me.

'You're always busy,' he said one night,

when I was reading in bed.

'Takes one to know one,' I said.

'But I'm less busy now,' he said.

'Not really.'

'Now that I'm not practicing at night when I'm watching the boys.'

'And do you sit around missing me?'

'I kind of do.'

'Well that's a good thing, isn't it?'

'Not for me.'

I liked the idea of him missing me. I liked the idea of a little longing entering the picture, though, in truth, Peter gone all day and me gone all night did not seem like the best recipe for marital success. I remember thinking that we'd have to figure it out sometime. Funny to think that, at that moment, 'sometime' seemed soon enough.

19

It was inevitable, I suppose, that Amanda would invite us all over to her house some night for dinner, and, at the beginning of October, she did. She liked to entertain. And, as sympathetic as she tried to be about my dealing with three boys all day, she didn't get it. Not really. How could she? She had the most obedient, pliable, self-entertaining child in the world: Gracin.

Gracin was a total girl. She wore pink. She had neatly brushed hair, parted on the side, always with a bow barrette. She wore cotton hand-smocked dresses — now with little cardigan sweaters over them — and Mary Janes with kneesocks.

And the thing was, such clothes were just right for her, because mostly what she did was sit. She sat at the picnic table and had her snack. She perched on the edge of the sandbox. She kneeled on the sidewalk and drew with chalk. She dangled on the swings (and did not need to be pushed because she knew how to pump her legs).

She was quiet, cheerful, obedient, and articulate. When Amanda brought her to the park, she also brought a stack of magazines or a book, because she knew she'd have nothing else to do.

I, in contrast, ran around the entire time. I crisscrossed the park constantly: pulling the boys out of trees, separating them when they fought, helping them up to the top of the jungle gym, fetching a ball that had gone under the fence, stopping Toby from picking up the dead pigeon near the tennis court, stopping Toby from trying to pet the feral cat, stopping Toby from eating an old lollipop he found next to the trash can, and — most often, what seemed like every day — shadowing Toby whenever he was giving off the biting vibe.

As anxious as I was about the fact that Baby Sam, now over a year old was still not crawling — or walking, either — I confess that some part of me did not know what I would do with three boys to chase when he started moving around on his own.

'We'll just build a cage for them,' Peter had suggested. 'When they fuss, we'll toss in cookies.'

I squinted my eyes like I'd heard that suggestion somewhere before. 'Is that Dr. Spock,' I'd asked, 'or Dr. Sears?'

Sometimes Amanda was a tiny bit judgmental about my parenting choices. After many afternoons at the park now, for example, she'd seen Toby bite several other kids. He had apparently discovered, after that first bite on our first day here, that biting was fun. Every time he did it, we packed up and left the park in shame, tossing apologies in the general direction of the wounded as we scurried away. Toby was building up quite a roster of victims, and I always hoped they wouldn't show up at the park again when we were there.

It was hands down the worst behavioral problem I'd encountered with my kids so far. I really had no idea how to stop him from doing it.

'Bite him back,' Amanda had suggested one day when I was fretting about it, without looking up from her magazine.

'I think they call that child abuse,' I said.

'He keeps doing it because you let him do it,' she said, as if it were the simplest equation in the world.

I'd been on the Internet about it, printing out article after article on 'biters.' It appeared that there wasn't much to be done. Some kids just liked to bite. You had to discipline them for it, sure, but you also had to know in advance that it wasn't likely to go away until they were talking. Nobody was quite sure what the connection was between biting and speech, other than the fact that both involved the mouth, but everybody agreed that once children started talking, they stopped biting. Of course, Toby was only two. He had months, at least, to go before he was talking in paragraphs, or even long sentences. So the prospects for our immediate future were pretty bleak.

'If you're not going to bite him, you should at least spank him,' Amanda said.

'Do you spank Gracin?' I asked.

'She doesn't bite people,' Amanda said.

'But if she did,' I pushed, 'would you?'

'Sure,' Amanda said.

But it was ridiculous to speculate. It was so easy to come up with solutions to other people's problems. To watch them struggle through parenting in a self-satisfied way and believe that if you were in their shoes, you'd have it all figured out. With friends back home, I'd noticed it over and again. Observations like, 'That child is so shy. His mother needs to get him some friends!' As if a few playdates would change a child's entire personality. As if better parenting could make something like shyness disappear.

I did it, too. There was something so delicious about reviewing other moms' struggles — the boy who ate dirt, the baby who was afraid of the bath, the girl who screamed whenever she saw a squirrel — and analyzing and solving their problems. If only the mother of that boy who ate dirt would give him an iron supplement, you'd say, he'd be fine. He was seeking out iron! Didn't everybody know that? What kind of mother hadn't read that? It was comforting to be an expert, to know that you, yourself, would never be stumped by such things.

Because the truth was, there was a dark underbelly of terror to motherhood. You loved your children with such an overwhelming fierceness that you were absolutely vulnerable at every moment of every day: They could be taken from you. Somehow, you could lose them. You could stop at the corner to buy a newspaper when a drunk driver veered onto the sidewalk. You could feed your child an E. coli-tainted hamburger. You could turn your head for a second while one darted out into the street. The threats to your child were infinite. And the thing was, if any of your children's lives were ruined, even a little bit, yours would be, too.

So there was some kind of perverse pleasure that came from criticizing others, or from hearing about their disasters. Because those people weren't you. It was a reassurance, in a time when such reassurances were hard to come by, that you, for the moment, were okay.

I tried to take a parent-and-let-parent approach to people and their kids. I had become far less judgmental over the years. Within a certain range of acceptability, we were all just doing the best we could and, really, given a basic foundation of love and some Richard Scarry books, kids would be okay. In the broader picture, issues like organic fruit versus conventional, wooden toys versus plastic, and co-sleeping versus crib sleeping just didn't matter all that much.

That was, after all, how my parents had parented. My mom just turned my brothers and me out in the yard to play. She did not dog-ear parenting books or put us in therapy. She did not sit around staring at us, searching for signs of pathology. She picked up the house and cooked dinner and chatted on the phone with friends, and if we needed her, we gave a shout through the screen door.

There was a time, just before Alexander was born, when I thought I could show her a thing or two. I thought if I read enough books and did a great deal of thinking, I could come up with a coherent philosophy of child-rearing that would take all the guesswork out of it. I thought that if I applied myself to the task, I would excel.

What I hadn't taken into consideration back then was the kids themselves. In those early days, I thought it was all about parenting. I thought that if parents made the right choices, followed the proper philosophy, and were, above all, consistent and wise, the proof would show up in the pudding. What I didn't believe was what just about every experienced parent I'd ever met had said to me: Babies are who they are from the moment they arrive.

Amanda had no idea what it was like to be with children like mine. She did not know what it felt like to be challenged by a child, or overwhelmed, or unsure of what to do next. It's easy to be smug when you've had it easy. I would much rather have been judged by a mom who'd had some challenges. But, of course, a mom who'd had challenges would know better.

I liked Amanda, though. And I was in no position to be choosy. The biting situation had made it hard for me to make friends in Cambridge. I was always watching Toby, following him, trying to anticipate his next move. I couldn't go chat with the other parents. I couldn't carry on a conversation at all — let alone an interesting one. It was intensely isolating.

And so when Amanda invited us over for a

Sunday supper at her house, I said, 'Fantastic!'

'I want to meet Peter,' she said. 'And I want you to meet Grey.'

'Peter really wants to meet you,' I said, which was not exactly true. He knew very little about her, other than her name. And all I could think about when I imagined meeting Grey was the adultery question. Was he cheating? Would I be able to tell when I looked at him? Would there be a faint lipstick smear on his collar, or would he have a kind of guilty shadow to his eyes? I was sure I must have known adulterers, since cheating was so common — but I'd never known about it at the time. Knowing that he might be cheating, and that he didn't know Amanda suspected, and that Amanda didn't know I had told Peter — it all felt a little too close for comfort.

The day we showed up, Grey did not hunch down guiltily and refuse to meet our eyes, as I'd half-suspected he would. But, even more surprising, he was not gorgeous, as Amanda had claimed. He was the opposite of gorgeous. He was stocky and pink-faced, with a turned-up snout that looked like it might start oinking any minute. Amanda was at least six inches taller than he was — in flats. When Grey first opened the door, I thought he couldn't be the husband. He had to be someone else: the butler, the gardener, a visiting fraternity brother, the family pet. But he was who he was. Amanda, who held herself to the most excruciating standards of beauty of any friend I'd ever had, was married to a truffle pig.

But he was likable. I hadn't been at their house fifteen minutes before I put the cheating question to rest. He was too nice. He chatted with Peter a little, and I watched him, thinking about the certainty with which Amanda had assured me that he was gorgeous. Grey was bright and friendly, wearing a polo shirt and khaki shorts. He made Peter laugh over and over again. Attractive, I could see. But gorgeous? Had she been lying? Had she been drinking? What kind of delirious person marries a frog thinking he's a prince?

★ ★ ★

Their house was an absolute Martha Stewart dream. We learned later that it was built in the 1830s and had belonged to three different Massachusetts state senators. It was in a leafy neighborhood, on a deep lot. The front yard was small and hunched up next to the road, in that quaint northeastern way, but the backyard seemed to go on forever — down a gentle hill to a ravine with a creek.

We started out in the backyard. They had giant piles of just-raked leaves in their yard, and the boys jumped in them while the rest of us stood in the late afternoon sun in our sweaters as Grey grilled salmon steaks with the confidence and flair of a TV chef.

Amanda chatted with Peter, asking him all about life in the classical music biz, thinking of questions that even I'd never asked. I half-listened as I held Baby Sam and watched the boys move down near the creek, reminding them over and over that they were not — absolutely not — allowed to go in the water.

It was amazing to hear the answers that Amanda got out of Peter. I was learning countless things about how he composed, and how he practiced, and what he thought about his graduate program, that I'd never even thought about. It really made me regret the way Peter and I kept forgetting to talk to each other. It also made me a little jealous of Amanda's backyard, thinking that if we had a giant yard and a creek to send the boys off to, we might be able to work in a conversation of substance from time to time, too.

It was a given that the boys were going to fall into the water at some point. If I'd known about the creek in advance, I would have brought extra clothes and shoes. But Amanda hadn't mentioned it. Maybe she thought everybody had a creek. Maybe Gracin was so docile that she'd never tried to go in. Even as the boys played, Gracin just stood pleasantly by in her frock.

But the water was far too much temptation for the boys. First, Alexander wanted to step on the mossy rocks. I curtailed that by threatening a time-out in the car. Then, he tried to poke Gracin with a stick. I threatened a spanking for that one. And then, just as the salmon steaks were done, and just as Amanda was saying to the adults, 'Why don't we head inside?' Alexander saw a frog.

He couldn't resist. Clearly, at that moment, no threat was enough to hold him back. He charged into the creek to grab it, and Toby, of course, followed.

I saw it happen. I heard Alexander draw in a sharp breath of delight and shout, 'Frog!' and I moved fast — tossing the baby to Peter, who almost dropped his beer — because I'd been through a variation of this stimulus-response scenario now with these boys a hundred times, at least. I was fast, but not fast enough. By the time I got down there, Alexander was down on his knees with his paws in the mud and Toby, who had slipped on the moss just as I reached the bank, had landed facedown in the icy water.

Peter, who had bounced Baby Sam over to Amanda like a hot potato, was a few steps behind me, and I pulled Toby out as he grabbed Alexander. Both boys were sopping wet, and Toby had a cut on his face from the fall, which was bleeding like crazy all down his cheek. Toby was screaming so loudly — more scared from going underwater than hurt — that I thought somebody would surely call the cops. Amanda held the baby like she'd never seen one before, saying, 'Oh, my God! Oh, my God!' Gracin burst into tears. And Grey disappeared into the house to get towels.

Turns out, the only towels in the Mr. and Mrs. Grey Boatman home were white, plush, and thick as blankets. If you'd seen these towels hanging up in their guest bath, you'd have wiped your hands on your pants. But within minutes, we had them soaked in mud and moss and dirty water and blood. Grey went back in for hydrogen peroxide and Band-Aids for Toby, and we moved to the patio to strip the boys out of their wet clothes.

That's how my kids wound up naked in Amanda's house. All Amanda had for Gracin were dresses — a closet full, crisply ironed.

Amanda insisted on washing and drying the boys' things — shoes and all — so they could put them back on. So Alexander ate dinner completely nude, and Toby ate in a Band-Aid and a diaper. We put garbage bags over the seat cushions.

Amanda's house was perfection. Once everybody was calm, and we were committed to resuming the dinner, Amanda took me on a light-speed tour while the dads got the children settled at the table. She had modern pieces mixed seamlessly with antiques. She had throw blankets tossed artfully over sofas and chairs. She had mood-setting paintings on the walls. She had dimmer switches. It was warm and sophisticated and comfortable all at the same time. And not a scratch on the wall. Not a scuff on the floor. The place could have been in *Architectural Digest*. A little too perfect, but perfect all the same. I loved everything about it, and I was consumed with house envy.

But it was not a house for kids. There were no toys anywhere, and nothing was child-proofed. No latches on cabinets, beautiful crystal and china figurines out on coffee and side tables, silk curtains, and, most frightening of all — white linen upholstery. Her sofas were white, her chairs were white, her ottomans were white. Every now and then she had a chair covered in a coffee-colored linen. But mostly, it was white, white, white.

I thought about our own sofa, a garish floral from the Furniture City Floor Sample Closeout, chosen specifically for the purpose of hiding Popsicle stains. Then I thought about our apartment, and the trucks and blocks and train pieces everywhere — not to mention the newspapers stacked up that we didn't have time to read and the dishes that we didn't have the motivation to wash. I loved this clean, grown-up home. I wanted to move in.

'I love your husband,' Amanda said in the entry hall.

'Yeah,' I said, ogling the antique sideboard. 'He's pretty great.'

'No,' she said, touching her fingers to my forearm. 'I'm *in love* with your husband.' She was teasing, but then she gave me a serious look. 'He's amazing.'

I shrugged, just as the guys were calling us in to dinner, and thought about what it was like to meet Peter for the first time — how handsome he was, and his strong, straight nose, and the way he bent his head down a little when he smiled. Of course he was amazing. And how strange that I didn't think about it every single minute. 'I guess he is,' I said. And then, a white lie: 'Grey seems great, too.'

She pulled in a big breath. 'We're both very lucky,' she said, turning back toward the dining room.

★ ★ ★

The kids lost interest in dinner after about three bites. Amanda had wanted to serve them on her wedding china until I talked her out of it. I forced her to dig through the pantry and find some paper plates, and, even after she did, I got the feeling it bugged her that I'd ruined the look of the table.

The meal was asparagus risotto with braised mushrooms arranged on top of the salmon steaks. That's what the grownups were served, and that's also what the kids were served. The boys didn't know what to do with the risotto, and at one point, I saw my naked Alexander pull a spoonful of it back as if he were going to catapult it across the table at Toby. I reached his arm across the table and said in the lowest and most threatening voice I could muster, 'If you throw one piece of food in this house, you will never see any of your trucks again.'

After a bit, Grey took the kids off to the playroom, over my protests. I wanted to send Peter up to watch them, but Grey and Amanda insisted that we stay at the table. 'It's totally kid-proof up there,' Amanda said. 'They can't do any damage.'

'There's a gate on the door,' Grey insisted. 'If they need us, they'll call.'

Amazingly, they didn't. They were completely happy upstairs by themselves for almost an hour. I remember wondering if the playroom had white upholstery, too.

Baby Sam, who had not napped that day, had fallen asleep on my shoulder, and so we were as close to having an adult dinner with other adults as we'd been in years. Aside from the grass, mud, and blood stains on our shirts, we suddenly felt very adult. The conversation bopped along, all of us far wittier in adult company. The food, I noticed once I was no longer on parenting duty, was so good that I couldn't help but make little moans of happiness as I ate. I had been anxious when we first came in to get the kids' clothes washed and dried and back on them. But now that they were in the kid-proof playroom, and I had a belly full of risotto, and I had made it to the bottom of my glass of merlot, I stopped worrying about it. They were fine.

And something about the *tink* of the silverware against Amanda's wedding china, or maybe the candle sheen on the wine-glasses, seemed to loop time around a little and bring me close to some younger version of myself. As if a twenty-year-old me were within shouting distance, just on the other side of the swinging door, say, in her overalls with paint smudges on her fingers. I could almost feel her there, the way you can tongue the memory of the grit in the hot dogs you used to grill on the beach in childhood. That night, in Amanda's house, maybe for the first time, it hit me that I'd lost something since having kids — no matter how much I had also gained. I suddenly understood what it was, exactly, people longed for when they longed for their youth. And the bittersweetness of that longing. Sometimes it's worse to remember a thing than to forget it entirely.

When Grey and Amanda asked us about how we met, I listened to Peter tell the story of the time he had watched me spill a bowl of vegetable soup in the cafeteria.

'I never did that!' I said.

'You did,' he insisted. 'Your hair was down, and you were wearing a T-shirt that said KISS ME. And after I saw you that day at lunch, I spent the rest of the day wondering if anybody had kissed you. Read that shirt and just walked up and done it.'

I didn't remember spilling the soup, but I did remember the shirt. I had gotten a couple of kisses from that shirt, actually. But only on the cheek. Nothing good.

'Was this before or after we bumped into each other in the library?'

Peter just looked at me.

'That day?' I prompted. 'In the library? You were wearing your peacoat? You were with your girlfriend?'

Peter shook his head.

'You slammed into me!' I said. 'You don't remember?'

'I just remember the soup,' Peter said. 'And the shirt. And the fact that I decided if you ever wore it again, I was going to go up and kiss you. But you never did.'

'I think my roommate stole it,' I said. 'Maybe you kissed her instead.'

'I'm pretty sure I could tell the difference,' Peter said. 'It would have been a hell of a kiss.'

'I don't doubt it.'

Amanda stood up. 'This is too cute,' she said. 'You people are making me sick.' She headed to the kitchen to move the boys' clothes to the dryer, calling behind her, 'I'll be back when I'm finished barfing. Please change the topic quickly.'

In the silence that followed, Grey knocked back the last of his wine, and in a voice much lower and darker than the entertaining voice he'd used all night, gave us this little non sequitur: 'Amanda had to practically break my arm for that ring on her finger. But here we are.'

And at that moment, before I'd had time to prod Grey for a little more information that Amanda and I could've analyzed at the park the next day, we heard Alexander's voice from the top of the stairs.

'Mom?' he shouted.

'What it is, Alexander?' I answered, trying not to startle Baby Sam awake.

'Toby just grabbed a piece of his poop.'

Peter and I checked the panic in each other's faces to see if we'd both heard the same thing just as Amanda reappeared in the kitchen doorway and caught our strangled expressions. 'What did he say?' she asked, looking nervous. But she got no answer, because Peter was already halfway up their staircase, and I was right behind him.

Working backward, we pieced the events together. Apparently Toby, wanting to be naked like Alexander, had taken off his diaper in the playroom. We found it in one of Gracin's doll beds. Then, it appeared, at some later point, Alexander had boasted to Gracin that he could open the gate on the playroom door, and, even though the gate latch was sold as 'impossible' to figure out, our brilliant boy had applied himself to the task with remarkable patience until the latch came free. Then, with the upstairs as their oyster, the kids decided to go exploring. And, in a kind of grand finale, smack in the middle of Grey and Amanda's Seagrass-carpeted bedroom, our naked Toby had pooped a log for the *Guinness Book*, stepped in it with his bare feet, and then climbed up onto the white, hemstitched, starched-linen bedspread to lead, from all appearances, a marathon session of naked jumping.

20

A few days later, Amanda showed up at the park with a white gift bag for me. She was late, and the coffee I'd brought her was already cold. She was wearing a white midriff top under her jacket, which was unbuttoned, and I could see the skin of her abs. She looked tan and smooth. My blue jeans and non-midriff T-shirt and sweater, in contrast, were covered in mud, spilled apple juice, and blackberry jam. Seeing Amanda walk up in all her stylish glory made me cringe again over what my kids had done to her home.

'We're paying to clean that carpet,' I insisted, for the tenth time, as she walked up.

'We needed to have it replaced anyway,' she said, waving the topic away. She didn't want to talk about the carpet. She didn't even want to talk about the gift bag in her hand. She had far more important news that took priority.

'I have to tell you something,' she said, sitting next to me on the bench and looking a little dazed.

'What?'

'I just saw Princess Diana.'

'On TV?'

'No. I just saw her.'

I frowned a little. 'Saw her?'

'On the street! Just now!'

'You saw her?'

'Yes!'

I decided to go with the obvious. 'Amanda, she's dead.'

'That's the thing,' Amanda said. 'She's not.'

'She's not?'

'No,' Amanda said. 'Because I just saw her on the street.' She shrugged. 'She's dyed her hair brown, and she's gained some weight. But she looks good. She looks happy. She had a cashmere scarf.'

'Are you saying she staged that car crash?'

'Yes,' Amanda said.

'Why would she do that?'

'Because,' Amanda said. 'Her marriage ruined her life. She was trapped. She wanted out. She wanted to start over and be free.'

I nodded.

'The fairy tale,' Amanda went on, 'wasn't what she thought it would be.'

I shook my head. 'Isn't that always the way.'

'So she staged the whole thing,' Amanda went on, 'and then she disappeared. Only her boys know how to find her.'

'And she's living here in Cambridge?'

Amanda shrugged. 'Who knows? She could just be visiting.'

I wasn't quite sure where to go from there. 'I cried on the day she died,' I offered.

'Me, too,' Amanda said.

We watched the kids for a little bit. Then I went with the subject change. 'What's in the bag?' I asked.

'Oh!' Amanda said, remembering. 'A present.' She handed it to me.

'Why are you giving me a present?' I asked.

'Now that I know what your life with those kids is really like,' she said, 'I think you could use one.'

The bag was stuffed with pink tissue paper and tied with an organza bow. Tucked into the tissue was a little card with Amanda's monogram that read, on the inside, in her hand-writing: 'Sex toys for beginners!'

'Oh, no,' I said.

'Oh, yes!' she said.

I pulled out the tissue and there, at the bottom, was a pile of kinky things that seemed somehow even kinkier here at a park filled with children: handcuffs, fruit-flavored body paints, stiletto heels, fishnet hose, lingerie so tiny it looked like it'd been made for Barbie, a little black whip with rhine-stones, a DVD called *A Hundred Naughty Ways to Spice Up Your Sex Life*, and, of course, some crotchless panties.

'You have got to be kidding me,' I said. My face must have been purple.

Amanda was literally bouncing up and down with excitement. 'You guys have a DVD player, right?'

'I hope you didn't take Gracin with you to buy these,' I said.

'I left her with the nanny.'

Of course. They had a nanny. I knew that. 'You know,' I said, covering the stash inside the bag with the tissue paper. 'I'm just not sure I'm a kinky sex kind of a girl.'

'Honey,' she said. 'This isn't kinky. This isn't even close!'

I wrinkled my nose. 'This stuff just doesn't appeal to me.'

'It's not for you,' she said. 'It's for Peter.'

'I'm not sure it appeals to him, either.'

'I promise you,' she said, 'it does.'

I hesitated.

'Take the bag home,' Amanda said. 'Try the stuff out.'

I eyed the bag.

Amanda could not believe what a chicken I was. 'Just take it,' she said, pushing it a little closer to me. 'Give whatever you don't want to Goodwill.'

I frowned at the bag while Baby Sam, still on my hip, swiped at it and missed. I thought about all the different types of sex out there. Goofing-around-laughing sex. Just-went-to-Victoria's-Secret sex. Three-glasses-of-wine-on-a-dinner-date sex. We-were-up-all-night-with-the-baby-but-if-we-stay-focused-we-can-be-asleep-in-twenty-minutes sex. Sex that started out as a backrub. Sex that started out as a peck on the cheek. Sex to make a baby. Sex on a lunch hour. Hotel sex. Motel sex. Car sex. Picnic blanket sex. There were thousands, and each variety had its charms. But the truth was, the best kind was the hardest to come by.

'What?' Amanda said, watching me hesitate.

'I'm just looking for passion,' I said. 'Not you-look-like-a-hot-hooker passion. More like I-want-to-consume-you passion.'

'Sure,' Amanda said. 'Who isn't?'

'You don't think that kind of sex happens in real life?'

'I guess it does,' Amanda said. 'Every few years or so.'

'You know what I want?' I said. 'I want Peter to put his hand behind my head when we kiss.' I looked at her. 'Do you know the kind of kiss I mean?'

She nodded, and then said, 'Men don't kiss like that in real life. Have you ever had a kiss like that?'

I couldn't remember. I'd had some great kisses. But the architecture of them was starting to fade.

'I'm going to teach Peter how to kiss like that.'

'If you have to teach him,' Amanda said, 'it won't be the same.'

★ ★ ★

That night, I skipped the photography lab and came straight home from the gym. Peter, who never stayed at the gym as long as I did, had already showered. I wanted to show him the bag Amanda had given me. I guessed he'd either think it was funny and we'd laugh at it together, or he'd find it inspiring and throw me down on the bed. Either way, I figured, it was win-win.

I arrived to find Josh and Nora watching *Gandhi* on our sofa — complete with cups of soda pop and a bowl of popcorn.

'I'd never seen it,' Nora said with a shrug.

This was, apparently, the inaugural night of Josh and Nora's new movie club. She had mentioned to him, the night before when he was fixing the stuck handle on my toilet, that she didn't really like movies.

'That's impossible,' Josh had said. 'Everybody likes movies.'

'I don't hate them,' she explained. 'I just don't like them.'

'You just haven't seen the right movies,' he said.

And so he was renting his top ten to show her. *Gandhi* was number one. Also on the list were *The Godfather, Three Kings, China-town, Citizen Kane, Midnight Cowboy,* and *E.T.* Josh had thrown in *When Harry Met Sally* as well, calling it 'a little something for the ladies.' Nora had veto power, but she wasn't vetoing anything, as long as he stuck to her general guidelines: no serial killers, no war movies, and nothing about cancer.

They were sitting next to each other on the sofa that night, shoulders almost touching, when I walked in.

'Where's Peter?' I asked.

Nora pointed at his office. 'Working.'

'He's supposed to be listening for the kids,' I said.

'I've got them,' she said. 'I told him to go work.'

So Peter was working and I had every other person who lived in my building in my living room. It didn't seem like the best moment to bust out the crotchless panties. I took a shower instead and then watched the end of the movie with Nora and Josh.

Josh was absolutely lovelorn over Nora. It

was palpable. When he was near her, he was practically panting. It had taken me awhile to figure it out, but now that I saw it, I could see nothing else.

'He's in love with her,' I said to Peter after they left.

Peter was at his keyboard, one headphone on. 'In love with who?'

'Nora!'

'She's, like, twice his age,' Peter said.

'Part of the attraction,' I said.

'And she has a mean streak.'

'Part of the attraction.'

'And she still wears her dead husband's bathrobe.'

'Not anymore.'

'What are you saying?'

'I'm saying I think old Josh might have a shot.'

'No way,' Peter said. 'No way.'

'I'm rooting for him.'

'Okay,' he said. 'Then I'm rooting for her.'

'Rooting for him is rooting for her,' I said.

He was starting to eye his music again. It was pulling him back to the keyboard. But I didn't want to let him go.

'Peter,' I said, really just hoping to get his attention. 'Did I ever tell you that Josh saw me naked one time?'

I could tell from Peter's face that I had not.

I could also tell from his face that I had gotten his attention. He set his pencil down and looked at me. 'When was this?'

I had thrown it out as a kind of fun little flirty thing. A way of trying to tickle a little jealousy out of him. But it was clear at this moment he wasn't tickled.

'Oh,' I said, changing gears and starting to downplay. 'It was ages ago. The kids stole my towel while I was showering.'

'Why was Josh in the apartment when you were showering?'

'He wasn't!' I said. 'He was outside painting.'

'That asshole,' Peter said, looking really kind of angry.

'It was an accident!' I said.

'Why are you telling me about this?'

'I don't know,' I said. 'I just thought you'd think it was funny.'

'It's not funny.'

'I guess not.'

'Why didn't you tell me about it when it happened?'

I shrugged, and then I gave him the truest answer I had. 'I was embarrassed.'

The flash of jealousy had surprised me. Peter was usually so laid-back.

I walked over to where he was sitting and started to kiss the back of his neck. After a minute, I could feel him relax. I pulled him up to face me so I could give him a real kiss — an apology for upsetting him.

Most of our kisses these days happened on the way to something else. Have-a-good-day kisses, or how-was-your-afternoon kisses or good-night kisses. But this kiss was an end in itself. It was something akin to delicious, and I let it last as long as I could before I tugged on his shirt, pulling him backward into the bedroom, toward the bed, until we fell back on it.

'Don't ever let Josh see you naked again,' Peter said. 'Even by accident.'

'I won't,' I said, and we started to kiss again, this time with more purpose, unbuttoning buttons and untucking shirts. Peter was just working on my bra hook when we heard the bedroom door squeak open. We both froze and turned to look. It was Alexander.

'Mom?' he said.

'What is it, babe?' I said, playing it cool.

'I'm thirsty,' he said. 'Could you just bring me a splash of water?'

★　★　★

When I got back to our room, Peter was in his pajamas already. He was moving slow and rubbing his forearms, which were always sore. The moment had been lost. And though I couldn't imagine this was actually true, I couldn't help but feel that our children had some kind of sixth sense for moments when Peter and I were focusing on each other. Even sleeping, they could tell when we turned our thoughts, even momentarily, away from them. It was discouraging. And Peter looked discouraged, too.

'I keep thinking,' Peter said, as I put on my own pajamas, 'about how they're here to replace us.'

'Who?' I asked.

'The next generation.'

I blinked at him.

'I just keep thinking that, as far as evolution is concerned, we're obsolete.'

'Well,' I said, sitting on the bed and taking one of his arms to massage. 'We still have to raise them.'

'But it's not about us anymore. It's about them. We're supposed to give everything we have to them. We're supposed to empty ourselves out.'

'This is why we're too tired for sex?'

'This is why we're too tired for everything.'

It was true. If we didn't have children, Peter would be kicking ass in grad school. As it was, every minute he wasn't teaching or

242

taking classes, he was with the kids. It must have been agony for a guy like Peter to be doing anything half-assed.

'Peter?' I said, deciding we needed a change of subject. 'Do you know why I came home early?'

He hadn't noticed that I'd come home early.

'I have something I want to show you,' I said.

He leaned back against the pillow. 'Okay,' he said, rubbing his eyes.

I went into the closet and grabbed Amanda's bag, walked over to him and pulled out the least silly thing in there, the thing I thought would most likely get his attention: the lingerie.

It did get his attention. His eyes, which had been almost closed, opened right up. 'What is that?'

'Amanda gave it to me,' I said.

'As a thank-you gift for her carpet?'

'I think more as a consolation prize.'

Peter was totally baffled. 'Girls give each other lingerie?'

'It's not just lingerie,' I said, dumping the bag out on the bedspread. 'It's a potpourri of sex toys.'

He went through the stash while I repeated Amanda's instructions for each item. His eyes still looked tired, but he did seem to be in a much better mood.

'Do you think these things are ridiculous?' I asked. 'Or do you think they're sexy?'

He took a good long look at the pile of naughty things on the bed. It was a big question. Finally, he said, with a such-is-life shrug, 'Both.'

21

That next Friday, a delivery guy knocked on our building's door with a bouquet of roses for Nora. Josh answered the door. In fact, he signed for the flowers and carried them up to Nora's apartment. Nora told me about it later.

'I think Josh might be interested in me,' she said.

I tried to come up with something better, but all I could say was, 'Duh.'

Nora had agreed to go on a date with an old boyfriend, Gary, who had heard through the grapevine that she was free. He had called a few days before, out of nowhere it seemed, saying he'd be in town Friday night and asking if she wanted to get dinner with him — and now, suddenly, it was Friday. Of all days.

'What the hell is this?' Nora asked Josh when she opened the door.

Josh set the flowers on her dining table. 'You tell me,' he said.

She read the card, which was from Gary and said something like, 'Can't wait to see you tonight.' And she made the little smile people make when reading cards like that.

'Can I see?' Josh asked.

'No,' Nora said, tucking it in her pocket.

'You're going on a date or something?' he asked, walking over to check some work he'd done on her kitchen faucet.

'Kind of,' she said, studying the flowers.

'So,' he said as he flipped on the faucet and ran his finger under the tap. 'You're ready to start dating again?'

She picked up the flowers to add some water to the vase. 'No,' she said. 'But I'm going anyway.'

She walked to the sink, set the flowers in it, stood right next to Josh — who did not move — and waited for the vase to fill. Josh was at just the right angle for Nora to feel his breath on her ear, to hear the sound of the air rushing from his body, to feel the motion of his chest as he pulled in air and pushed it out. They were that close.

And she got this crazy feeling that he wasn't watching the vase fill with water, as she was, but, instead, was watching her profile. She'd always liked her profile — her long no-nonsense nose and the plumpness of her lips, and as she felt him watching her, she was suddenly imagining what he was looking at, what could be holding his attention. She could feel his eyes almost the way she felt his breath, and the tenderness of his gaze caused her to see herself in a different light.

With Viktor, they had been together for so long that they hadn't even needed to really look at each other anymore. They knew what there was to see. But here in her kitchen with this young man, this *guy*, she knew she was being studied. Every curve, every lash, every laugh line. He was looking at her in a way that she never even looked at herself.

He was a little nervous, she could tell, from being so close and from letting his eyes travel all over her like that. It made her feel nervous, as well. Her hair had been tucked behind her ear, and then it fell forward against her cheek. She was afraid to reach up to move it back, afraid, really of breaking the spell of this moment, which she suddenly wanted to last as long as possible. This kind of electricity was so different from the heavy air that had collected in her apartment since Viktor died.

Nora wondered what she would do when the water had reached the top of the vase and she had no reason to stand there anymore. And, just exactly as it did, Josh reached up and pushed the tuft of hair back behind her ear, brushing the pads of his long fingers along her cheekbone. She was so absorbed that she did not think to turn off the water, and it ran over into the sink.

Suddenly, she felt silly. She hit the faucet, poured off the extra water, picked up the vase — much heavier full than it had been empty — and started to take it back to the table. Josh moved to help her. 'I got it,' he said, but his hands overshot the distance, and he wound up pushing the vase out of her grasp. It fell to the floor and shattered, flowers and glass and water going everywhere.

'Shit,' Josh said. Nora went to get some towels, and they piled the roses up on the counter and stepped around the hunks of glass.

Nora wasn't sure why she had accepted this date with Gary in the first place. At first, it had just been too awkward to say no. Then, as they continued to chat on the phone, she remembered his voice. It had been almost thirty years since she had spoken to him, but the sound of his voice, the feel of it against her eardrum, was so familiar. It took her back the way an old song can. It sparked some kind of visceral memory of what it felt like to be so very young and have the future waiting for her somewhere up ahead.

They had broken up because she was spending the summer in Stockholm with an aunt. And it was a few weeks later that she met Viktor, who was ten years older and already teaching classes at the university where she was taking a summer course. She'd walked into Viktor's class by mistake and then wound up staying. By the end of the summer, she and Viktor were engaged. It was that easy.

Their careers were that easy, too. She turned out to be just as smart as he was, got multiple degrees of her own in his same field, published three books, got an adjunct faculty position next to his tenure track, and team-taught thousands of students with the love of her life for twenty years. In the summers, they traveled, their suitcases stuffed full of books, and in the winters, they worked in bed side by side, legs tangled in the comforter. They had been happy with each other. They hadn't needed other people. They hadn't needed children. They had been truly lucky.

And now Viktor was gone, and all her expertise about grief was no help, and she was alone.

But then Gary showed up again. As if he'd been waiting, and all those years with Viktor had been an interlude. Something about that interpretation felt so appealing — as if things were only about to begin.

'I have to get dressed,' Nora told Josh, when the floor was clean.

'Need some help?'

'I think I can handle it.'

'I was coming up anyway to open that stuck window,' he said. 'Before the roses.'

Nora hesitated. She had wanted to focus on her date, and getting ready, and all the little switches in her mind she was going to have to flip to make a date of any kind seem okay. But Josh was here. He might as well stay. 'Okay,' she said.

And then Josh, standing closer to Nora than she'd realized, reached down to the bottom of his T-shirt and, in one motion, pulled it up over his head, revealing a twenty-something torso that was lean and muscular in the way only young men's bodies are.

Nora turned her head away. 'Put your clothes back on!' she said.

But Josh just grinned and shook his head. He had shaken her up. 'Nope,' he said. 'I'm hot.'

And that's how Josh came to open Nora's door for Gary with no shirt on. Gary, in a bad suit with a bad tie, apologized and backed up to check the apartment number. But Josh said, 'She's almost ready.'

'Are you her son?' Gary asked.

'He's my landlord,' Nora called from down the hallway, her heels clicking on the floor and one hand at her ear, fastening a last

250

earring. She stepped up to them in a black cocktail dress that she hadn't worn in years. Josh's mouth fell open a little when he saw her. He had gotten used to her in Viktor's bathrobe.

★ ★ ★

The date was a disaster. Nora had been acutely uncomfortable about Gary's teeth, which he had bleached to a glow-in-the-dark white. He had taken her to a sports bar for dinner. 'It wasn't Bennigan's,' she told me, 'but it was close.'

'What did you eat?' I asked.

'I don't want to talk about it,' she said.

Gary had been divorced twice and had two children. His ex-wives were now in a book club together and had become great friends. He was living in Phoenix but had just taken a marketing position that would have him flying to Boston a couple of times a month.

'What does he do for a living?' I'd asked.

Nora had shrugged. 'Business.'

Gary had told Nora he was looking to have some fun.

'I try not to have fun,' Nora had replied, 'if I can help it.'

In the end, he'd had too much to drink and became weepy at the memory of her as a younger woman. Then he had railed against the tyranny of his alimony payments, lamented the fact that Nora was no longer nineteen years old, and propositioned the waitress for a threesome at his hotel — at which point Nora walked out of the restaurant, intending to call a cab. But then, worried he would mow down a pedestrian if he got behind the wheel, she turned and went back in.

She drove Gary back to his hotel, elbowing him away as he groped her. When she finally pulled up in front of the lobby, she got out of the car and walked away, driver's door still open, engine still running, Gary befuddled by his seat belt clasp. She was so angry, she was actually stomping the ground as she walked. Everything about this evening had been an insult to Viktor's memory, and she should have known the minute Gary showed up in his maroon tie. Honestly! What the hell had she been thinking?

It was chilly out, and it was ten blocks from the hotel to home. Nora's coat wasn't warm enough, but there it was. She wanted so badly to tell Viktor about her date. She found herself longing to call him on the phone, longing to hear that rich voice as he teased her for thinking that a date with that bozo would have made anything better. Before long, she had tears on her face.

She started up the steps of our building to find Josh waiting for her on the top one. He had wrapped a thick wool blanket around himself. His nose was a little pink.

'That guy's an idiot,' he said.

'You think?' Nora said, sitting down next to him.

'What were you thinking?' Josh asked.

'Somewhere very far away,' Nora said, 'Viktor is rolling his eyes at me.'

Josh didn't say anything to that, but a few minutes later, he unwrapped the blanket from around him and put it around Nora's shoulders. She thought about making him take it back, but she didn't. She just let herself enjoy the weight of it for a little while as they watched the cars go by on the road.

'So,' Josh said. 'You're dating again.'

'Not anymore.'

'I'd ask you out myself,' Josh added, after a little bit. 'But my grandparents would freak out.'

Nora suddenly felt irritated. It was not thoughtful of him to kick her when she was down. The last thing she needed tonight was a conversation about how young he was in comparison to her. That was it. She was going inside. She didn't have to follow one stupid man with another. It made her want to yell at him. Then, spoiling for a fight, she asked, 'Why? Because I'm twice your age?'

Josh frowned over at her like that hadn't occurred to him. 'No,' he said simply. 'Because you're a shiksa.'

22

A few weeks later, on the first snowy day of the year, Peter had a surprise vasectomy.

We'd talked many times — most notably, just before Baby Sam was conceived — about how I had borne, literally, the brunt of all birth-control-related issues in our lives for as long as we'd known each other, and that at the first reasonable moment in our reproductive lives, it would be Peter's turn.

Peter agreed with me on every point. There was no good birth control: The synthetic hormones of the Pill were creepy, the IUD gave me two-week periods, I didn't have time to get the Shot. We had been diaphragm people for a long time, but I finally threw in the towel on it when, after many internal injuries from the cold, slippery thing snapping open before it was in place, one night it slipped out of my fingers and spurted into the toilet like a fish. I stood there for a long time, trying to decide if the humiliation of the plumber pulling it out of our sewer cleanout the next day would be worse than having to stick my hand in the toilet at that moment. In the end, I fished it out with a pair of salad tongs, but that was it for me. It, and the tongs, went right into the trash can. And we'd been riding bareback ever since.

Peter had said he was willing, even eager, to get snipped. And yet, somehow, he hadn't gotten to it. Even inspirational stories about guys we knew who'd taken the plunge didn't spur him on. When I wrote the phone number down for him, he lost it. When I tossed the V-word into conversation, he scowled. I had pressed the topic not too long before, and he'd confessed to having mixed feelings.

Peter put it this way: 'I'm just not so sure I'm comfortable with the idea of it.'

'You know,' I said, by way of encouragement, 'I had a similar feeling about giving birth. Three times. But I sucked it up. Okay?'

We had left it at that, Peter looking slightly sick to his stomach and me feeling a little more feisty and insensitive than necessary. It was his body, after all. Part of me thought it was uncool to push him. But another part of me was ready to be done with spermicides and latex and period-counting and worrying. Besides, once you've had procreational sex, which on so many levels is the best kind, it's hard to go back.

So that morning, when Peter said he'd canceled his lessons for the morning and was going to Planned Parenthood, I said, 'You are?'

He looked very proud of himself. 'Yup.'

'Did you make an appointment?'

He gave me a look that said, 'obviously,' and then said, 'Yup.'

I gave him a high five. 'You rock!'

Then, as if to remind himself of the perks of going under the knife in this way, he pulled me over to him and said, 'So there better be something for me in Amanda's Bag of Treats when I get back.'

'Babe,' I said. 'Your whole life is going to be a Bag of Treats.'

In truth, there was no bag of treats for him when he got back. Just a Bag of Frozen Peas (for the swelling) and some Tylenol with codeine. He said it didn't hurt, but he walked a little bit like one of those dogs whose front and back legs were not aligned quite right. The boys and I made a stack of snowballs with maple syrup on top for Peter to snack on. For lunch, we brought him a giant pizza from Sal's down the block — and left again quickly before anyone started jumping on the bed.

Alexander wanted to know why Daddy had peas on his noodle, and I said that he had a noodle boo-boo. We spent the afternoon drawing get-well cards with dictated messages like, 'Hope your noodle feels better!' and 'Get well soon!' and 'Eat your peas!'

The surprise vasectomy earned Peter some booty points. I felt so grateful to him, and so touched that he'd pushed past his fears in honor of our gasping sex life, that I decided to do something for him. I was going to give him a little time to recuperate and then, on the night before he left for California, which happened to be just before our ninth wedding anniversary, I was going to thank him. Properly. I wanted him to know that I would never see frozen peas the same way again.

His timing was just about perfect. He fixed our birth control problem right at the time I was arriving back in my body after a long absence. I had been like an empty house whose owners were on vacation, an occasional friend stopping by to turn on the porch light or bring in the paper. But now I was home, and ready to crank up the stereo with some Sarah Vaughn and invite in some company.

Because I felt different. I felt like a person who could squeeze into her pre-pregnancy jeans, if not button them. I felt like a person who could make changes. I felt *new 'n' improved*. I didn't feel perfect, but, in a way I'd never anticipated, I didn't need to feel perfect. I wasn't trying to pretend that the childbearing years and the stretch marks and the wetting my pants when I sneezed had never happened. I would always have those ridges on my stomach where the skin had pulled apart. I would never be the person I had been before these babies had ravaged my life. But I didn't want to be.

★   ★   ★

The next morning, Amanda called while I was changing Baby Sam's diaper. I held Baby Sam with one hand and stretched to grab the cordless with the other, resolving to spray the phone down with Lysol later.

'You should say that you love me now,' Amanda said right off, 'because you'll be too excited to say it after I tell you.'

'I love you,' I said into the phone, making Peter's eyebrows go up.

'Okay,' she said. 'My friend Anna Belkin has a very hip café in Somerville, and she hangs art for sale on the walls.'

'Uh-huh?' I said.

'And she's looking for photographs.'

Baby Sam was flailing his legs all over the place, rolling in the poopy diaper and kicking his heels into it. I wasn't entirely listening.

'Are you listening?' Amanda asked.

'Not really,' I said.

Amanda sighed. This was not how she had pictured our conversation. 'She wants you to hang your photographs in her café,' she shouted. 'For sale!'

'Why?' I asked.

'I told her you were a freelancer for *National Geographic*.'

I dropped the phone. Baby Sam rolled for the edge of the changing table. I caught him just in time and then set him down with a truck to play at my feet, clean but naked, noting, in a resigned way, that he'd probably wind up peeing on the floor. I picked up the phone. 'You did what?'

'Just to get her attention!' Amanda said. 'Then I showed her the photos you took of me.' She paused. 'She loved them!'

'But I'm not a freelancer for *National Geographic*.'

'You're missing the point,' Amanda said.

'But you lied about me!'

'A white lie.'

'But who is going to tell her the truth?'

'She doesn't want the truth. She just wants your photos on her wall.'

At this point in the semester, with only one class to go, I was taking two kinds of photographs. Portraits, for my book about beauty — and I had yet to break the news to

Amanda that she was likely too convention-
ally beautiful for me to include her — and
candids, taken both at the park and all over
town, as I went on my rounds with the boys
in the stroller. The photos I was taking had a
snapshot quality to them that gave them a
bittersweet feel. Anna Belkin thought they
would sell like hotcakes. And she'd take a 10
percent commission.

Anna Belkin wanted big photographs, so I
had to learn how to print them big — and
fast. Peter was leaving for the Hamilton
Fellowship in just over a week. And once he
was gone, it would be all me all the time with
the kids. I'd have to do all my work before he
left. I'd be way too exhausted after he was
gone. I'd been in denial about Peter leaving
— by choice. It seemed like the best way.
Thinking about his leaving brought up a
hurricane of emotions in me: I was proud of
him, happy for him, and wanted to support
him, but I was also jealous of him, resentful
that he got to go off and pursue his interests
unfettered, and anxious about how on earth I
would manage for that long without him.
And, to boot, he was going to be out of town
on our anniversary.

That night in the darkroom, Nelson
showed me where the giant plastic tubs were,
explained I'd have to fill them on the floor,

and helped me mix the chemicals. He had brought a six-pack and came in after hours to help me. I wound up with two-foot-by-two-foot images, printed in black and white with good contrast and a black line around the edge. Nelson was a big fan of the black line. A black line showed you hadn't cropped anything, and he felt like part of taking good photos was framing them right in the moment that you clicked the shutter. Cropping after the fact was basically cheating.

Nelson was a little irritated at my good fortune.

'That's how it works, I guess,' he kept saying. 'It's all who you know.'

'It's not all who you know, Nelson,' I said. 'If she hadn't liked the photographs, she wouldn't have asked me.'

We were leaving the darkroom after cleaning up and it was already late. I'd printed all the photos Anna Belkin had room for while Nelson looked on. The next step would be to frame them, which Nelson would also help me with. He had a friend at a framing gallery who would give us some free stuff.

As we stepped into the revolving door that kept light out of the darkroom, Nelson was saying that he liked my photographs. That he thought I really had something. 'You're just one of those people everything always comes easy to,' he said as he pulled the door closed.

'Nothing comes easy to me, Nelson,' I said. 'Except photography.' And just as I said it, we heard a *thunk*. The revolving door, which usually spun easily around to open up on the other side, had hit something or snagged on something or gone off its track. It was, at any rate, not moving.

'Hey,' Nelson said. 'Hey!'

It was pitch-black inside, but I could hear Nelson pushing on the handle and banging against the door with his palms. When he couldn't get the door to budge, I started working on it.

'This thing's a piece of shit,' Nelson said.

I didn't respond. I was pushing on the handle with all my body weight.

'It's very flimsy,' Nelson insisted. 'I bet we could stab our way out with a pencil or something.'

I wasn't good in emergencies. I wasn't a quick thinker. But, after we'd had a few minutes of standing next to each other in total blackness, I said, 'MacGyver? Do you have a cell phone?'

It turns out he did, and we called Maintenance, who said they were sending someone right over.

We sat on the floor and waited, and Nelson kept trying to hand me his beer bottle for sips. 'No thanks again, Nelson,' I kept saying.

Nelson told me about a photography show he'd been to earlier that week for a woman who took pictures of plastic hula-girl dolls in different locations around the world. He said he hadn't expected to like them, but one photo in particular — a hula girl on the dashboard of a car in a snowstorm — had brought tears to his eyes, though he couldn't say why.

As Maintenance took their sweet time, Nelson said he had something else to tell me.

'I'm interested in somebody,' he said.

'Someone other than your ex-wife?'

'Someone other than my ex-wife.'

'That's great, Nelson,' I said.

'Except for one thing,' he said.

'What's that?'

'She doesn't like me.'

'She doesn't like you romantically, or she doesn't like you at all?'

Nelson paused for a long time. Then he said, 'She doesn't like me at all.'

Half an hour later, we were out. It turned out that the door was so stuck, Maintenance had to take it apart to get us out. I wondered what I would say to Peter when I got home. He'd surely want to know why I was so late. I felt bad, as I puttered home in the Subaru with the heater blasting, about worrying him. And I found myself wishing over and over that I could have been trapped all that time in a tiny dark space with Peter. But there was no way, of course, that I could have been that lucky.

When I walked into our bedroom, he was lying awake in the dark.

'Where the hell have you been?' he asked, sitting up. 'It's one in the morning.'

'I got trapped in the revolving door,' I said, heading to the dresser to find some PJs.

It was really late. I knew that. Peter didn't have to tell me all the things that were wrong with me coming home after the whole city had gone to bed. I could have been dead. I could have been hurt. I should, at the very least, have called.

'I thought you were asleep,' I said, pulling a T-shirt over my head.

But the truth was, I hadn't thought he was asleep. I hadn't really thought about him much at all until I was driving home. I had just been thinking about me. I had forgotten to be thoughtful. I felt a little guilty about it, and that must have played into my answer somehow when he asked about what had happened. 'You got trapped in the revolving door?'

'Yes,' I said. 'It froze, and I had to wait for Maintenance to take it off the tracks.' There was really no reason that I didn't mention that Nelson had been in there with me, other than I knew that Peter wouldn't like it. And I knew Nelson *had* liked it. And with one week before Peter left for the fellowship, I didn't want to fight. I just wanted to crawl in next to him and turn off the light. I felt guilty for a lot of things these days — from being a tired mama for my kids, to the piles of laundry that I hadn't quite gotten to — but one thing I felt guilty for that I hadn't thought about until just that moment was that, on some level that really shouldn't have meant anything, I was enjoying Nelson's little crush on me. It was just nice to feel like a person someone — anyone — would have a crush on.

'You were trapped in there alone?'

Of course Peter would ask this question. And now, in that one almost imperceptible moment, without ever intending to, I'd accidentally given Peter something to worry about.

'No,' I said. 'I wasn't alone. My photography teacher was trapped in there, too.'

Peter took that in. 'Okay,' he said. 'And what's her name?'

I climbed into bed and pulled up the sheets. 'His name,' I said, 'is Nelson. And he's the goofball at the gym in the flip-flops.'

Peter thought about it. 'I've never seen anybody in flip-flops at the gym.'

It made sense that Peter wouldn't have noticed Nelson. The two weren't even in the same league.

23

The photographs were printed, pressed, framed, and finally ready for hanging on the night before Peter was leaving for California, which also happened to be the Night of Romance I'd been planning for weeks. I had picked up a bottle of champagne and, in a tribute to Amanda's ingenuity, gift-wrapped a little box of naughty kitchen utensils as a thanks-for-the-surgery, glad-you're-all-better, let's-get-down-and-dirty, hold-on-tight-and-enjoy-the-ride après-operation gift. My plan was to get him a little tipsy, thank him earnestly for being such a great man, and spend the rest of the night doing things to him that would make it impossible for him to forget me while he was gone. Amanda had been coaching me for weeks, and I was ready to take him down.

I was intending to get the photos up fast and get home. Nelson picked me up outside my apartment in the Extension School art van, and I promised Peter I'd be back in an hour. Nelson had already loaded the photos up himself, and I worried quietly on the drive over that he might have dropped, cracked, or otherwise ruined them. But he had insisted on doing it all. He didn't charge me for his time, but I had paid for it. I'd paid for it all semester in conversation — listening end-lessly to stories about his ex-wife, who he was now stalking a little bit, but not in a scary way, just in a sad, sitting-outside-her-house-in-his-car, watching-her-do-dishes-through-the-mini-blinds way. On the way to the café, Nelson told me she'd just thrown out her old pair of yellow dish gloves in exchange for some that were sky blue, which was his favor-ite color.

'I love to watch her do the dishes,' he said. 'She's so efficient.'

'Nelson,' I said. 'You need to take up swing dancing or start playing golf or teach yourself macrame. Do not park outside your ex-wife's house.'

'I only do it while I eat,' he said. Then he gave a shrug. 'You gotta eat, right?'

'Take a cooking class, Nelson,' I said. 'Get cable. Go after that girl who doesn't like you.'

Outside of class, and not counting imaginary conversations with his ex, I was the only woman Nelson talked to. He was just lonely. And though he was in, shall we say, a low spot in his life, he really was a great photographer. Even his pet portraits had something really happening in them. He was a disaster, but in a good-natured way, and somewhere under that bad hairdo was a real artist.

And he'd come to think of me as his discovery. He came with me that night to deliver the photographs in part, I think, so he could take some credit. He was completely sober that afternoon, and I found myself wishing he were that way all the time. He helped me carry the photos in, and we hung them easily on big nails in the exposed brick walls. Then we stood back to admire our work.

'Did you drink when you were married?' I asked, just to make chitchat.

'Sure,' Nelson said.

'But not like now.'

'No,' he said. 'Now I'm on a bender.'

'I like you better sober,' I said.

'I wish I did,' he said.

Just as we were leaving, Anna Belkin herself — tall and swanky with straight-across bangs and cat glasses — came in. She lavished praise on me until Nelson had a coughing fit, and then wanted to know what prices I had put on the photos.

I shrugged. I wasn't sure. Then I squinted: 'Fifty bucks?'

'Oh, Lord, no,' she said. 'You can't charge fifty. Nobody charges fifty.'

I felt embarrassed, suddenly, and greedy. 'Twenty-five?' I suggested.

At that number, she laughed so hard, she snorted. 'Wrong way!' she said. She was going to start them at $350. But if they moved too fast, she was bumping them up to $400.

I looked at Nelson. Nelson looked at me.

Finally, I said, 'You're the boss.'

On the way back to the art van, I was glad to be heading home. Nelson had a pregnant quality to his pauses that evening, as if he were wanting to ask me something or tell me something, and, though I chose not to imagine what it might be, I knew for sure that I did not want to hear it.

It was clear and cold, though not snowing. Nelson was elated at my success with the photos and was far more articulate than I was used to. 'You've really got a way of seeing things,' he said, 'an instinct for when to snap.' I was lapping up the praise like a puppy, and it was hard to know if I suddenly liked him more because he was sober or because of all the praise. He grinned at me from the driver's seat. 'From total beginner to café artiste in one semester,' he said. 'I must really be one hell of a teacher.'

'It's all you, Nelson,' I said.

He had shaved that morning, and I found myself thinking he'd be a pretty decent man if he could be at his best all the time. But, of course, no one can do that. Nelson made it seem like he was drinking because his wife left him. But it was most likely the other way around. I studied him until he glanced over and saw me doing it, then I turned my eyes to the road.

'Can I tell you something?' he asked then.

'Sure.'

'I quit drinking yesterday.'

'Oh,' I said. 'I noticed you seemed different.'

'Showered and shaved, for one.'

'But also, you know, sober,' I added.

We both nodded as the streets moved past the windows.

Finally, I said, 'How's it going?'

'It's okay, so far,' he said. 'Tonight'll be the real test.'

'Why tonight?'

He seemed thoughtful. 'Usually,' he said, 'the first night, I'm full of gumption. I am inspired. I am committed to change and self-improvement.' He waited to enter a roundabout. 'By the second night, all that's worn off.'

'Are you going to get the shakes or anything?' I asked.

'A little,' he said, shrugging.

'You already have them,' I guessed.

He nodded. 'And the headache. And the nausea. And the vomiting.'

'You should get somebody to stay with you tonight,' I said.

'Well,' he said, 'actually, I was wondering if you might do it.'

This was it. This was the question he had been not asking me all night.

'Nelson, I can't,' I said. He knew Peter was leaving for three weeks the next morning. It was an insane question. He never should have asked it.

'I'm sorry,' he said, as he pulled the van up in front of my building and put it in park. 'I just wasn't sure who else to ask.'

'You should go to AA,' I said, but he wasn't listening.

'There's one more thing,' he said, looking at the steering wheel.

'Okay,' I said. 'But I need to get going.'

'I'm in love with you.'

24

I can't say that hearing those words didn't get to me. Even though Nelson had clearly fixated on me as some kind of exit strategy from the life he'd dug for himself. Even though he had that crazy hair and was so irritable and was not my type at all. Even though I should have seen it coming. It affected me to hear it. Words like that are powerful. They make you feel wide awake. They make you stop with your fingers on the door handle.

'Nelson,' I said, a nervous tightness in my chest. 'That's just not practical.'

'I know,' he said. 'And I know you don't feel the same way.'

'Not even remotely,' I said.

'I know,' he said again. 'But that doesn't change my situation.'

'I'm sorry about that, Nelson,' I said.

I was just about to open my door and escape when Nelson pulled a folded piece of paper out of his jacket.

'What is this?' I asked, taking it.

'It's a recommendation letter,' he said.

I unfolded the paper. It really was a

recommendation letter. For Nelson. From his ex-wife.

I looked at him for an explanation.

'She called me to meet her for coffee the other day — ' he started.

'Good,' I said. That sounded promising.

'To tell me that she was getting married.'

'Oh.'

'She thought I was crazy when I asked for the letter, but then she gave in when I told her about you.'

'What did you tell her about me?'

'That I thought you could save me.'

It should have been creepy. Grown people don't think like that about other people. But somehow it wasn't. Something about his face as he said it reminded me of Alexander's. His expression carried a hopefulness that made me feel tender toward him.

'I can't save you, Nelson,' I said. And then, as gently as I could, 'And I'm not going to try.'

It was time to get out. I wanted to get to Peter and turn this moment as quickly as possible into something that had already happened instead of something that was still happening. I opened the door then and turned to say good-night, but Nelson was out of the van already, waiting for me on the sidewalk. I walked around to him and said,

'Please tell me you will find someone to be with you tonight,' I said.

'I'll do my best,' he said.

And then it was awkward. A hug, after his proclamation, seemed too intimate. A hand-shake seemed cold. I decided on a little 'bye-bye' wave, but Nelson wanted to shake, and when I gave him my hand, he pulled me toward him and — with astonishing agility from a man I'd seen lolling around the photography studio for months — moved in to me, put his other arm around my waist, and kissed me.

There are no words to describe how shocked I was. Nelson was not exactly a man of action. By the time it occurred to me to push away, I had already been released. All I remember at that moment, as I stumbled back across the snow-packed side-walk, was Nelson's face, looking pleased with himself and like he'd accomplished a very impressive thing. And then, right after that, I remember Peter, appearing out of nowhere and shoving Nelson in the chest, almost knocking him over.

'What the hell was that?' Peter wanted to know.

'Peter,' I said, 'it's nothing.'

But Peter wasn't looking at me. I'm not even sure he heard me.

'What the hell was that?' he asked Nelson again. 'What the hell was that?'

Nelson was blinking at Peter with his mouth a little open. Peter was waiting for an answer. I couldn't figure out what to do or say. Even at this point, I was still hoping to resolve this whole thing quickly and get on with our real lives, skimming my mind for an answer that would put things back where they should have been. I had candles and champagne upstairs!

And then, in a moment of exceptional stupidity, Nelson piped up with an explanation that I guess he thought would clear the whole thing up. 'I'm in love with her, man.'

If we'd been in a movie, Peter might have given an exasperated look to the camera. 'I'm in love with her' was bad enough. But, really, adding 'man' to the end was just asking for it.

Nelson asked for it, and he got it. Peter didn't have a choice but to hit him. You can't say something like that to a man about his wife — even if he is a classical musician with a KILL YOUR TELEVISION bumper sticker on his car — and not get punched. All I can guess is that Nelson must have wanted Peter to hit him.

What amazed me about that first punch, and the couple that followed, was the sound. I'd seen enough fistfights in the movies to have a set of expectations. But the punch didn't have a great *smack*. It sounded more like a slap. It sounded small.

But it was big enough to knock Nelson down. As unbelievable as it sounds, he wasn't expecting it. Peter got him in the jaw with his fist, and Nelson hit the ground. And that was the next sound: the wheeze of air as Nelson's rib cage hit the sidewalk.

For the second time in two minutes, I was frozen in disbelief. I watched Peter tackle Nelson and punch him in the face at least two more times before I came to my senses and started shoving against Peter, trying to push him off. In the next instant, Josh was there, too, and together we knocked Peter over into the berm of snow along the sidewalk, and that was enough to break his momentum.

When Peter stood up, he was out of breath and his face was so contorted in rage and heartbreak that he did not even look like himself. He panted on the sidewalk, glaring at me for a minute, and then, without a word, went inside.

I had never once seen Peter hurt anyone. There was nothing about him that was violent or mean. Even stray insects inside the house were more likely to find themselves scooped up and tossed out the back door than squished.

I ran after Peter. But he was not talking to me. I followed him up the stairs, saying all the things that people who've been caught kissing people they weren't supposed to kiss say. *It wasn't what it looked like! I don't even like him! He just grabbed me! I didn't even see it coming.*

I followed Peter into the bedroom. His bags were already packed. The kids were already asleep.

'This is insane,' I said. After a certain point, it was all I could say. 'Peter,' I said. 'This is insane.'

Peter didn't say anything. His knuckle was bleeding, and he went into the bathroom to rinse it under cold water.

Peter's face was so hard, I felt terrified. I'd made him mad a hundred times. Maybe a thousand. But not mad like this. I kept talking a mile a minute trying to make him see how totally insignificant that moment on the sidewalk had been — how, if Peter hadn't been there, it would be over by now, only an uncomfortable memory that was already fading. But Peter didn't say anything. And the more I talked, the more I explained, the more I went on about Nelson and his ex-wife and his rumpled shirts, the more useless my words felt.

If he had at least said something, at least

argued with me, I would have felt better. But for the first time in all our years together, he wouldn't speak. He bandaged up his hand while I fluttered around him like a humming-bird, and then he walked over to his side of the bed, picked up his duffel bag and his backpack, and walked out the door.

I followed him. Down three flights of stairs, out the front door, onto the sidewalk. The art van was gone now. There was blood in the snow on the sidewalk. I followed along behind Peter, leaving the boys alone upstairs and asking a whole series of questions that he did not answer: 'Where are you going? What are you doing? Where will you stay? Don't you want to tell the boys good-bye?' I started grabbing at his arms. I ran around in front of him and tried to stop him with my body, but he shoved me away with a force I'd never even thought he was capable of.

I could only follow Peter for so long before I had to get back to the boys. Finally, I gave up. I stopped walking and gave it one last try. 'Peter!' I called again, as if this time he would hear me. 'This is insane.' I watched him keep walking, thinking there was no way we had really come to this point, that this absolutely had to be a nightmare because it simply could not be happening in my waking life. And then, Peter turned around.

I watched him walk back toward me, and I was completely motionless, except for my chest rising and falling with each breath, waiting to see what he would do. It seemed like the course of my whole life would be determined by what he said when he got close enough. I hoped like anything that this was the moment when we would both start laughing.

But it wasn't. Peter stopped just inches from my face. He couldn't even meet my eyes. When he spoke, his voice was a whisper. 'Don't call me in California,' he said. 'Don't fuck that up for me, too.'

25

Back in college, Peter had just gotten his cast off when Connor invited both him and me to her twenty-first birthday party. It was the week before the end of school. Her parents owned a cabin on a lake about half an hour from campus, and around thirty people were heading out there to spend the night.

Connor let me know that Peter probably wouldn't have made the cut if it weren't for me. She didn't know him that well, after all. But she'd asked him the night before in the common bathroom while they were both brushing their teeth, and he'd said yes.

'He totally wants to hook up with you,' she said.

'You got that from 'yes'?'

She gave me a look. 'It's a hunch.'

Peter was going to catch a ride with Connor's ex-boyfriend, a history major with flags of different countries tacked up all over his room and who Connor still slept with from time to time just so she didn't fall out of practice. Technically, they were 'just good friends.' She didn't even particularly like him, she'd told me once, but she thought they'd probably get married.

'Why?' I'd asked her.

'That's just how things seem to work for me,' she'd said.

Connor's family's cabin had been built in the twenties, as had most of the cabins on the lake — except for a batch of recent mega-mansions that were generally regarded as eyesores. Down the shore from the cabin was a stone clubhouse with a fireplace and a deck overlooking the water. Connor's parents were hosting a dinner there for us that night — complete with champagne — and then everybody was going to spend the night at the cabin. Their next-door neighbors had offered to let the boys stay at their house to help keep things civilized.

I drove out with Connor. Her mother had already put sheets on all the beds and pushed back the furniture to make room for sleeping bags. Her parents were not staying the night. They claimed they trusted us to behave.

At the dinner, there were bottles and bottles of wine. We sat at long tables with white cloths and told crazy stories about Connor: the time she threw a watermelon off the second-floor balcony, the time she tried to dye her hair like an American flag, the time she set the dorm kitchen on fire. I watched her up at the head of the table and felt happy to have her for a friend. But not that happy. Because Peter hadn't shown up, and there was an empty chair for him — and a little place card, truth be told — next to me.

★ ★ ★

I got up to go to the bathroom just before dessert, and when I came back, I actually gasped out loud to see that Peter's chair, which had been empty all night, suddenly had someone in it.

But it wasn't Peter. It was Connor's non-boyfriend, the guy Peter was supposed to have arrived with. He had been seated right next to Connor but had clearly felt an urge to wander around. He was a tall, beer-drinking, baseball-cap-wearing guy, and everybody called him by his last name, Callaghan.

'You're not dating anybody,' he asked as I sat down, 'are you?'

'Not that I know of,' I said.

I wanted to ask him why Peter hadn't come, but I didn't know how to do it without pulling back the curtain on my quivering, anxious heart. I finally decided on: 'You got here kind of late, didn't you?'

'I was supposed to give a guy a ride,' he said. 'But he never showed up.'

'Weird,' I said.

'Fuckin' weird.'

Callaghan stayed next to me through the birthday cake and the candles and the singing. I couldn't figure out why he had come to sit next to me. If he was trying to make Connor jealous, he was succeeding. If he was trying to escape her, he was failing in a big way. Connor was staring at us like she was watching TV, and occasionally tossing broccoli stalks at us, and shouting out inappropriate things, like, 'She's taken, Callaghan! Or she'd like to be.'

She was so drunk. And there, halfway through my chocolate layer cake with raspberry drizzle, I watched my idea of what the night could have been disintegrate. The grounds were so beautiful, with hydrangea bushes and tall fir trees. The club-house itself felt like a movie set. It was a perfect night for dancing, and flirting, and kissing. I had envisioned slow-dancing with Peter, or maybe taking a walk along the shore. But after Connor hit me in the temple with a half-eaten biscotti off her plate, I knew for sure: There was no possibility for romance that night. I was going to spend it — I suddenly just knew — in the toilet with Connor, holding her hair while she threw up. It was my birthday-at-the-lake destiny.

But I decided to fight it. I was ready for romance. I had blow-dried my hair! I had new lip gloss! I had remembered to bring my hoop earrings, and I was wearing a fragrance called 'Passion!'

I tried to will Peter to show up. I had this hope I couldn't shake that he'd wind up coming anyway, even though he'd missed most of the party already. I did the things that always seemed to prompt romantic encounters in the movies: I strolled by the lake. I stood at the railing on the dock. I flirted with other guys. I joined the truth or dare game that was gathering in the lounge.

And then he arrived. I had just been dared to suck on the earlobe of my freshman-year roommate's ex-boyfriend when Peter appeared in the doorway — without his crutches or his cast, standing on his two feet and scanning the circle until he saw me.

Then he said, 'Lanie, can I see you a minute?'

My freshman-year roommate's ex-boyfriend protested. 'She's supposed to suck on my ear.'

There was a pause, until a girl with a nose ring said, 'I'll suck on your ear.' And I was released.

Peter and I walked down toward the boathouse. There was lightning flashing in the sky, and occasional deep rumbles of thunder, but no rain yet. Peter's doctor had just taken off his cast on Friday, and Peter still walked a little gingerly. Not the walk I was used to.

'I'm late,' he said.

'I noticed,' I said.

'I forgot to meet my ride,' he said.

'You forgot?'

'I was writing music,' he said. 'Did you know I play piano?'

'I did know that,' I said.

'Well,' he said, 'if music comes into my head, I can't think about anything else until it's on the page. I can't function, actually, until I've written it down.'

'Weird,' I said.

'It's horrible,' he said, like he needed to lay it all out for me. 'I forget to eat. I forget to sleep. I miss classes. It's like being possessed.'

'Wow,' I said.

And then he got to his confession. 'It makes me a bad boyfriend.' He met my eyes. 'I've stood up every girlfriend I've ever had. I missed my prom because I was composing. My girlfriend waited two hours in her dress and heels before driving there by herself. And I didn't even apologize for two days.'

'Because you were still writing music?' I asked.

'Because I was still writing music.'

We had reached the water, and we sat down on a dock. I felt so grateful to Peter for arriving at last.

Then I said, 'This party's been a little bit like a prom.'

'I don't doubt it,' he said.

'And you've missed most of it.'

'But not all.'

'Well,' I said, 'I'm glad you made it.'

Peter gazed at me until I felt nervous. 'Me, too,' he said. He was watching my eyes. 'Because I was hoping to see you.' He looked down at the water, then, and asked a question I never would have expected him to ask. 'Were you hoping to see me?'

And here, in this moment, I was brave. I'm not sure if I was just tired of the uncertainty, or if I was encouraged enough to hope for the best, or discouraged enough not to care, but I only hesitated for a second before laying it on the line. I met his eyes and did not blink. 'I hope to see you every day.'

I thought he might kiss me then, but instead he said, 'I need to tell you something else.'

'What?'

'The music I wrote today is a rhapsody. And it's for you.'

And that's when I grabbed the fabric of his T-shirt and pulled him closer. As it started to rain, I brought his mouth to mine and gave him the very first of a lifetime of kisses.

26

The morning after Peter left for L.A. — or possibly just *left* — was a zoo. Children, as they say, are very intuitive, and they always seem to know when you are aching for a few minutes of calm to clear your head — and that's when they really let you have it.

Everything should have stood still without Peter, but, instead, life seemed to speed up. From the moment I woke up, I was troubleshooting one disaster after another. There I was, on duty alone from six in the morning on, in my PJs, no bra, teeth not even brushed, eyes still puffy from a long night of weeping and writing Peter long letters I eventually threw away.

Before we'd even had breakfast, Alexander had broken a slat under the bed he'd been jumping on and then almost crushed himself by tumbling over the chest of drawers in his room. Toby had spilled a full glass of ice-cold water all over my lap and fallen headfirst into the empty bathtub. And Baby Sam, ready to outdo everybody, had poked me in the eye with a fork, thrown a bowl of cereal and milk across the kitchen, and — unbelievably —

started walking and crawling within the same five minutes.

Baby Sam had been able to sit up on his own, of course, for many months. Then a few weeks back, he'd added pulling up to a stand. He'd teeter next to the couch and watch everybody go by and wail in frustration until somebody moved him to a new spot. He did not, however, show the slightest interest in moving his own feet or in using his body to get places. Until that day.

His wispy hair was going everywhere that morning. He was pretty calm, but his brothers were all over the place. I kept having to pull Toby down off the kitchen table, and then Alexander locked himself in the bathroom and needed help *right away*. And meanwhile, Baby Sam decided he wanted this little wind-up car across the kitchen. He reached for it, screeching like an eel, but instead of being a mother who responded promptly to such noises of distress, as I usually tried to be, on this morning I just kept saying, 'Work with me, Baby Sam. I'll get to you when I can.' Finally, Baby Sam just got tired of waiting. The shrieking disappeared, and, only a few minutes after I had picked the bathroom lock with a paring knife, I noticed the house was quiet and saw him standing on the other side of the room.

'Baby Sam! What did you do?' I asked.

He lifted up the toy car so I could see —
and then he took about six steps in my
direction, fell over and, undaunted, continued
toward me by crawling. It was unprec-
edented. Walking and crawling on the same
day! In the same five minutes! I would have
given anything to have had Peter there with
me at that moment. To have had a witness,
and not just anybody, but Peter, to share it
with and go over and over the minute details
with later. But it was just me. I jumped up
and down and clapped, and I tried to get
Alexander and Toby to do the same, but they
had other things going on.

So then the worry that I'd been toting with
me about Baby Sam for so many months just
kind of disintegrated, there in the kitchen. I
closed my eyes and tried to feel waves of relief
washing up against me. But I couldn't.
Because, as often happened, before I'd gotten
rid of one worry, a bigger one had already
taken its place.

I tried to analyze everything that had
happened the night before. I tried to diagram
Nelson's kiss in my mind. How long had it
lasted? It couldn't have been more than two
seconds. He got in, he got out. His timing,
really, was pretty good. It was too short a kiss
for me to, say, rack him. But it was long

enough to make an impression.

And what had I been thinking during the kiss? Most likely, something like: 'Holy shit! Nelson is kissing me!' But I truly couldn't remember. I just kept obsessing over those two seconds. Short as they were, they were one second too long. Surely, during the first second, my brain was just catching up to what was happening. But what was going on during the second one? It should have been a reflex action: Nelson grabs me, I push him away. And yet, though I'm confident I would have pushed him away eventually, I hadn't — at least not in reflex time.

It wasn't that I doubted myself or my motives. I was not, on any level, attracted to Nelson. I had not waited passively through that second second because I was enjoying myself, or trying him out, or hoping for more.

Partly, as crazy as it sounds, I didn't want to be rude. I didn't want to hurt his feelings. The man had just quit drinking and declared his love, for crying out loud. It didn't seem supportive to reject him harshly. Pushing him away mid-kiss would have added humiliation to his rejection, and I certainly didn't want him to get in the art van and head straight to a bar.

Part of that second second also had to do with just not knowing what to do or how to put a stop to things. Shove him? Kick him? Scream? I didn't actually have time to form a strategy. For a person like me — a worrier who liked to take a full forty-eight-hour period to stew over just about any decision — having to formulate and execute a response in one second was a tall order.

And then, if I was really honest, I'd admit there was another reason I hadn't pushed Nelson away more quickly. I was worried, in that short moment, that I'd done something to bring the kiss on. I'd figured out Nelson's crush months before, and I hadn't done anything to put him off. I didn't encourage him, either, though. To be fair, there might not have been that much I could have done, since his feelings were unspoken. I could not, for example, have marched over to Nelson during a photo critique and said, 'I sense that you have a crush on me and you must shut it down right now.' On some level, my only option might have been to continue on as I had. I hadn't flirted with him or promised him anything or even been terribly friendly. But I had liked that he liked me. It had seemed harmless enough as time went along. But right at that moment of the kiss, I suddenly wondered if he'd known that I liked it, had felt it somehow, and had taken my liking being liked as my liking him. When the two things really had very little to do with each other.

On the night I married Peter, my dad gave me his best advice about how to make it last. He said, 'Put protecting the marriage before everything else.' I had taken his advice to heart, and, in response, I never consciously did anything that might put my marriage in jeopardy. I did not flirt with people. I did not go out drinking at bars. I did not develop close friendships with guys who were not Peter. Except, of course, these days, for Nelson — sort of. Nelson had kind of snuck up on me. It had never occurred to me that a man as goofy as Nelson could be a threat to anyone other than himself.

But seeing it from Peter's view, I realized that he might, as impossible as it seemed, actually be thinking that I'd been having an affair with Nelson. I was, without question, obsessed with photography and that class. It was true, I realized with a little jolt of horror, that I spent more time with Nelson these days than I did with Peter. I had stayed at the studio until midnight at least four nights a week for months. I could easily have been having an affair. It would have been a perfect cover. And Peter didn't know Nelson well enough, or possibly even me anymore, for that matter, to rule out something even that ridiculous.

27

In the early morning hours, that first day without Peter, I'd tried to call my mother. At 5:15, while I'd been nursing Baby Sam and panicking about how I was going to make it through the day, she was the only person I could reach out to. After all, Dubai was nine hours ahead of us, so she'd be awake. She wasn't home, of course. I just got her cell phone voice mail.

And so I just started talking to it, glad we had a family calling plan that wouldn't charge me, as if I were writing a long letter. When it cut me off, I hit 'redial' and continued talking. I started at the beginning, with the first photos I took with her camera, and ended with the vision of Peter's angry back as he strode away on the packed sidewalk snow. All in all, I left fourteen messages on my mother's phone. By the last one, I was in tears again, and my voice had a frenzied, hoarse quality that caused even Baby Sam to keep a wild eye on me.

These were my first fourteen phone calls of the morning. The next one, hours later, was an incoming. It was Amanda, on her way to my house, with some news of her own. Grey, in a stealth move that not even Amanda had anticipated, had just asked her for a divorce. After a home-cooked breakfast of poached eggs and rosemary new potatoes.

'Grey just left you?' I said.

'Uh-huh,' she said.

'This morning?'

'Uh-huh.'

And then in a tone of voice that sounded almost delighted, as if we had bought the same shoes on the same day or chosen the same nail polish color at a mani-pedi, I said, 'Peter just left me last night!'

Amanda paused to correct me. 'Left for the *fellowship*.'

'Yes,' I said. 'But also possibly *left me*, as well.'

She couldn't imagine what I was talking about. I gave her the two-minute summary, and then said, 'So I'm not sure if he left me, or if he *left me* left me.'

'He caught you smooching your art teacher,' Amanda said, unwilling to engage in ambiguity. 'He left you.'

'I wasn't smooching anybody,' I said. But we had to marvel at the timing. It was incredible. The two of our marriages breaking apart within hours of each other. 'What are the odds?' I said.

'Not good.'

Grey and Amanda were supposed to be leaving that morning for a weeklong trip to Santa Fe. Her bag was packed, as was his, and she'd bought a new winter scarf — a scarlet color that would have looked great among the adobe.

Instead, their plane took off with them still at home, arguing in hushed voices while the housekeeper pretreated the laundry. Grey seemed irritated that Amanda had kept him there so long, as if his leaving had been a foregone conclusion. As if she were petulantly delaying the inevitable the way a child delays bedtime.

Amanda told me she'd been half-joking when she worried about Grey's affair. She'd worried about every man she'd ever been with cheating on her. She believed it was the things you didn't worry about that always got you in the end, so she hedged her bets by worrying a little about everything she could think of.

But without meaning to, she'd hit on something. Though Grey denied the affair — and she'd never found any proof of it, despite hours of searching — he was leaving her nonetheless. No couples counseling, no trial separation. He was happy to give her full custody of Gracin, who he still wanted to try to see 'as often as possible.' He was thinking about taking a job in Chicago and apparently had been mulling it over for a month without even saying a thing.

They had gone out to the movies the night before, as they did every Friday night, to see the new James Bond, which was, apparently, the nail in the coffin on their marriage. Watching Bond Jet Ski through a shark-infested ocean and wind up at the side of his lady love, Grey had had an epiphany: His life lacked excitement.

'His life lacks excitement,' Amanda said, skipping the greeting, as I opened my door. Her eyes were smudged with dissolved mascara. Minutes later, she was on my sofa with a compact open, cleaning herself up. I, on the other hand, was dashing around the apartment, pulling Toby down off the toilet tank, guarding Baby Sam as he teetered around the living room, warning Alexander not to throw any more cold spaghetti noodles at anyone, especially Amanda. Gracin was at school, so Amanda could do exactly what I would have done, if I'd had the option: She curled up on the sofa.

'Grey left you to become James Bond?' I asked.

'It looks that way,' she said. Then she looked right up at me. 'But he's never going to get any action. He's so homely.'

I was completely shocked. 'I thought you thought he was gorgeous.'

'He was gorgeous,' she said, 'when I loved him.' She picked a spaghetti noodle off the arm of the sofa. 'People are always beautiful when you love them.'

While Grey was ending their marriage, Amanda had kept glancing at her chipped nails, thinking about what lovely hands she'd wound up with, and how much they looked like her mother's, and how she really needed a manicure and ought to take better care of them.

'You can't leave me,' she finally said. 'That's not going to work.'

He gave her such a patronizing look, then, that she had been tempted to throw the butter knife at him. And he said, in a voice far too matter-of-fact, 'You can't make me stay.'

That was the moment she believed him. After fifty-five minutes, she finally believed him. He was leaving her. She determined that she wouldn't give him the satisfaction of seeing her cry. If he didn't love her, then she didn't love him. If he could walk away, then she could, too. She made her voice very calm. She started cleaning the kitchen, pulling clean silverware out of the washer basket and putting it in the drawer. She kept it together at that moment. She was being left by her short, pug-nosed husband, but she was far too fabulous to care.

And then their conversation shifted into logistics. He would take the bags he'd packed for the trip and come back in a few days for the rest. He'd be staying at a hotel over the weekend. He was sorry to miss the trip, and he hoped she'd go anyway later in the afternoon and 'take a little time.' The sitter was coming, he pointed out, and the relaxation, he added in an insultingly tender voice, might do her good.

That was when she lost it. The faux-sympathy got her. 'Don't fucking talk about what will do me good!' She slammed the silverware drawer closed so hard that a piece of wood at the corner popped off. It felt good to slam something that hard. She had always loved to throw things when she got angry, and this morning was no exception.

She threw the silverware basket on the floor and watched the forks and knives scatter. She slammed the cabinets closed over and over with increasing frustration as they popped back open each time. She took a dish off the counter and shattered it. She picked up one of the breakfast chairs and smashed it down against the floor, knocking off one of its legs. She'd never broken a piece of furniture in anger before. The destruction, in that moment, felt great — even though that chair was an antique that had taken her two years of searching to find.

And all the while she was shouting any words that came into her head: 'Don't talk to me about what would do me good! You selfish prick! You don't get to walk out on your wife of seven years and hand out tidbits of wisdom for living as you skip out the door! You don't get to take up residence in a hotel and turn into Dr. Phil! Don't tell me what to do! It would do me good to have a husband! It would do me good to have a person who loves me best in the world! A person who keeps his promises! Who takes me to dinner! Who takes out the trash! Who changes the lightbulbs! Who brings me Starbucks! Who wants to know how my day was! Who holds my hand at the movies! Who goes with me to Santa Fe! That would do me some fucking good!'

She paused to stare him down. She was breathing hard and feeling a little triumphant. As if she'd really let him have it. As if this were any kind of argument that she could win.

'That's the thing,' he said. 'I don't want to take out the trash. I don't want to change the lightbulbs.' He moved toward the door. 'And

I don't want to go with you to Santa Fe.'

It was hard to top the smashing of the breakfast chair, but she saw a chance, and she took it. She picked up the orange juice pitcher on the table — Tiffany crystal that had been a wedding gift — and without thinking about the fact that the pattern had been discontinued or how much she'd miss that pitcher after it was gone, she smashed it on the floor, aiming straight at Grey's feet and managing to soak his suit up to the knees with juice.

He walked out the kitchen door after that, leaving her alone. She stood for just a second, watching orange juice drip down the low panes of the French doors. But then she took a deep breath and held it and turned to head out herself. That little rodent was not going to make her cry.

By the time she showed up at our apartment, of course, she was crying. And on top of that, she'd broken a nail during her tantrum.

'He said he wanted passion,' she told me on the sofa. 'He said he was bored.'

'You've got passion!' I said. 'You've got passion to spare!'

But the truth, and Amanda and I both knew it, was that if passion was what he really wanted, if he really needed thrills and excitement and uncertainty, if he really wanted to be James Bond, he might just have to go somewhere else. Because being married — and raising kids, especially — was about stability, about certainty, about patterns and expectations. It had to be that way, for the kids if nothing else.

Grey had said he felt suffocated, and not in a metaphorical way — physically suffocated. He said he couldn't breathe sometimes in their house, the way it's hard to breathe in a smoky kitchen, and that he'd come home for supper and have to stop at the front door and take deep breaths before he stepped over the threshold. Amanda and I knew that feeling. It wasn't a reason to leave. It was just part of parenting.

But he was tired of parenting, and marriage, and 'the whole thing.' There was, as he put it, 'too much shit work.'

And there was nothing to say to that. Some aspects of marriage were shit work. And many aspects of parenting were. Literally. But the payoff for the drudgery — the laundry folding, the toilet plunging, the prescription filling, the trips to the dry cleaners — in theory, at least, was intimacy. Something you could not buy, or pick up at a bar, or have a one-night stand with. Something you could earn only by putting in the man-hours.

'Did you point that out to him?' I asked.

'I did,' she said.

'Well, what did he say to that?'

Amanda had her cell phone out and was poised to dial. Within the hour, she'd be at the nail salon, starting fresh with a dark raspberry color she'd never tried before called 'You Wish.' She took a deep breath. 'He said, 'You know as well as I do that intimacy is overrated.''

★ ★ ★

The next call of the day just after Amanda left was Nelson, apologizing.

'You're not drunk,' I noted.

'Not yet,' he said.

'I thought for sure you'd fall off the wagon.'

'Thanks for the vote of confidence.'

In fact, Josh had driven him home in the art van. And stayed with him overnight. And given him some good books to read. And talked to him about the Twelve Steps. And agreed to be his sponsor. And listened to some Steely Dan on vinyl. And turned out to be a poster boy for turning your life around. 'He really knows his shit,' Nelson said.

'I'm glad,' I told him.

There was a pause, and then Nelson said, 'I'm sorry about last night.'

I took a deep breath as he said it. I knew that Nelson was not a bad guy. And I knew that he posed no threat to Peter. But I also knew that this would be the last time I'd ever talk to him.

I said, 'Nelson, I know you're sorry. But now I can't talk to you anymore.'

'Hold on — ' he started, but I was already gone. And that was it. After all the ways we'd gotten tangled in each other's lives, I untangled us like that. I'd find a new photo lab, and, possibly, a new gym. But I wouldn't talk to him again. Even if he passed me on the street.

Just as I hung up with Nelson, Nora, who had heard the news about Peter from Josh, knocked on the door, wanting to check on me.

'He left,' I said. 'He left last night.'

'He left for his fellowship, or he left you?'

'The consensus so far,' I said, 'is probably both.'

Next thing, she was running me a hot shower. She called Josh to take the two big boys down to his place — and he was glad to do it: He had some packing peanuts they could jump in — so I could take a minute to pull myself together.

'It's going to take a lot longer than a minute,' I said.

'Wash your hair,' she said. 'When you can't do anything else, you can do that.'

One of Nora's books on grief had been a national bestseller in the eighties. My mother even owned a copy, and Josh had a signed first edition he'd found on eBay. But Nora didn't write about grief anymore. Or teach classes. Or claim to know anything. She decided, after Viktor died, that she'd had no idea what she was talking about — and she'd gone on sabbatical. She did, however, after a year and a half without Viktor, have some advice for me about how to get through the day alone.

'Shower every day,' she said. 'Brush and floss. Blow-dry your hair and wear something nice. Don't forget lipstick and mascara, at the very least. Do not look at old photos. Do not hold articles of his clothing to your face. Do not close your eyes and try to pretend that he is sitting across the room reading the paper just so that you can feel okay again, even for a second. Do not sit in his desk chair, put on his glasses, put his shaving cream on your face, or carry his toothbrush around in your pocket. Do not read his books. Do not stand among the clothes in his closet. Do not write letters to him at night. Stay in the present, or, if at all possible, in the future. There's nowhere else you can go.'

I didn't ask about the bathrobe. I just nodded and took it all in.

After my shower, I helped Baby Sam toddle around the kitchen while Nora made French toast. I gave her the whole Nelson story, too, and she listened as she cooked. By the time we were sitting at the table, Baby Sam on my lap, she was convinced about what to do. 'When we finish eating,' she said, 'we're buying you a plane ticket to California.'

'I can't go to California,' I said. 'I don't have any money.'

And then, in a way that never seemed to happen, the universe came to my rescue. The phone rang, and it was Amanda, on her cell, with a new manicure, giving me the scoop that Anna Belkin had decided last night, while she was closing up the café, to buy one of my photographs herself. The one of Gracin in all her Band-Aids next to the tree with the gnarled trunk. 'She's leaving a check at the register,' Amanda said, 'for three hundred and fifty dollars. Less her ten percent commission.'

'That's a ticket to California,' Nora said, when I hung up, as if that settled the matter. 'That's exactly what they cost.'

'Yes,' I said, 'but I would need four tickets

to California.' I pointed at Baby Sam, who had crawled up under my T-shirt to nurse.

'Leave them here,' Nora said. 'I'll watch them.'

But I wasn't leaving them with Nora. Babysitting three sleeping children for a couple of hours with their parents at the end of the block was one thing. Babysitting three children for an entire weekend with their parents on the other side of the country — especially my three feisty children — was too much.

'I'll think about it,' I said. But I wasn't going to think about it. I couldn't leave them. I'd have to figure out this thing with Peter some other way.

28

The next morning, I couldn't find my phone. I went to check for a message from Peter, and it wasn't hooked up to the charger. When I thought back, I couldn't even remember hooking it up to the charger. And so I looked everywhere. I started with my purse and worked my way out. I spent the morning peering into the refrigerator with a flashlight and waving my arm behind bookshelves. After five hours, I called it: It was lost.

I packed up the boys and we hiked over to the cell phone store. The boys knocked over displays and crawled between customers' legs while the salesman explained to me that it was going to be $189 to replace it. If I'd had insurance, a lost or broken phone would have been free. But as things were, it would be $189. 'That's why it's a good idea to take out insurance,' he said. 'For when you lose your phone.'

'But I never lose my phone,' I protested.

The salesmen looked at the boys, then back at me. 'Well,' he said. 'Sometimes you do.'

I forked over the money, and I could almost hear our savings account gurgle like a bathtub drain. But it had to be done. We didn't have another phone. It was important to be smart with money, but it was more important to keep the line open for Peter. On the walk home, I checked my messages — none of which were from Peter — and then tossed the new phone in my bag.

It was freezing out, and when we got home, I went to the kitchen to heat up some soup and try to put together a salad. I later calculated that my bag couldn't have been sitting in the entryway longer than about three or four minutes before Baby Sam toddled over and found it unzipped. Maybe less.

I barely had the soup on the burner when Alexander came into the kitchen. 'Mom,' he said, 'can I tell you something?'

I was rooting in the fridge for salad ingredients, though most everything was looking limp. 'In just a second,' I said.

'Just a quick thing?' Alexander said.

'I just need one minute to focus here, babe.'

'It's really quick.'

I yanked my head out of the fridge and slammed the door closed. I turned to Alexander and put a hand on my hip. 'What?'

'Baby Sam just dropped your new phone in the toilet.'

It wasn't broken. I fished it out and shook it for a while. Then I blotted it with towels and even blew it with a hair dryer. When I'd done everything I could do, I squinted and pressed the power button. The screen came on, and the sound. I dialed Amanda and got her voice mail. I air-kissed the phone to thank it for being so resilient and thanked my lucky stars that it still worked. Which it did. For the most part.

★   ★   ★

For the next few days, the boys and I spent as much time as we could at the park, in our parkas, scarves, and hats. I did not want to be in the house. I called Amanda every couple of hours to compare notes on abandonment. And Nora made me promise to stomp on her ceiling if I felt desperate in the middle of the night.

The truth was, if I tilted my head a little, I could pretend that Peter was still up in the practice room. But, of course, he wasn't. He had said not to call him, so I hadn't. It seemed like the least I could do. He needed time to concentrate and, dammit, I was going to be the kind of wife who would give it to him. He thought I was selfish, and I would prove him wrong if it killed me. Or our relationship. I would do my penance by leaving him alone. Even if it meant he decided against me. I didn't see any other choice. If I couldn't respect this one request, he'd decide against me for sure.

But he should have called me by now, at least. I was expecting my phone to ring every minute, and I'd flipped it open to check a hundred times. And nothing. No one, in fact, was calling me at all.

Just when I was starting to feel really lonesome, my mother showed up in Cambridge. She had mentioned to me awhile back that she'd been thinking about coming for Christmas. And then she came.

The boys and I spotted her down the street on our way back from the park, and soon they were all shouting their version of her name, Marita: 'Mita! Mita! Mita!' When, pregnant with Alexander, I had given her a choice between Nani and Gani for a grandmother name, she had said, 'Neither.'

'What is he supposed to call you?' I said.

'Marita,' she said. 'Like everybody else.'

When we got to our building, where her bags were resting on the steps, Alexander was all over her, and though Toby, at this point, wasn't quite sure who she was, he wanted to do what Alexander was doing, and so before I knew it, she was crouching on the front steps with the boys all over her. My mom, in her wrinkle-free slacks and ladylike traveling sneakers, was up for it. Even Baby Sam toddled over to get in on the action, and I found myself feeling so relieved that she had shown up when she did, as if my mom — who could find any toy, earring, or book report that was ever lost, who could fix anything that was ever broken — could piece Peter and me back together again.

At first I thought she must have gotten my messages, recognized my distress, and hopped on the first plane to offer support. 'Did you get my messages?' I asked.

'What messages?' she said, dusting off her pants as the boys ran circles around her.

'I left a bunch of messages on your cell phone.'

'I lost that phone weeks ago,' she said. 'I dropped it in the ocean.'

Of course she had. 'How many cell phones does that make, now?'

'I don't know,' she said, gesturing at Josh to get her bag. 'Five? Six?'

Turns out, it was just great timing. Over fish sticks and frozen veggies at supper, she told me that she had tried to call me a few times to firm up our plans from the club phone, but no luck. She had been about to send one of her signature e-mails when my dad had suggested she surprise me. She suddenly got this proud, flushed look on her face as she thought about him, and then she said, 'Isn't he adorable?' As if she were a teenager talking about a beau! In that moment, I felt so jealous to think that they still had it so good after all these years. And I also felt a little irritated that they felt my life was so uneventful that she could just show up from the Middle East unannounced and expect me to be free.

'Mom!' I said. 'What if I'd been busy? What if I'd had plans?'

My mother gave me a look and said, 'When was the last time you had plans?'

What was I going to do, argue? 'So here you are,' I said.

She raised her eyebrows and said, 'Surprise!'

She said my dad and my brothers were coming, too, in a few days.

'Where is everybody staying?' I asked.

'Here,' she said, looking around our two-bedroom, one-bath shotgun apartment. 'We can fit.'

Having my mom suddenly here was a great distraction. I showed her the apartment, which seemed far dirtier when I viewed it through her eyes. We put fresh sheets on my bed for her while the boys got underneath and we pretended to look for them. We did the bedtime routine together, my mother lapping up every minute of bath, pajama, and story time. Watching her, I had to believe that she loved nothing more than being around us. She was like a thirsty sponge drinking us in, and I found myself wondering how I ever would have made it through this first week alone without her.

Boys asleep, my mother and I drank cups of decaf in the kitchen, and she told me all about the exciting life in Dubai she and my dad were living. She had enrolled in a sushi-making class, she'd taken up horseback riding, and she was learning to ski. Leave it to my mother to take up skiing in the desert.

'Snow skiing?' I asked.

'Yes.'

'In the desert?'

'They have a snow machine,' she said. It was an indoor slope on a spiral, and the ski instructor could change the angle from green to blue to black. There were trompe l'oeil paintings of snow and mountains and Swiss chalets on every wall. They kept the place at forty-eight degrees. It was, she insisted, almost like being there.

'Do you wear a parka?' I had to ask.

'I wear a sweater,' she said, 'with little snowflakes on it.'

She was insistently upbeat and kept flashing me the prim smile she always gives when she is making things seem better than they are. But my mom wasn't one for laying it all out. If I'd asked her what was wrong, she'd have said, 'Nothing,' and been irritated at the question. So I didn't ask.

When she ran out of sunny things to say, she turned the focus onto me. 'And what's going on with you?' she asked, leaning in, ready to bond. 'You look fantastic.' Something about her chummy manner suddenly irritated me. It was ridiculous that I was going to have to fill her in on the past five months of my life. I suddenly felt, in a totally irrational way, like she'd abandoned me.

But she wasn't having it. 'You,' she said, 'were the one who left first.'

'But I didn't want to leave.'

Her eyes flashed, and then she said something she probably regretted even as she was saying it: 'Well, neither did I.'

I didn't say anything to that. With my mom, it was important to know when to quit.

She stood up and dumped her coffee in the sink. Then she grabbed a sponge and started wiping crumbs off the counter.

'I'm here now, aren't I?' she pointed out, starting on the dishes. Then she let out a short sigh. 'What can I tell you, Elena? I've left you messages. I've sent you e-mails. I'm just not a long-distance person.'

It's so easy to think of your parents as existing solely for you — to see their actions only in terms of how well they address your needs. Even as an adult, it's hard to think of your parents as people with goals and circumstances different from your own. As I sat at the table, pouting, I suddenly thought about all the things my mother had lost when she and my father moved: her garden, her home, her friends, the life she'd worked so long to build. Even her furniture was in storage. Her photo albums, her books, the kitchen clock with the ladybugs on it, the Blue Willow china she'd been collecting for twenty years that matched her mother's. And, of course, the last time she'd moved anywhere it had been to leave her entire family behind and set up a new life in America. So this move with my dad must have been a pretty big deal. It only hit me at this moment: It had been a tough five months for my mother. She needed to do some things for herself. And I could relate to that. I could really relate to that.

I got up and joined her at the sink. We worked together quietly for a few minutes, and then I filled her in on the whole story, from Khaki Pants to Amanda's pooped-on rug to how much I loved the cameras.

By the time I got to the part about Nelson, we were making up the sofa in the living room for me to sleep on. 'Why did you let him kiss you?' she asked, shaking out the bottom sheet.

'I didn't let him kiss me,' I said. 'He just grabbed me.'

'And you haven't heard from Peter since?'

I shook my head. 'He left a stack of letters for the boys,' I told her. 'One for each day.' I'd been reading the letters to them each morning after we woke up. They were short, and they usually had little stick pictures for the boys to look at, and he'd sealed them in envelopes, so we took turns ripping them open. The boys loved the letters, and even Baby Sam listened with bright eyes as we read. Sometimes when I read them, I'd think about what a good man Peter was to provide for us in this way. And sometimes I'd wonder what I would do with the letters if he didn't come back. I couldn't just read the last one, dust my hands off, and say, 'Well, that's the last of Daddy!' It seemed clear that I'd have to start writing them myself. But the idea of doing that made me feel short of breath.

'But nothing for you?' my mother asked. 'He hasn't called once?'

'Maybe he's not a long-distance person,' I

said, giving her a look.

She ignored me and, dropping a pillow into its case, said, 'Well, you'll have to go after him.' She told me to go to California, and, this time, when the suggestion came from her, I said okay.

I could just afford a deal on a red-eye flight, which would get me into L.A. on the last day of Peter's fellowship, the night of his concert, when he would play, along with the other two honorees, for the largest crowd of his life. It was my plan to meet him before the concert, win back his love, sit adoringly in the audience while he played, and then spend a little time with him sans children, frolicking and reclaiming our youth before returning home. It was a wildly optimistic plan.

And so I went online and bought a ticket with my $315 from Anna Belkin. My mom was the only person in the world I'd have left the boys with, and, bless her, she agreed to extend her trip a week so I could do just that. My dad could make it back to Dubai and manage for a week without her. And her sushi class could wait. With help from Nora and Josh, my mom would do fine. She could run a household far better than I could. I was sure that when I got back and walked in the door, the boys would have put away their toys, had their hair cut, and be eating spinach for supper like it was the vegetable they'd been waiting for all their lives.

★　★　★

When Peter had accepted the fellowship, I'd been convinced that I'd be spending Christmas Day alone with the boys in our apartment.

Instead, Amanda and Gracin spent the night, as they had done many times since Grey left, without even calling — just showing up with matching overnight bags. Something about the pandemonium of my life appealed to Amanda in those early weeks without him. She didn't want a life so organized that she could spot everything that was missing. She wanted chaos. She wanted confusion. She wanted to move in with us.

And we had chaos to spare, because my father arrived the week of Christmas, as did my two brothers, and everybody set up shop in my apartment. My dad and my mother took my bedroom. My brothers brought sleeping bags and slept on the floor in the boys' room. And Amanda and Gracin brought their own queen-size AeroBed and five-hundred-thread-count linens and slept together in the living room with me. It was far too crowded. We were like animals in a barn.

But nobody was willing to leave. Nobody, I'd remark to myself when I was feeling cranky, except Peter.

My parents had sprung for a tree, which we had decorated with our little stash of homemade ornaments — though only the top half, because Baby Sam, now King of Toddling, kept taking the ornaments off and eating, throwing, or stomping on them. Still, it was festive. We put the tree in the kitchen, where we had the most room.

My brothers — neither of them married, both of them over thirty now but still boys themselves in many ways — kept my three guys busy from dawn until dusk. They built forts, tossed balls around, raced Matchbox cars, told stories, sledded down the stairs on trash-can lids. My mother cooked for all of us, and at night, when the kids had fallen asleep, we sat around the kitchen table drinking decaf and catching up.

Christmas Day, I had planned to give the boys, as we did every year, one present from Santa and one present from Mom and Dad. The present from Santa was always something new, and the present from us was most often from a thrift shop. But this year, my brothers each had presents for the boys. My parents had presents for the boys. And Amanda and Gracin had spent a whole afternoon in the boys' section of FAO Schwarz, gathering every yo-yo, water gun, slingshot, Lego set, truck, train car, and Nerf ball they could find. It was total debauchery. You could not see the floor for the toys.

But the best present that day was from Nora, for me. She had wrapped up a good-size box and inside was just a little piece of paper. It read, 'Coupon for Date Night babysitting — every Saturday for one year.'

'Every single Saturday night?'

'Sure,' Nora said. 'What else do I have to do?'

I suspected that she'd find something better to do at some point, but I figured we'd cross that bridge when we came to it. For now, I just said, 'Thank you.' It was an optimistic gesture from a true pessimist. It said Nora believed that Peter would come home, and that he'd still like me enough when he did for us to redeem that coupon over and over.

That night, my mother cooked a giant turkey with stuffing for supper, and Nora came up to join us. Josh did, too, and he brought two things with him: a menorah, since Hanukkah and Christmas overlapped that year, and a date, who looked like she could have been in high school, to whom Nora was very polite. It was a loud, messy, chaotic holiday — the very best kind. It was almost loud, messy, and chaotic enough for me not to miss Peter. But not quite.

As soon as everyone who was going home had gone home, I raced down to Nora's place to get the scoop on Josh's date. It turns out, Nora and Josh had been in a fight for over a week. Nora told me about it, shouting over the noise, while she vacuumed her apartment.

Josh had walked Nora down to her door after a special Ladies' Nite Movie Night, which had been a showing of *Out of Africa*, and there, on the landing, he'd kissed her. She'd felt it coming, and she had let him, and had even wanted him to do it, since their shoulders had been brushing against each other all evening long, and since the movie had put them both in that kind of mood. It hadn't seemed like a bad idea to her at the moment.

But when his lips actually touched hers, even though she had expected and even wanted them to, when she actually felt the soft warmth of his mouth — a mouth that was not Viktor's — she pulled away and slapped him.

'You slapped him?' I shrieked when she told me. 'That's so Bette Davis! I love it.'

Josh had shouted, 'Hey!' when she did it, and he pulled back, his eyes bright with tears.

Then he rested his hand on his face for a minute, and when he looked up, his expression told her that he wasn't likely to try to kiss her again. 'Okay,' he'd said, as if she had said something out loud. 'Okay.' And he went downstairs.

Two nights later, Josh had not shown up at my place, even though *Raising Arizona* was on the schedule — one of his very favorites. And then, the next morning, when Nora shuffled down for the paper in her new robe — pale green silk with Chinese embroidery — there was a girl leaving Josh's apartment. A twenty-something girl with a tattoo on her slender hand that read 'Knucklehead.' She was standing in Josh's doorway, clearly headed home after a long night, fingering Josh's belt buckle as she talked to him. She seemed like a nice enough person.

'At least he had clothes on,' I said.

Nora shook her head. 'Only pants,' she said.

Nora had wanted to disappear back up the stairs as soon as she saw them. But they'd seen her, too, so she just waved, totally poker-faced, and went out to the front steps.

'Was the poker face convincing?' I asked.

'It was utterly convincing,' she said, not looking too happy about it. 'You'd have thought I'd never even met him before.'

Out on the front steps that morning, Nora had tried to think of a reason not to go back into the building, but there wasn't one. She pulled the door open just as the girl was coming out. They smiled at each other. And Nora stepped into the hallway just as Josh's door slammed closed.

'Juvenile,' I declared, when Nora finished the story.

'Of course,' she shouted, as if she were reminding herself. 'He's practically a teenager.' Then she flipped the vacuum off. 'I shouldn't have slapped him, though,' she said in a softer voice. She closed her eyes for a second before looking up at me. 'It was a great kiss.'

29

The day after Christmas, Amanda sat me down and said, 'We've got work to do.'

'Work?' I asked.

And then she rattled off a list of improvements I needed before I saw Peter — or, more accurately, before he saw me: haircut, mani-pedi, new clothes, new shoes, dentist, eyebrow plucking, new bras.

Haircut first, she said, at a tiny boutique in Harvard Square that had a three-week waiting list. (Amanda had told them I was about to be on *Good Morning America*). Then: clothes and shoes — and, just as vital, toes, eyebrows, teeth, and hands.

'Like the song,' I said.

'What song?'

And so I sang 'toes, eyebrows, teeth, and hands' to the tune of 'Head, Shoulders, Knees, and Toes,' pointing out each thing as I went. How could she be a mother of a four-year-old and not know that song?

'Oh,' Amanda said. 'She does all that stuff at school.'

Amanda clearly needed a project. She was doing her best to regroup. Grey had been back to the house twice since he left, both times while she was out. He spent Christmas in New York City, 'for a change of pace.'

'New York City?' I asked.

'With his girlfriend,' she said. And then, before I could react: 'I don't want to talk about it.' What she did want to talk about was me. And Peter. And what we could do to save our marriage. 'I don't want you to wind up alone like me,' she kept saying.

Amanda came with me to get my haircut, and when I sat in the chair, she launched into a stupefyingly detailed conversation with the stylist (named Tangy, 'like the fruit') about options for my 'look.' Left to my own devices, I would have asked her to trim two inches and then flipped through a magazine until she was done. But Amanda was using words like 'lift' and 'roots,' 'gradation' and 'perimeter.' Tangy had washed my hair and combed it all down over my face.

From underneath, I said to Amanda, 'You sure know a lot about hair.'

'I love hair,' Amanda said. Then she confessed that often, when people were talking to her, she was imagining new hairstyles for them. She'd try a short bob, for example, on a chubby grocery checker with a ponytail. A bob done right, she told us, could mimic cheekbones and slenderize anybody. If the bob didn't do the trick, she'd lighten it a little. 'Everybody looks better blond,' she said. In this way, she improved the world around her. New hairstyles, swankier clothes, and better makeup. 'It's very distracting,' she said.

It was decided that my thick, straight, dark hair needed to be 'chipped' and 'razored' into a layered shoulder-length 'drape' that was long enough to be sexy but not so long that it lost its joie de vivre. Highlights were considered and rejected because we were going to run with my exoticism. 'I'd like to be able to put it in a ponytail,' I offered, but realized almost as soon as I'd said it that usability was not the primary consideration. I was no longer in a wash 'n' go world.

After two and a half hours, I left the place with a shopping bag of hair products, a round styling brush, a professional comb — when I asked Tangy what made it 'professional,' she said, 'This plastic was developed at NASA' — a $100 blow dryer (with diffuser), and a giant helmet of hair worthy of a TV news anchor.

'I can't afford any of this,' I said, as Amanda piled products on my lap. 'I can't even afford' — I picked up the smallest vial — 'this.'

'It's my treat,' Amanda said, and when I

started to argue, she said, 'Actually, it's Grey's,' and held up a credit card with his name on it.

Part two of our Beauty Bonanza was makeup, by way of an eyebrow-shaping session. The beautician, at the nail place next door, who had a great Persian accent, explained to me quite cheerfully that she was going to rip out every errant hair on my face with a piece of twisted thread.

Amanda nodded to me. 'It's an incredible technique.'

I hadn't thought too specifically about the concept of 'shaping' until that moment. 'It sounds like it's going to hurt,' I said.

The beautician smiled gently, sorry to have to break the news. The thread wrapped around her pointer was already pinching a little. 'Of course, sweet lady,' she said. 'All beauty hurts.'

Tears were still running out of my eyes as we walked across the square to a department store. 'Are you crying?' Amanda asked. 'Or is it just your eyes?'

'Just my eyes,' I said.

I perched on a stool at the only open makeup counter. The makeup lady, Vanessa, said, 'She needs everything?'

Amanda closed her eyes for emphasis before saying, 'Everything.'

329

So Vanessa went to work, Amanda standing behind her shoulder with arms crossed, frowning in concentration. 'You're using the Mink?' she asked. 'You don't think Black Taffeta?'

'Mink's a little smokier,' Vanessa said.

'But the Taffeta has more mystery.'

'But the Mink is more come-hither.'

'But the Taffeta is more I'm-going-to-throw-you-on-the-ground-and-show-you-who's-boss. ' Amanda glanced at me. 'In a good way.'

They were dead serious. Colleagues at work on a problem as important as, say, the restoration of the Sistine Chapel or the retrieval of ancient Egyptian artifacts.

Vanessa moisturized me, then evened out my tone with foundation, then spent what seemed like an eternity brushing makeup onto my eyes. All I could think about was Camille Martin from sixth grade, who got an eye infection from a makeover at the mall. 'Is this sanitary?' I asked.

'We keep everything very clean,' Vanessa assured me.

I didn't see how, but I didn't ask. I was not in charge today. I just had to cross my fingers and hope for the best, though I couldn't help imagining how useless the effect of all this makeup would be if I arrived in L.A. with pus oozing out of my eyes.

I must confess, on some level, I was hoping for a transformation. I was hoping, as Amanda had promised, to look into the mirror and see a new version of myself — beauty I had never even known was there. Instead, when I looked in the mirror, I just saw me. Me with a lot of makeup. Me like a kid with face paint on. But still, just me.

Vanessa and Amanda gasped when I shook my hair out and turned to them. Vanessa, there in the middle of all those makeup counters, shouted, in a voice that seemed to erupt from genuine enthusiasm: 'Foxy!'

When I got home, the boys — all five of them, plus my dad — had built a spaceship out of the bunk beds. Alexander spotted me through the doorway and said, 'What happened to your face?'

'I got it painted,' I said. 'Like you did at the zoo that time.'

'What type of animal are you supposed to be?'

Before I could answer, my mom, passing me in the hall with a stack of folded laundry, piped up: 'A prostitute.'

Alexander frowned. He knew something was up. We'd read a lot of books about animals, and he'd never seen a picture of a prostitute. He looked at me for the straight dope. 'What kind of animal is that?'

What was I supposed to do? I shouted, 'Thanks, Mom!' over my shoulder. Then I said, 'It's a bird that lives at the North Pole. With Santa.'

30

Two days before I was supposed to leave for L.A., I found myself, after the boys were asleep, in Peter's practice room. My father and brothers had left, and Amanda and Gracin had gone home. My mother was in the kitchen organizing for her time alone with the boys. The house felt very quiet.

I hadn't been in Peter's practice room since he'd been gone. I hadn't wanted to go in. But now, as time was approaching for me to see him again, I found myself eyeing the door, glancing at it as I folded laundry, touching the handle as I walked by. Finally, I went in.

The room felt like him. The file cabinet he'd dragged with him everywhere since college, the framed poster of a Maurice Sendak print, the mandolin hanging on the wall, the woven Mexican rug on the floor. The combined effect of his things, together in a kind of landscape, left such a strong impression of him that soon a wave of longing had me leaning against his desk for balance.

He'd left in a rush, and the place was a wreck. He'd knocked over a chair on his way out that'd had a stack of papers on it, and they'd fanned out all over the floor.

I didn't want him coming home to this mess. I didn't want him coming home to anything that would remind him of that crazy night with Nelson. I righted the knocked-over chair. I emptied his trash can. I started picking up the papers on the floor and stacking them back up.

And that's when I noticed my name at the top of one of them. It was a sheet of unfinished music, which I couldn't read, but, at the top, it said: 'For Elena. Again.'

He'd written music for me before. He wrote the music we got married to, as well as many other things, from that first rhapsody to sonatas to spare little modern clinky-sounding things. But it had been a while. A long while, in fact. Until that moment, I'd thought he hadn't written anything for me since before we had kids.

But this page didn't look familiar. A third of a page of notes, and then blank. I picked it up to look a little closer, and there was another one underneath it. This one said, 'For Elena, who made me French toast this morning.' It was also unfinished.

I picked that one up. There was another one underneath: 'For Elena, whose hair is as black as feathers.' I started picking up the pages faster and faster. They were all pieces that Peter had written, and they were all unfinished, and they were all — every single one of them — dedicated to me. And this had been a tall stack of papers on his chair. I'm telling you, there were hundreds. Each with a slightly different thing to say: 'For Elena, who is taking care of a sick baby.' 'For Elena, who kissed me in the middle of the night.' 'For Elena, so far from home.'

The last piece I picked up was the one that had fluttered the farthest away. By then, I had a stack of sheet music a foot high on the chair. The date on the top of this last one was the night Peter had left. This one had maybe ten notes total. And under the date, it said: 'For Elena, who I will miss every day.'

I held it up to my face, as if it might feel good to be close to the page, as if some lingering aura of Peter might still be there. Then I tried to smell it, looking for some remnant of him. And then at last I carried it with me out to our bed, where I hadn't slept since my mother had arrived, and curled up there on my side and held it.

He still hadn't called me. It had been two and a half weeks, and nothing. At first, my mother arriving was a good distraction. And then seeing my brothers and my dad, and then Amanda and Gracin moving in. But with almost everybody gone now, with things settled down, there was no way not to obsess over it. Peter hadn't called. I had not gone two weeks without talking to Peter since I'd known him.

'Maybe he's just punishing you,' Amanda had offered earlier in the week.

'He's not that mean,' I said.

'Maybe he's testing you to see if you'll break down and call him.'

'He's not that messed up.'

It seemed to me that the only explanation for his not calling was that he didn't particularly care. For four years, we'd been straining to keep ourselves, our kids, our minds, and our marriage together. And now, it seemed possible that one bizarre and ridiculous moment had caused everything to unravel.

And that was the notion that had me curled up on the bed. Before the thing with Nelson, Peter was writing music for me — or trying to, at least. After, he didn't seem to be thinking of me at all. Suddenly, I felt stupid flying all the way across the country to see him. I felt desperate and undeserving and greedy. I was hoping this gesture of mine — plus a few artfully applied cosmetics and a new wardrobe — would make it all better. I was hoping to get him back. But there on the bed it occurred to me that it just might not work.

A marriage is such a fragile web of promises — to take out the trash; to pick up tomatoes at the market; to take the kids so the other can nap; to love, honor, and cherish; to *not kiss anyone else.*

At that, I started crying, and then I couldn't stop. I cried myself to sleep. I cried the next morning as I made breakfast for the boys. I cried off and on all day. I cried so many tears that I actually started to worry I might get dehydrated, and I sat down around four o'clock and drank three glasses of water.

My mother told me to pull myself together. That I was going to disturb the boys. That mothers didn't get to sit around crying all day, no matter how much they felt like it.

But Alexander was the only one of my boys who was disturbed.

'Why are you doing that?' he kept asking.

'It's just my eyes,' I said.

'But not your heart?'

I faked it for him. 'Not my heart, just my eyes.'

He wasn't sure if he believed me.

'They'll feel better once they're done,' I said.

But it didn't feel like they'd ever be done. I realized now, in a way I never could have

337

imagined only a month before, that my marriage might be over. And for no reason at all.

★ ★ ★

Amanda drove me to the airport that night in her Mercedes with heated seats. I had pulled myself together some by dinner-time, but saying good-bye to the boys got me going again. In four years, I had not been away from them even once.

They all held on to me on the front steps — two on my legs and Baby Sam's arms around my neck. I had to peel myself away. Everyone was crying as I scurried down the walk — except for Alexander, who instructed me to 'go get Daddy and bring him home.'

'Mama!' he shouted after me, until I turned. 'Don't forget to get Daddy!'

'I won't,' I said. I was at the curb now, moving away. Amanda was waiting for me in her shiny car. I was almost on my way.

But Alexander had one more thing to say. 'Mama!' he shouted.

What could I do? I turned around.

His face was so cheerful. He knew about compliments now. He'd learned that he could tell women at the store that he liked their earrings or their shoes and their faces would shift into big smiles of pleasure. My own face must have been wrinkled with worry as I tried to get out of there. He must have sensed how much I needed a little boost. When I looked up, he gave me the biggest compliment he could think of. He blew me a kiss and said, 'You look even plumper today than you usually do.'

'Thanks, babe,' I said.

★ ★ ★

On the highway, Amanda's inlaid dashboard polished to a high sheen, Amanda was impatient. She said, 'You simply have to stop crying. You're making your eyes puffy.' Then she said she had something to tell me.

'What?'

'I did a crazy thing last night.'

That got my attention. 'Please don't tell me you slept with that dog walker who followed you home,' I said.

'Crazier,' she said.

I turned to look at her.

She went on. 'I called Peter,' she said.

'Peter who?'

'Your Peter.'

'My Peter?'

She nodded.

'When?'

'Last night.'

'Why?'

'Because you weren't allowed to,' she said, as if it made all the sense in the world.

'Did you tell him I was coming to L.A.?'

'No!' Amanda said, shocked I would even ask. It had been her concept for me to surprise him in the first place. She believed that surprise was the first thing that went missing in married life. A surprise was important. It was not something she would fumble.

'Amanda,' I said, getting nervous. 'What did you say?'

'First, let me say,' she began, 'that I was only trying to help.' Then she confessed that she'd been out on a very bad first date that night and, on top of that, it had been her wedding anniversary, and she'd had maybe a glass of wine too many.

'How did you even get his number?' I asked.

'I had it in my BlackBerry,' she said, like that detail should have been obvious. 'From his flyer.'

I waited for her to continue. So she began.

'I wanted to remind him how great you are, just in case he had forgotten. And I wanted to know why he hadn't called you.'

'Why hasn't he called me?'

'We never got to that part.'

She really had just wanted to smooth the way for me. To butter him up a little, and remind him to be sweet to me, and remind him that I was not as tough as I seemed. She wanted to sing my praises and let him know how hard these weeks had been for me. In case he was still angry. She wanted to help bring him around. But, she confessed, she might have gone a little overboard. 'But no matter what he says,' she said then, 'I did not actually use the word 'suicide.''

Suicide! 'Who was committing suicide?' I asked.

'You were,' Amanda said.

'I was committing suicide?'

'Just toying with it,' Amanda said.

'You told Peter this?'

'No!' Amanda said. 'I just hinted at it.'

Amanda's reasoning for hinting to Peter that I was thinking about suicide went like this: Peter should have called me. He was taking me for granted. He should know how lucky he was to have me. And, to sum up: 'Life is short and love is precious.'

'But I am not toying with suicide.'

'No,' Amanda agreed. 'But Peter won't know what he's got until it's gone.' I suddenly realized that she did not feel the least bit guilty about lying to Peter. She grinned at me. 'It's my Christmas gift to you. Trust me, sweetheart. Fear and passion are, like, practically the same thing. There will be some good loving waiting for you in California.'

Then Amanda told me she was sorry about something else. She had spilled the beans about the miscarriage.

'About the what?'

'About the miscarriage.'

It took me a second to catch up, and by the time I did she was already explaining: 'He said nothing I was saying really sounded like you. And so I had to bring out the big guns. I said he'd really broken your heart storming off like that — especially when you were still depressed about the miscarriage.' She gave me a minute to register that before she added, 'I had no idea you hadn't told him.'

And then, before I thought it through, I just said, 'I hadn't told him because it never happened.'

Amanda didn't follow.

'I wasn't pregnant that day at the park.'

'Why did you say you were?'

'Because that mom in the khaki pants asked me when I was due.'

Honestly, I had not planned to come clean about that low moment in my life — ever. Some secrets are okay to keep. But here we were.

'Unbelievable!' Amanda shouted, and smacked the steering wheel with the palm of her hand. For a second I wondered if my lie had somehow been worse than hers. We were at the airport. Amanda took an exit for the passenger drop-off. Then she said, 'She asked you that?'

I nodded. 'She did.'

'Why did you say yes?'

'Because it was easier than saying no.' I shrugged. 'And she was making me feel frumpy.'

Amanda's face got serious, just as she pulled to a stop in front of the skycaps. 'You shouldn't have lied to her,' she said, and I nodded in agreement, ready to take my scolding. Then she said, 'You're way better looking than she is.'

And I couldn't be mad at her after that. She had called my estranged husband without asking me and told him I was suicidal because of my fictional miscarriage — which was, any way you sliced it, inappropriate behavior. But she meant well. And, maybe most important: She thought I was prettier than Khaki Pants.

I hugged her. And then it was time to call Peter and set him straight. But I'd lent my phone to my mother, who had, of course, lost it. 'Give me your phone,' I told Amanda, as I reached into her purse. We were at the terminal, and we'd been parked at the passenger drop-off too long. It was time for me to get out. And there, with airport security waving us on, I dialed Peter's number for the first time in two weeks.

But no answer. It went straight to voice mail. And I did not leave a message because in that moment, with Amanda staring at me and airport security now approaching the car, I did not know what on earth I could possibly say.

31

I could tell you everything there was to know about Peter. His favorite fries were the little hard ones down at the bottom of the bag. He cleaned his ears every night before bed with Q-tips. He was afraid of vampires. He had a recurrent nightmare about a giant hand trying to grab him. He liked lemons, but not limes; cilantro, but not parsley; and cake, but not icing. He could read a three-hundred-page novel in an hour. He slept on his stomach. His favorite fruit was pineapple. Green peppers made him throw up.

But I couldn't seem to index all my trivia about him into any meaningful pattern. It was useless information. The only thing I cared about was what he was thinking now and what he would say in seven hours, when I showed up at his door. If I were a computer, I might have been able to plug that information into some kind of an algorithm that could predict something about our future. But as it was, it was just me. I could tell you that he still had the Darth Vader piggy bank he'd begged for on his sixth birthday, but I couldn't tell you if he still loved me or not.

At Amanda's insistence, I did not wear any mascara on the flight to L.A. — or any eye makeup at all. And, as she had predicted, I cried much of the way there. When I wasn't crying, I was wearing a 'soothing eye mask' filled with cold jelly to keep the puffiness down — a present from Amanda before I left. 'This thing'll stay cold for ten hours,' she said proudly as she handed it to me. They developed it — '

And then I cut in: 'At NASA?'

'That's right,' she said.

'NASA really turned out to be a great beauty investment.'

I wasn't sure if the mask was helping. I checked my reflection a couple of times in the bathroom, but I mostly just looked red and puffy. I kept it on, though. What else was I going to do? My whole plan of looking so fabulous that Peter couldn't help but forgive me was in serious jeopardy. Though Amanda had pointed out that I had another great advantage now, thanks to her help. 'You're not dead.'

I wondered what Peter would see when he saw me today — after all my study with Amanda to turn myself into something irresistible, to claim that power beautiful

346

women have. I wanted to be beautiful. I wanted Peter to feel a thrill to see me. I wanted to find the passion that had been lost at the bottom of the toy bin for so long. And more than any of that, I wanted to find a way to keep Peter close. I had no idea how to make any of those things happen. But just for now, for one weekend, I wanted to clean up pretty good.

When the long flight landed, I wheeled my carry-on toward baggage claim. Here was the plan: To collect my suitcase full of beauty supplies and find a bathroom where, per Amanda's instructions, I could 'get gorgeous' before arriving at Peter's dorm room. My first job was to change into the black jeans and red shirt she'd picked out. Next, I was supposed to shake my head upside down and squirt hair spray into the roots to 'reinfuse it with lift.' Then: Do a couple of jumping jacks, splash my face with cold water, brush my teeth, apply some Visine if necessary, and follow every step of the makeup recipe Vanessa had concocted for me. Then, walk quickly and confidently to the taxi station while repeating personal affirmations (Amanda's suggestions: 'I am a badass wife and mother,' 'I am fierce and feisty,' 'I am a force of nature,' or 'Every man in this airport wishes I were naked' — none of which felt remotely true), then proceed to Peter's place, without picking at my new manicure, and take that man by storm. It was eight in the morning.

But before I made it to my bag, as I was walking out past the long line of shoeless people waiting to get in at the security checkpoint on the other side of the glass, I slipped in one of my new platform wedges: in particular, the pair that, when I tried them on, had inspired Amanda to touch her finger to my ass and make a sizzling noise. After years of sneakers and flip-flops, high-heeled wedges were, perhaps, a bit ambitious. But they'd made me feel tall at a time when, most days, I felt the opposite.

I hit the floor and almost tripped the business commuter behind me. A security guard with the name tag EDUARDO helped me out of the flow of traffic and leaned me against the wall so I could put my shoe back on. It felt good to lean against something, and I took a minute to regroup.

There is no better people-watching than at the airport: the whole world packed into such a tight space, moving fast with all their essentials in their rolling bags. And what caught my attention, as I took a few breaths and lay my eyes on the crowds, were all the imperfections. Everybody had them. Every single person that walked past me had some kind of flaw. Bushy eyebrows, moles, flared nostrils, crooked teeth, crows'-feet, hunched backs, dowagers' humps, double chins, floppy earlobes, nose hairs, potbellies, scars, nicotine stains, upper arm fat, trick knees, saddlebags, collapsed arches, bruises, warts, puffy eyes, pimples. Nobody was perfect. Not even close. And everybody had wrinkles from smiling and squinting and craning their necks. Everybody had marks on their bodies from years of living — a trail of life left on them, evidence of all the adventures and sleepless nights and practical jokes and heartbreaks that had made them who they were.

In that moment, I suddenly loved us all the more for our flaws, for being broken and human, for being embarrassed and lonely, for being hopeful or tired or disappointed or sick or brave or angry. For being who we were, for making the world interesting. It was a good reminder that the human condition is imperfection. And that's how it's supposed to be.

That said, it was time to find a bathroom so I could get gorgeous. It was going to take at least an hour. But before I could find one, I found something else. I found Peter. In the airport. Of all places. Going somewhere with his duffel bag across his chest like a messenger.

But he had a concert in L.A. that night, and not just a concert: *the* concert that the whole fellowship, and in fact even his whole life — had been building toward. Where, exactly, was Peter going? I couldn't imagine. And I suddenly didn't want to know. I felt, in that moment, like somehow I was prying into Peter's life, like I shouldn't have been there. I felt a strong urge to step behind that doughnut-bodied security guy and hide.

But just then, as if he felt me watching him, Peter turned all the way around and met my eyes. He looked terrible. He hadn't shaved, and his eyes were bloodshot and red, like he hadn't slept. He held my gaze like that for a good few minutes, his mouth a little open, as if he didn't trust his eyes.

And, of course, I looked terrible, too, after a day of crying, no sleep, and the longest plane ride I had ever taken. I certainly looked nothing like the fancy girl who'd had her makeup, hair, and clothes coordinated by Amanda at the mall. But it was okay. It hit me at that moment that Peter wasn't looking at my eye shadow, or lack thereof, or my lipstick, or lack thereof. He was looking at me. I didn't have to try so hard to stand out. I stood out, in this sea of travelers, simply because I was me.

I was near the end of the glass partition that separated the people coming from the people going. Peter was on the other side. We watched each other through the glass. Peter's line moved forward, but he didn't move with it. When the guy behind him nudged him, Peter stepped out of line, without dropping my eyes, and started walking toward me. He didn't look away once, just walked with a steady purpose right to where I was. I felt frozen, and, as Peter rounded the glass, when he was just two steps away from me, Eduardo the security guy said, in a sharp voice, 'Hey! You can't go this way!' But Peter didn't even seem to hear him, and I worried, suddenly, that Eduardo might hit him with his nightstick.

Two steps later, though, Peter was right up in front of me. I hadn't been able to read his face. I wasn't used to his expression. Was he angry? I'd never seen him so disheveled. His shirt was untucked, and his clothes looked like he'd slept in them. I held very still as he stepped up to me. I was afraid to move. Was he going to yell at me? Leave me? Tell me he was moving to Mexico and throw divorce papers in my face?

'Hey!' Eduardo said again.

But Peter didn't even pause. Without even

dropping his duffel, he reached right up to cup the back of my head with his hands and brought my mouth to his. I did not have time to think about the fact that it was exactly the kind of kiss I'd been wanting to teach him weeks before. He was moving on instinct, his body an expression of his thoughts. And then we were pressed against the airport wall, kissing, Peter's focus so intense it seemed like he wanted to crawl inside my body — with Eduardo the security guy looking on.

I'm sure I've had kisses that good before. But I can't remember even one.

We made out like teenagers against that wall. And when Peter came up for a breath, he stared at my face like he'd never seen it before, and said, 'Why are you here?'

'Why are *you* here?' I countered.

'I was going home to find you,' he said.

'I was coming here to find you,' I said.

Peter touched his forehead to mine and took a deep breath, as if he were trying to breathe me in. And I remember feeling like I never wanted to move from that spot, not even caring that Eduardo was keeping a wary eye on us.

Peter pulled back again to meet my eyes. 'You're okay?'

'I'm okay,' I said. 'I'm okay if you're okay.'

'I'm okay,' Peter said. 'Are we okay?'

I nodded. 'I hope so,' I said. 'I can't tell you how much I hope so.'

And then, when Peter kissed me again, I realized something — or maybe it was that night, at the concert, as Peter rocked the piano and I fought the urge to point out the 'For Elena: who kisses with her hands' in the program to the person next to me; or maybe it was even the next day, as we ate take-out Chinese in bed out of the cartons, still naked at lunchtime; or maybe it was even on the plane ride home, after we'd begged seats next to each other and while Peter slept with his head on my shoulder: I realized that nothing about that kiss could have been as good if I didn't know Peter backward and forward and inside out. If I hadn't watched him shave a thousand times, or poked him in the middle of the night for snoring, or watched him pace the hallways with each of our wakeful newborns. And, also, if I didn't know that he knew me the same way and had seen me at my worst as often as at my best. If we didn't know each other precisely that well, and hadn't been disappointed and dismayed time and again, and breathed each other's breath, and become so woven into every minute of each other's lives, and even come to take each other for granted in the way that you only can when you've seen years and years of day-in and day-out, it wouldn't have been the same.

I realized something else, too, seeing Peter again after all that time: As much as that kiss felt exactly like the ones from college I'd remembered so many times, there was something new between us right then in the airport, some real sense of discovery. Everything was just as it had always been, and, at the same time, everything was brand-new. And, despite it all — everything, more than anything, felt exactly like home.

Epilogue

Amanda would later say that my bumping into Peter like that was too impossible and that I was making it up. She insisted that nobody's luck was that good. She also insisted that Peter changing his plane ticket home five minutes after she called him was totally unbelievable as well. But that's what he'd done. And the first flight that wasn't full took off two hours after mine landed. And he stayed up all night worrying, trying to call my lost cell phone and, when that failed, Amanda's. She slept through the ringing. And though she did see his cell number ten times in her missed calls the next day, she still didn't believe any of it.

'There is no man on the planet,' she said, 'who would have left town like that on the morning of the biggest concert of his life.'

No man, it appears, except Peter.

I would also find out later that Peter had not stayed angry with me when he was in L.A. Quite the opposite. He hadn't been gone two days before it hit him that I hadn't wanted that kiss from Nelson.

That night, Peter had been brooding

about the kiss, as he'd done at least a thousand times since it happened, while he ate a PB&J for supper, alone in his little dorm room. He was studying the image of Nelson kissing me in his head, again, and he noticed something that he hadn't before: my arms were at my sides the whole time. They just dangled. And that's when Peter knew for sure that I hadn't wanted Nelson to kiss me. 'That's not the way you kiss,' Peter said later. He said that I kissed with my hands, ran them everywhere, put them in his hair, stroked his neck. That settled it for him, right then. He suddenly, in that great optimistic way that Peter had, felt better. In that one moment, I was forgiven.

He had picked up the phone right away and called me. He left a long message detailing his epiphany and apologizing for being a jealous asshole. Then he asked me to call him back. He said, 'Call me, okay? I want you to call me.'

But I didn't call him. Over the next few days, he called at least five times — maybe more. But I never called him back. Turns out, being dropped in the toilet had broken the phone a little bit. Not too much. But just enough. I couldn't receive any calls. And I guess I received few enough calls in general that I didn't even notice.

Peter thought it was my turn to be mad. He thought I was giving him the cold shoulder. But before he could come up with a way to get back on my good side, something else happened: Peter woke up with music in his head. Loud music. Urgent music. And, as always, he couldn't do anything at all — couldn't even function — until he'd written it down. He later described it like an explosion in his head. And it was, if this makes sense, a letter to me. In music. All the things he'd meant to say for the past four years, all the dreams he'd wanted to tell me about, or the funny stories that happened while he was at school, or the thoughts he'd wanted to share but that had been lost, as so many things are, in the everyday hustle. Those things started coming back to him, as if they'd been waiting all that time for their chance, and as soon as things got quiet, they all took it — at once.

He wrote like a maniac after that. He didn't even realize time was passing. He played so much his fingers got blisters. He forgot to eat. He forgot to sleep. Sometimes, if he couldn't stand it, he'd crawl under the piano to nap so he didn't have to waste time in transit. It was as close to going crazy as he ever hoped to get, and, on the other side of it, he had a massive piece of music to play at the final concert that would absolutely blow all the other musicians out of the water. When Peter finished playing, the audience didn't just clap, they cheered. They didn't just stand, they jumped to their feet. The roar in the auditorium was so loud, it sounded like people were stomping on the floor. And they may well have been.

Being away from the noise and the kids and the craziness of life in our house had cleared Peter's head — and out of the silence emerged the piece of music that he'd been trying to write all semester. It was, in truth, the piece of music he'd been trying to write all his life.

Everything came out that next day in his dorm room. We spent the whole day in bed — ate, fooled around, and talked and talked and talked. I came clean about my non-pregnancy, my non-miscarriage, and my non-suicidal feelings. He apologized for taking me away from home and for leaving me at the holidays and for overreacting about Nelson. Every few minutes, we marveled over how easy it was to talk to each other when we were alone.

★ ★ ★

The music he wrote during that fellowship landed Peter, among other things, a tenure-track job at Boston University. So we didn't have to move. We stayed in our little apartment building for several years after that, as did Nora and Josh, who spent a lot of time with our kids — and each other.

Just about the time Josh had given up on Nora for good, she had showed up at his door. She took his hand when he answered and led him upstairs without a word, into her apartment, into her room. He stayed that night and didn't sleep in his own apartment again even once after that. By the next fall, he and Nora were both back in school — as student and teacher — and they rode their bikes to campus together.

When my parents' three years were up, they moved back to Houston and sank much of the money they'd made on our old house into a new house just a few blocks away. My mother went to work on the garden, strolled over to visit our old neighbors every afternoon, and continued with her cooking lessons. My dad spent his retirement planning elaborate vacations for the two of them all over the world, though, he promised, they'd never move away again.

Amanda had sat down the same weekend I was in L.A. and typed up a list for herself of things to accomplish in her post-divorce year. It was four pages long, single-spaced, and included things like take tap-dancing lessons, change hair color, go deep-sea diving, learn to ski, have eyebrows tinted, kiss a total stranger, sleep in a tent, and read *Heidi* to Gracin. By the end of the year, she had only checked three things off the list, but one of them was *Heidi*. It turned out Amanda was great at reading, and Gracin was great at listening. They curled up under Gracin's comforter in their PJs every night and read until past bedtime. After *Heidi*, they read *James and the Giant Peach*, *The Cricket in Times Square*, and *Alice's Adventures in Wonderland*. Pretty soon, Gracin's whole bookshelf was full.

As for getting skinny, I never really made it. After all those months of working so hard to bring myself back into my body, after trying so relentlessly to recover that lost version of myself that I couldn't stop mourning, I finally found a stopping place — and settled out at a mom size. Not a high-school-girl size, not a college-girl size, but a mature, woman's, now-I-really-get-it size. I got stronger, and maybe trimmer, but I never actually returned — as I confess I'd been hoping — to my pre-mom self. Which made sense. Because I was not that self anymore, and I was no longer even close to that self. In the end, that was a good thing.

But I kept going to the gym. I established a rhythm — a deeply syncopated one, but nonetheless: an hour at the gym and an hour in the darkroom every weeknight between the kids' bedtime and mine. One hour for my body and one hour for my soul — as if those two things are somehow not the same. Time set aside to strive for that impossible balance between excitement and exhaustion, between longing for and having, between giving yourself away and hanging on to yourself, between how things are and how they ought to be. And then, once a week: I ate my beautiful piece of chocolate cake. And every Saturday: Peter and I hit the town on our hell-or-high-water Date Night.

Really, when I look back on it, I did exactly what I had set out to do. I changed my life. I woke myself up. I rediscovered passions of every variety. I forced myself to take a little time. I found a way to bring some of who I used to be into who I was.

And I took lots of pictures. I haunted parks and accosted women at the post office until I had 103 good ones. I took pictures of Nora and Amanda and the redhead at the gym. I took pictures of grocery checkers and bookstore clerks and women standing on the street corner with polka dot umbrellas. I spent four years taking photos of every woman who caught my eye, and then, in the darkroom we built when Peter moved his office to the university, I developed them.

And here, after all that, is what I have come to believe about beauty: Laughter is beautiful. Kindness is beautiful. Cellulite is beautiful. Softness and plumpness and roundness are beautiful. It's more important to be interesting, to be vivid, and to be adventurous, than to sit pretty for pictures. A woman's soft tummy is a miracle of nature. Beauty comes from tenderness. Beauty comes from variety, from specificity, from the fact that no person in the world looks exactly like anyone else. Beauty comes from the tragedy that each person's life is destined to be lost to time. I believe women are too hard on themselves. I believe that when you love someone, she becomes beautiful to you. I believe the eyes see everything through the heart — and nothing in the world feels as good as resting them on someone you love. I have trained my eyes to look for beauty, and I've gotten very good at finding it. You can argue and tell me it's not true, but I really don't care what anyone says. I have come, at last, to believe in the title I came up with for the book: *Everyone Is Beautiful.*

Acknowledgments

Before anything, I have to thank the many people who helped me nurture, feed, and amuse my sweet children while I was writing this second book. My amazing husband, Gordon, has been the King of Dads this year, and I can't thank him enough for all the storytelling, grocery-shopping, and car-washing he's done. And my beautiful mom has been the Grande Dame of Helping Out (tiara is forthcoming) — from meals to sleepovers to taking on any babysitting challenge, she has stepped up time and again. Many hugs to our family friend Maria Cruz — and her beautiful daughters, Mimi, Carmen, and Anna, and to Rebecca (and her handsome son, Daniel) Rios — for countless kindnesses (and *pupusas*) this year! Thanks also to our ever happy-to-help neighbors Mary and Jeff Harper.

I am also in such awe of my phenomenal agent, Helen Breitweiser, and my brilliant editor at Random House, Laura Ford, who make it all possible. It's an honor and a pleasure to know them. My publicist, Kate Blum, got my first book out there in a big and beautiful way. Robbin Schiff and Julia

Kushnirsky designed the gorgeous cover for this book, and Dana Leigh Blanchette designed the pages. Many thanks also to Libby McGuire, Kim Hovey, Janet Wygal, and Christina Coleman for all their help and support. A special thanks to Christina's aunt Renee for putting together a charm bracelet for me!

Thanks also to the musicians and composers who've educated me about the musical life: Molly Hammond, John Stone, and my dear friend Sam Nichols.

My hometown of Houston is lucky to have a thriving literary community, which has been so great to me this year. Many thanks to Fritz Lanham and the *Houston Chronicle*, Jane Moser and the folks at Brazos Bookstore, Valerie Koehler and the crew at Blue Willow Bookshop, Rich Levy and Sis Johnson and the good people at Inprint Houston, Robin Reagler and Writers In the Schools, and Greg Oaks and the literary gang at Poison Girl bar.

I have been so grateful this year to meet the Kirtsy chicks: Laura Mayes and her two brilliant friends, Gabrielle Blair of Design Mom and Laurie Smithwick of Leap Design. I also had the great fortune to correspond with Catherine Newman, who posted about my book on her amazing blog, and to become buddies with the fabulous Brené

Brown, whose Ordinary Courage blog is a true feast. I wish I could mail hugs of gratitude to the authors who offered blurbs for *Bright Side,* and all the bloggers and reviewers and readers who have helped spread the word! Thanks, also, to Ben Affleck, who accidentally walked past a reading I gave in L.A., let me give him a book, and then got himself photographed by the paparazzi. Thanks, Ben!

Brett Chisholm took my glamorous author photo and Ryan Rice featured me on his blog. The fabulous Jill Smith designed my snazzy website, and her husband, Wooch Graff, offered great enthusiasm about the book and crucial info about fist-fighting. Mike Roberts is a star for all his fast and furious web programming. Gene Graham is a saint for letting me get some writing done at her heartbreakingly lovely hill-country house.

I've been beyond lucky to have so many great people who have helped support my first book: Peter Roussel and the Houston Intown Chamber of Commerce, Susan Bischoff with the Houston Public Library Foundation, First Lady of Houston Andrea White, Jenny Lawson, Susan Lieberman, Liz Sullivan, the Debutante Ball, Lucy Chambers, Erica O'Grady, Rosa Glenn-Reilly,

Sarah Gish, Dusty Gilbert, Hillary Harmon, Cynthia Lescalleet, Kit Detering, Tracy Pesikoff, Dana Kervin, Katherine Weber, Dr. Linda Cook, Sherry Levy, Rebecca Rautio, the Houston Smith and Vassar clubs, and St. John's School.

And just a few other teachers I am grateful to have known growing up: Linda Woods, Jean Martin, Virginia Roeder, Rosie Beneritto, and Florence Harris — and the amazing Myrtle Sims, whom I've come to admire as an adult. Thanks, too, to my mommy group friends just for being awesome: Jenny Nelson, Erika Locke, Julia Smith Wellner, and Andrea Campbell. And a few other friends and family: Faye Robeson, Abigail Mayo, McNair Johnson, Philip Alter, Veronique Vaillaincourt, and Mimi and Herman Detering.

And again, as always, I want to thank my supersmart, so-excited family for the billions of ways they always help me out. More thanks and love than I can possibly express go to my beautiful sisters, Lizzie Pannill and Shelley Stein; my awesome brother-in-law, Matt; my niece, Yasmin; my parents-in-law, Ingrid and Al Center; Grandma Yetta Center; my very supportive dad, Bill Pannill; my wise and tolerant mom, Deborah Detering; my blue-ribbon husband, Gordon Center (thanks again, G! Sorry about all the pens in the bed!); and my two children, Anna and Thomas — who are so deliciously cute, they should be on cupcakes themselves!